The Ruined Duchess

The Scandalous Sisters

HELENE MATHESON

OLIVERHEBERBOOKS

The Ruined Duchess Copyright 2025 © Helene Matheson

Cover art by Dar Albert at Wicked Smart Designs

Published by Oliver-Heber Books

0 9 8 7 6 5 4 3 2 1

Prologue

In Memoriam of the 7th Duke of Ross, James Edgar Harding

I am highly ~~put upon~~ honoured to be ~~forced~~ permitted by the Royal Historical Society ~~of snobs~~ to record the passing of my ~~depraved~~ loving father ~~not by blood~~, the 7th Duke of Ross. It is impossible for his countrymen to understand his ~~lack of~~ dedication and sacrifice for the Crown. He took a deep ~~personal~~ interest in the financial markets to improve ~~his own~~ the country's coffers. He held the interest of ~~his whores~~ the people at heart and ~~scoffed at~~ exemplified the meaning of self-sacrifice to improve conditions for the poor. He will ~~not~~ be dearly missed by his ~~beast of a~~ doting wife, the Duchess of Ross, and his only ~~bastard~~ son, Nashford Xavier Harding.

— *DRAFTED OBITUARY FOR JAMES EDGAR HARDING 7TH DUKE OF ROSS, SEVENTEENTH DAY OF MARCH 1803 WRITTEN BY THE NEW INEBRIATED DUKE OF ROSS, NASHFORD*

1

*XAVIER HARDING AND CORRECTED THE
NEXT DAY AFTER HE SOBERED FROM HIS
CELEBRATORY NIGHT OF DEBAUCHERY*

APRIL 1803

"Give it back. I don't want it."

His father's solicitor scurried along behind the new Duke of Ross as he marched through the great hall. "Your Grace, the estate is quite vast."

"It's falling apart. The rugs are threadbare, the furnishings tattered, the walls are dingy with—is that supposed to be art?" His lip turned up at the sight of a child's version of the Corra Linn, one of three waterfalls of Clyde painted directly on the walls in the hall. Before he could take his eyes off the monstrosity, something splattered on his head, seeping through his thick dark hair like an asp slithering through the overgrown fields around the loch.

He closed his eyes. The art wasn't the only ghastly thing occurring in this household. So help him God, if that was bird shite from doves roosting in the roof, he would get his rifle and blast holes through the birds and the roof.

He looked up at the dripping ceiling and breathed a sigh of relief to discover it was only water saturating his scalp. "And there's rain coming through the roof." The pails scattered around the hall should have made the problem evident. It was the shabbiest estate he'd ever seen, and the fields didn't look much better.

"The tenants pay their rent on time, and up until four years ago, the estate was doing quite well."

He stopped and the barrister nearly ran into his chest as he turned around. As it was, the scrawny man with spectacles slipping down his nose fumbled the stack of papers in his hands. Several floated to the floor as Mr. Bremble swatted at them like a swarm of bees in the garden. He missed every damned one.

"What happened four years ago?"

"The *lady* of the house gave birth, suffered an affliction, and never recovered." Bremble crouched to picked up the papers, but only succeeded in dropping more of his tiresome reports.

He should help him, calm the man's nerves at the very least. He did neither. He was a Duke. "And ..." He didn't see what Mrs. Blair's health had to do with the downfall of an estate. If it had been her husband's health, well, that would be understandable.

"Her ... ah ... her lover, Mr. Blair refused to leave her side."

Nash's left eyebrow rose of its own accord. Bremble had caught his attention ... for the moment. This was a part of the story he'd somehow missed. It was his understanding Lady Elizabeth Sinclair had scandalized the Ton when she'd married a mere mister some fifteen years ago. Mr. Duncan Blair had been a businessman who'd become wealthy at a young age and captured his bride's heart when they were both quite young. The couple had been head-over-heels in love according to his own mother, who wouldn't have known love if it bit her in the arse.

He searched his memory for an inkling of a scandal attached to the couple or the estate, but nothing came to mind. The estate had been built in the thirteenth century, or so the story went, and because of its location leading to the Highlands, it had been a vital piece of property to occupy in order to control Scotland. At least that's the way it had been in centuries past. The last battle to occupy Urquhart had been fought in 1689, when supporters of the Protestant monarchy of William and Mary held off the Jacobites. The Protestants subsequently blew the castle to the ground.

From what Nash could see, it should have been left that way.

He didn't want the blasted rubble. He turned away from the man who was trying to tell him he couldn't give back a gift from the King no matter how much he wanted to do so.

He stopped Bremble's tirade with the lift of his hand. "Lady Sinclair was married to Mr. Blair," he corrected the older man.

Bremble shoved his spectacles up the bridge of his nose with his middle finger.

"Actually, I was the one to discover the marriage was not legal."

"How is that possible?"

"That I determined it wasn't legal?"

Nash nearly growled. "That the marriage wasn't legal. We're in Scotland."

"But they were married in England."

He was about done with this ridiculous trip. It was a waste of his time. "So they got married in England. They were *married*."

"No bans were posted, and the vicar wasn't a vicar."

"Excuse me?" The man was talking nonsense.

"The couple was in a hurry to marry, and Mr. Blair acquired a special license from a questionable source. A friend of a friend who claimed a favor was due to him by the Crown—it was not. The license was forged. A 'lark,' the man confessed. If they had gone a few miles further to Gretna Green, the marriage would have been valid, but they stopped in Carlisle, where a town drunkard stumbled out of the rectory when they arrived and they mistook him for the vicar."

The story sounded ludicrous. "How could they mistake a drunk for a vicar?"

"In his intoxicated state, the man soiled his own attire and borrowed the real vicar's clothing. Since the vicar was his brother, there was no real crime—until he performed the marriage ceremony."

"You must be joking."

"I'm not, Your Grace."

"You're telling me that a self-made man of business believed he could obtain a special license, which he cannot as a mere mister, obtained the forged license, took his bride-to-be all the way to Carlisle to get married, stumbled across a drunk posing as a vicar, married the society miss, but not really." He had to take a breath before he could continue. "Then he traveled to Scotland and lived with her for over a decade as man and wife ... and it was only after their deaths that this came to light?"

"Yes, Your Grace."

"How could the man be so stupid and still live?" He winced. The only reason he was here was because the man's own stupidity had caused him to die, after becoming so inebriated he fell into the loch and drowned.

"They were said to be in love, Your Grace."

Nash rolled his eyes. It was more likely the man couldn't wait to get under the chit's skirts, and she had been holding out. He had no doubt Blair hadn't actually sat by her side while she succumbed to death and then mourned his wife's passing. It just wasn't done.

Nash knew the greed of self-made men seeking society misses with dowries. Mr. Blair had probably been celebrating his widow-hood with whores, and lost track of what was important—his estate. "How did you find out about this?"

"I demanded a copy of the marriage license when Mr. Blair died."

"Why would you do that?"

"Because the Duke held a standing IOU from Mr. Blair."

Nash blew out a breath. "Of course he did." Gambling was the one thing his father had done well. That and stealing what belonged to another.

"When I learned of Mr. Blair's death," Bremble continued, "your father instructed me to look into his background."

"I'm beginning to lose my patience, sir. Why would my father care about Mr. Blair's background?"

"I'm getting to that, Your Grace. Since the estate has brought in a tidy sum in the past, I suggested to your father that it could bring in a sizable profit once again if it were managed properly. I have always inquired upon the estates that would bring a tidy profit for the Duke when the Duke held an IOU. That's how your father acquired so many estates."

God save him from helpful solicitors. The man was more evil than his father.

He sighed and looked around the grand hall. He supposed the castle couldn't be considered a rubble since it was made of ancient stone and it was said to have been fought over repeatedly for its strategic position on the road to Inverness. The view of Loch Ness was beautiful. Some may want to live in such a place ... just not him. It would take far too much of his hard-earned money to repair the castle to its previous glory. He should decline to collect on the IOU and let the heirs of Mr. Blair keep the estate.

It was in his best interest. The road north was treacherous and his coach had thrown two wheels on the journey. He couldn't imagine many of his mistresses wanting to travel to a drafty old castle on a bitterly cold loch which could only boast of a brutal and biting wind. His current mistress, Cecily, had found the trip to be unbearable. Her weak stomach and the frequent stops they'd made to accommodate her had turned it into a tedious three-day trip from Dumfries. It had also made him painfully aware of his need to be closer to London in order get away from the unpleasant side of traveling with a woman. He'd rather travel *to* a woman in the future.

"You're saying Mr. Blair owed my father the price of the estate?"

Bremble shook his head vigorously. "No, Your Grace. Mr. Blair owed your father one hundred pounds."

"One hundred pounds? That's it? Then tell me exactly how I came to acquire the entire estate?" he asked, even though he didn't want the answer.

Bremble nearly preened as he stood up with his papers now neatly stacked in his arms. "Mr. Blair said there was no problem paying the debt, but he died and he didn't have an estate manager to pay his debts. Your father—"

At the sound of Nash's growl, the solicitor cleared his throat and started again. "The previous Duke instructed me to advise the

Crown of the debt owed, but when the Duke passed so suddenly, I was a bit busy to do anything about it. Then the King's man of affairs contacted my firm regarding compensating you for finding the King that wonderful horse. Of course, I remembered the debt, and the lack of a legitimate marriage, and I suggested this piece of property be compensation, since it was scheduled to go back to the Crown anyway."

Nash frowned. "Don't the Blairs have daughters? In Scotland, the estate transfers to the daughters if there are no heirs."

"Not to *bastard* daughters, it doesn't."

"Excuse me?" He seemed to be repeating himself, but Bremble didn't mind. If anything, the man was quite pleased to discuss *ad nauseum* the subject of how he stole the children's birthright.

"Lady Sinclair was not married to Mr. Blair. The six daughters were not born in the marriage bed."

A sick feeling knotted in his gut. "They're bastards," he clarified.

Bremble grinned. "They're bastards."

The man repeating his words made Nash suddenly understand his mistress's weak stomach all too well.

Wailing broke through the air like a clap of thunder rolling through the Highlands. He looked up the stairs to see six sets of eyes staring down upon them. Six orphaned girls. The youngest appeared to be the source of the disturbance and continued with the racket as if someone was pulling her hair out by the roots. From what Nash could see, not one of the other girls standing near her was causing her any pain. If anything, they were attempting to comfort her. Four of the girls, became so engrossed in the youngest's despair, they forgot about him and Bremble standing below.

The sixth set of eyes leading the pack, however, told another story. She couldn't have been a day over fourteen and she was ignoring her sisters. She was a child, really, with a wild mass of auburn curls that reflected the untamed flame alight in her green eyes. He knew the color because unlike her younger siblings, this girl was focused of their presence, and from the anger marring her perfect complexion, he'd bet she'd been listening in on their entire conversation.

He met all six girls at the bottom of the steps and bowed. The wailing stopped. "Ladies forgive me for making your acquaintance without a proper introduction. I am Nashford Harding, Duke of Ross."

All six girls stared at him now. The youngest one sniffled. Her hair was a bit darker than the rest without a hint of red in the long strands. The four girls consoling her had identical features with pale complexions and blond hair done up to make them look much older than what they actually were. Stick-figures that were currently all legs and arms, but no doubt would have captured many a buck's attention if they were introduced to society when they came of age—which would never happen thanks to him and the imbecile standing next to him.

It was the oldest one, however, who captured his attention. On the cusp of womanhood, she was a mere shadow of her future self. No doubt by the time she reached her majority, she would be the type of woman to command the attention of every man when she made her way into a ballroom. He could imagine her storming the entrance and causing such a disturbance, the Ton could only stand by in awe of her tempest spirit. Fire glistened in her auburn curls, and upon closer inspection, it seemed to hold every shade of her siblings' hair. As if the younger girls were but a small glimmer of her perfection ...

... And she would no longer be allowed to enter society. Thanks to him.

At the age of twenty, he was a Duke. The title and responsibilities were his alone. No one would ever be the wiser to his true birth ... and in turn, he had repaid the kindness of fate by ruining the lives of six young girls, all in the span of one month.

Bloody hell.

One

My Lord Duke,

I regret to be the bearer of such scandalous news. My cousin, your beloved goddaughter Lady Elizabeth Sinclair's marriage to Mr. Duncan Blair was not documented in the church registry. As a result, their six daughters have been declared illegitimate, and are no longer considered eligible heirs to Urquhart Castle and its holdings.

The estate was returned to the Crown, however, our King, in one of his bouts of generosity, has seen fit to bestow the estate to the new Duke of Ross as a personal gift to compensate for the debt owed by Mr. Blair to the Duke's late father. Lady Sinclair's children have been turned out of their childhood home and left destitute.

When I learned of their circumstances I wanted to help, but my husband's scandalous departure from this world has left me in a position of being unable to care for one, let alone six children. My standings in society would not help the black mark on their reputations, but rather doom them to a fate they do not deserve.

For the time being, I have sent the girls to live with their nanny, however, I implore you to assist the girls—they are in dire need of a champion.

Yours respectfully,
Lady Drake

—A letter to Edward Charles Hancock, Duke of Nithesdale, from Lady Phoebe Drake, written May 1803 after learning of her distant cousins' eviction.

Two

DECEMBER 1810

He was dying.

She should feel something. Anything. Sorrow at least for the Duke who had taken in a fourteen-year-old orphan, but as she walked down the long corridor to his bedchamber, the only thing Iseabail felt was a dose of panic, making her mouth dry up as if she had eaten a handful of flour in one gulp. She knew that feeling well. A childhood dare by her sisters had left her gasping for air as a voluminous white cloud spewed from her lips. Her sisters' laughter had echoed through their home. This, however, was not a childhood prank, and not one smirk of joy crossed the faces of the footmen she passed.

A Duke was dying.

Yet she could only stare at the massive doors to his bedchamber as if they were protecting her from the cruelty of fate. She twisted her clammy hands, feeling a sense of her future no longer being hers to control—as if history were repeating itself, and another Duke was stealing her destiny. This time, however, he would not live to see it. Nor was he doing it out of greed or a sense of entitlement, but rather death was taking him before he could deliver his promise.

Gone was her impending season. There would be no suitors to choose from. Or a dowry to speak of—unless the Duke of Nithesdale had bestowed a dowry upon her to save her family before he died. Or would she have to stand alone between the world and certain ruin once more? Fear of imminent doom caused a lump to form in her throat. It went down with a loud gulp.

Her mother would hate her display of fear. Her father would chide her for her weakness, and together they would show her the path to standing on her own two Blair feet ... a path she had not been able to locate in the past eight years without them.

Why the Duke of Nithesdale had chosen to take her in eight years ago was a mystery ... especially to her. He was her mother's godfather, to be certain, but he owed the Blair sisters nothing. For years she'd written off his generosity as a guilty sense of duty. Now, it seemed his generosity would be another unfulfilled promise, leaving her with a cruel tempting taste of what her life could have been.

The first time she'd approached Caerlaverock Castle and witnessed its opulence, Iseabail should have told the footman to turn the Duke's coach around and take her back to her nanny's cramped little cottage. The Ton was not known for its generosity, or for their forgiveness of those who had been foolish enough to squander their wealth, like her father had done in his grief. Nor did they forget ladies who married beneath them. It didn't matter her parents' marriage was a love match. Lady Elizabeth Sinclair had scandalously eloped and married Mr. Duncan Blair, a man of commerce.

Even the servants knew of the scandal, and upon Iseabail's arrival eight years ago, they had whispered in plain sight. "He's grooming the little chit to be his whore," one footman had said, as he leered at her in the most uncomfortable manner. Iseabail had learned his name before any other. Louis.

At the time she had no idea what his comment meant, but she knew by the look on his face he was someone to avoid. From that moment on, she did everything to avoid Louis and the few who'd nodded in agreement with his assessment of her character. *He's trouble of the worst kind,* her mother would have warned—if she'd been alive.

"Lady Ishbel," the housekeeper's harsh voice startled her out of her memories. Mrs. Hagerty pronounced her name as if it weren't Scottish at all.

For eight years it had nearly driven Iseabail mad, and she found herself whispering "Iseabail" with a Scottish brogue under her breath for the millionth time. "Yes, Mrs. Hagerty," she said, loud enough for woman to hear. Yet still, her voice sounded as strangled to her own ears as it had the day she arrived.

"You mustn't dawdle. His Grace doesn't have much time left on this earth. His periods of wakefulness are few. Hurry along." Mrs. Hagerty's hands swept the air as if she were shooing a flock of chickens in the yard, not that Mrs. Hagerty would be caught anywhere near the chickens. Iseabail stared at the door, and Mrs. Hagerty's tone hardened. "Go."

The footman didn't hesitate and gave Iseabail little opportunity to gather her courage before he opened the double doors to the grandest room she'd ever seen. Granted, the parlor at Caerlaverock was admirable, and the library was awe-inspiring. She'd always found the dining hall grandly cavernous, although if she hadn't always dined alone, perhaps she wouldn't find it so.

Iseabail took a fortifying breath as she walked across the threshold into His Grace's rooms. Inside, she paused, and had to wonder what the old bugger had been thinking to create such a space. It was a golden room fit for the King himself.

Good heavens, even the bedposts appeared to be made of gold.

What kind of man slept in a golden bed? Did he believe himself to be the monarch of the castle? She supposed he was regent of his own domain. Caerlaverock was his—but was it necessary to have wall panels embroidered with golden thread to obtain a peaceful night's rest? Did the royal-blue velvet draping on the bed and windows keep nightmares at bay? Iseabail's gaze traveled up the cobalt canopy. Only then did she realize there were angels on the ceiling, blowing horns and escorting a horse-drawn chariot driven by a warrior who looked remarkably similar to the Duke—thirty years ago.

Caerlaverock castle was grand and well-furnished, but the Duke's chambers ... well, there was grand, and there was *grand*. These rooms compared to the *galarie des glaces* at Versailles. Not that Iseabail had ever laid eyes on the French court's magnificence, but her mother had told her stories ...

A moist, rattling cough came from the bed. "Is that her?" the Duke rasped.

Iseabail's eyes stopped perusing the lavish decor. She stopped marveling at the large chandelier that glittered like a sky full of diamonds as it reflected the light of the crackling flames in the fireplace. Her gaze snapped to the large golden bed with the Duke's family crest embroidered upon the deep-blue canopy.

His Grace wasn't the only one seeking her out, the room was full of people looking at her. Assessing her.

"Yes, Your Grace." The well-endowed woman dressed in a rich, garnet gown which displayed her décolletage advantageously, leaned over the Duke and wiped his brow. Iseabail had seen numerous women of questionable repute enter the house, but this woman was different. Under different circumstances, she would call her family. Under these, she was a mere stranger she had seen from time to time. Yet still, her beauty was mesmerizing. She wore her rich auburn hair piled high upon her head in graceful curls. The fabric of her gown was satin, and her face was beautiful and smooth. She held herself as a lady would, and her movements were the epitome of refinement. Lady Drake was grace personified.

"Come here, girl," the Duke rasped.

Iseabail's footsteps fell soundlessly on the plush carpet as she approached the massive bed swallowing up the considerable frame of the Duke. The Duke's ragged attempts to breathe echoed throughout the palatial room, as the five individuals on the opposite side of a golden balustrade encircling his bed stared at her with varying degrees of judgement. She was quite certain three of the four men didn't hold her in high regard by the scowls they wore. The Duke's mistress, however, held her gaze, and smiled. She actually smiled. She always smiled and said kind words.

His mistress. Dear God, how was she supposed to address this woman? She was everything Iseabail had been instructed to ignore. Yet she was family, her mother's younger cousin, and she looked so much like Iseabail they could be sisters.

Unsure of the proper protocol in a situation such as this, Iseabail returned the greeting with a slight incline of her head. One of the men coughed and her eyes immediately flew to see which one didn't approve. It shouldn't matter. It didn't matter to Iseabail, but it would to society.

Because Dr. Wakefield would talk. Reverend Lacey, the local vicar, would preach about it on Sunday. She prayed the Duke's solicitor, Mr. Forrester, wasn't one to pass judgement. Despite his polite demeanor on every other occasion when she'd met him, today he seemed to distance himself. As if he wanted to deny any plausibility in a crime she was about to commit. She couldn't help but notice his eyes darting toward the fourth man. She didn't know for certain as to the man's identity, but she could guess.

"Take my seat, Lady Iseabail," the Duke's mistress said.

Her name rolled off the lady's tongue with a Scottish lilt. It was breathtaking in its beauty, and nearly brought tears to Iseabail's eyes.

"Th-thank you." It was all she could manage to blurt out and still not offend the gentlemen present. The woman stepped back and allowed her to approach the Duke from the left side of the bed. On the opposite side, the doctor appeared to be measuring out laudanum, an amount that was almost certain to put not just the Duke to sleep, but every last person in the room.

Standing at the Duke's bedside, Iseabail realized she was

shaking as she had at fourteen when she approached him in his study. The Duke had shown her mercy, and a modicum of fatherly affection through the years, yet she couldn't help but wonder why she was requested to attend this small gathering at his deathbed. The fourth man, whom she guessed to be the Duke's cousin and heir, Mr. Henry Jarvis, stood off to the side. Rounder than the Duke, with the same shock of ginger hair, Mr. Jarvis did not appear to be the type of person to show mercy. In fact, Iseabail was quite certain the gleam in his eyes was that of glee and greed, not grief for his dying relative.

He shouldn't be the next Duke of Nithesdale, she thought. The current one was still young enough to marry and sire an heir. No one had expected him to die, yet here he lay—dying, and Mr. Jarvis was next in line for the title. He would become the next Duke of Nithesdale once her Duke was dead. If the man's new clothing was any indication, the new Duke of Nithesdale was going to prance around town looking like a pregnant peacock. His stark white breeches displayed surprisingly scrawny legs, and his tight, claret-colored tailcoat and brightly stripped waistcoat did nothing but accentuate his fondness of food.

Iseabail gazed down at His Grace, who seemed to have deflated in size and stature since the last time she'd seen him two weeks earlier, during their monthly chess match. The doctor's expression was grave, and the Duke's solicitor refused to meet her gaze as the pastor flipped through the pages of his Bible, his lips moving as if he were reading the scriptures.

"Forrester." The Duke's voice commanded attention even in his weakened state, and his attorney with pleasant gray eyes surged forward.

"Yes, Your Grace."

"Send for Mrs. Hagerty and Paddington," the Duke wheezed. "It's important they understand who is in charge upon my demise."

"Of course, Your Grace." Forrester went for the door, even

though the errand should have been done by the footman standing beside it.

The physician attempted to hold the laudanum to the Duke's mouth, but he shook his head and pushed the doctor's hand away before closing his eyes. The Duke opened his eyes and spoke. "I am dying ... but not yet." He glared at the doctor as he raised the laudanum once more. "I don't want that odious concoction."

"But Your Grace—" The Duke's glare seemed to bore holes in the man's head, and the doctor stepped back. "Of course, Your Grace. I am here to serve."

Iseabail shook her head. "Everyone comes down with an ague from time to time," she assured him. "I'm certain you will be hale and hearty in no time. Then you will be ready for all manner of trouble—"

The housekeeper chose that moment to enter the room and gasped at Iseabail's statement. Dr. Wakefield turned away. Mr. Forrester froze. Mr. Jarvis narrowed his eyes and looked at her in a new light—one Iseabail didn't like in the least, and the Duke chuckled. Reverend Lacey's face turned a brighter shade of pink than her own.

She really hadn't meant it to sound as scandalous as all that. "I didn't mean—"

The Duke's mirth turned into a coughing spell that drew everyone's attention back to him. The doctor leaned over with the laudanum at hand, and the Duke slapped it away, choosing instead to take the handkerchief Iseabail offered.

"There's a reason I asked for you to come, Jarvis," the Duke finally said.

The man in question pressed forward from his position against the wall, eager to please the dying Duke. "Yes, Your Grace."

"I've acquired a special license."

Mr. Jarvis looked around as if one of the others present could explain what the Duke was speaking of ... or perhaps he sought affirmation the Duke was out of his mind in his last moments on earth. Getting no reaction from anyone else, because Iseabail certainly had no earthly clue as to what the Duke was talking about, Mr. Jarvis looked back to the Duke. "Your Grace?"

"I'm afraid you won't be the next Duke of Nithesdale upon my death."

Mr. Jarvis laughed as if the Duke had told a joke. His mirth died when not a single person met his gaze. Then he sputtered, "But I—I—I'm your heir."

The Duke raised his once beefy hand, which now looked feeble as it shook, and silenced any further protestations of Mr. Jarvis. "You know that Miss Iseabail Blair is my ward," he breathed.

Mr. Jarvis's gaze flew to Iseabail and then back to the Duke. "Surely you don't think I'm going to marry your whore? I'm already married."

The small intake of her breath was the only objection in the room.

The Duke ignored the insult. "What you don't know, is that when my heart gave out, I was in the act of ruining her."

Mr. Jarvis wasn't the only one to gasp—there was a chorus in every tone on the musical scale. At least that's what it sounded like to Iseabail's ringing ears. The Duke coughed once more and pointed a shaky finger to warn off the doctor before the man could approached with laudanum, but the doctor's feet appeared glued to the floor. She looked to Lady Drake for salvation. Surely she would save her from this disaster.

The woman stared at the intricate stitchings on her kerchief, attempting to blend into the furniture, as if that were possible in her crimson gown.

The Duke regained his voice, weak as it was. "Today, Miss Iseabail Blair will become my duchess." Mr. Jarvis sputtered again, but the Duke refused to be denied his declaration. "Obviously, we don't know if she is with child or not, but if she is, my son will be the next Duke of Nithesdale."

Mr. Jarvis turned on her and lunged, murder in his eyes. If it hadn't been for Mr. Forrester stepping in front of her, spreading his arms wide as if to protect her ... womb? Dear God, Mr. Forrester believed she had been with the Duke in ... in *that* manner.

Iseabail took a step back, her hands going to her midsection as the roiling of her stomach threatened to cast up her breakfast. Every man, woman, and servant in the room noticed the gesture. She immediately dropped her hands to her sides and clung to the folds of her gown as if they were her lifeline.

This could not be happening.

Mr. Jarvis stormed from the room, delivering a parting shot along the way. "I will be watching, whore."

It was exactly what her parents had wished to spare their daughters from hearing. *Whore* and *bastard*, yet it seemed the perceived sins of the mother were indeed going to be passed on to the daughters, despite their efforts. The insults were part of her destiny, thanks to the dying Duke in front of her.

"Come here, Iseabail," the Duke commanded, and she found herself obeying. She should have stormed from his chambers before Mr. Jarvis had a chance to utter a word. Called out the Duke and his blasted heir on her own. She could shoot as well, if not better than the lot of them. Instead, she found herself standing next to the Duke of Nithesdale with one question upon her lips.

"Why?"

The Duke reached for her hand and she let him grasp it, despite her own desire to swat his hand away as he had done to the laudanum. Perhaps with Jarvis gone, he would recant his claim or at least explain why he would shame her in such a fashion.

"You may begin Reverend, and don't fill the ceremony with fluff. I've not much time for this world."

Startled, Iseabail attempted to pull away, but the vicar's slapped hand down on top of hers, clamping it to the Duke's, and held fast. Before Iseabail could object, the sham of a ceremony had begun and everyone was waiting for her to say something. She looked to the vicar, the doctor, the solicitor, and lastly the mistress. All patiently waited for her to say something.

"Say it lass. Say you do, or your future is gone." Despite the shock of everything that had occurred in the past few minutes, Iseabail knew she had little choice. There was no escape. Her immediate future did not look promising without the utterance of two words. Two words that would give her a momentary reprieve —it was the only hope she had to save her sisters. Two words that were the most frightening thing she'd ever had to say in her life.

"I do."

Only when the minister had pronounced them man and wife did he release their hands. It was then the Duke pulled her hand to his mouth and kissed the back as he would to any other lady of the Ton. To the onlookers, it probably looked endearing, but then he crooked his finger in a gesture for Iseabail to bend toward him. Her heart hammered as she bent down to hear his warning.

"Get yourself pregnant, Duchess, and your future is set, whether it's a boy or a girl. Fail to do so, and in nine months' time you'll find yourself out in the cold, a ruined duchess the Ton will enjoy destroying."

The smack on her backside was so utterly shocking she nearly fell forward onto the bed as she gasped at the Duke, who lay grinning with a devilish gleam in his eyes. He'd never shown a hint of impropriety. Yet he seemed determined to add one last notch in his belt of sins before he died.

"Now, dear, if you would kindly prepare my bride." He waved a shaky hand at Lady Drake, who rushed forward. "I'd like to have a wedding night with my duchess." He winked and grazed the top of Lady Drake's breasts with his fingers.

Iseabail felt the blood drain from her face. The doctor sputtered.

"Y-Your Grace. You are not up—"

"Don't tell me what I'm up for, Wakefield." The Duke grinned.

Lady Drake blushed all the way down to her nearly exposed nipples.

"Paddington," the Duke called out.

"Yes, Your Grace." Paddington's face had been the only one to remain stoic throughout the entire scene. Iseabail wasn't sure if his expression would change if the Duke suddenly rose up, murdered her on the spot, ordered two footmen to remove her body, and left the mess for Mrs. Hagerty to clean up.

The Duke continued giving instructions to the butler as if nothing were amiss. "Please escort the good doctor and Reverend Lacey to the blue parlor so Mr. Forrester can advise them of my wishes." Although the Duke spoke slowly, not once did he struggle for a breath. If anything, he appeared invigorated. Whereas she'd been in a frozen state of shock since she was pronounced the Duchess of Nithesdale.

A duchess ...

She didn't feel like a duchess.

The Duke coughed and brought her thoughts back to the present. He cleared this throat, his breathing becoming labored once again. "Mrs. Hagerty, if you would see to tea."

"Yes, Your Grace," Mrs. Hagerty murmured, and left the room.

The gentlemen began to leave the room, with Lady Drake following behind Mr. Forrester, who once again refused to meet Iseabail's imploring gaze.

"Phoebe," the Duke called out, and Lady Drake froze. "Stay. My new bride doesn't have half the expertise in the art of pleasure as you, and I want to enjoy my wedding night."

The Duke's mistress paled. Iseabail grabbed hold of the golden bedside table as her legs nearly crumpled beneath her. Mr. Forrester glowered but continued out the door with a shocked Dr. Wakefield and a vicar who was vigorously wiping his brow.

The Duke was definitely going to hell, and he was taking Iseabail and Lady Drake along with him.

Three

My dearest Lady Drake,

I have found myself unable to fulfill the promise I made to you seven years ago. Unfortunately, our plan to bring young Iseabail together with the Duke of Ross has been thwarted by my failing heart. In this endeavor, I have enlisted my solicitor, Mr. Forrester, to bring an alternate plan to fruition. I will, however, require your assistance to see to Iseabail and Nashford's future happiness—if not together, then irrevocably bound by my heir. Here's what I require ...

Yours sincerely,
Nithesdale

—A letter from Edward Charles Hancock, 6th Duke of Nithesdale, to Lady Phoebe Drake, December 1810

Nashford Harding, Duke of Ross, was bored beyond measure. The tedium was expected. The constant parade of matchmaking mamas and title-seeking widows was enough to make a man never leave his home. Except they'd probably start seeking him out there if he avoided such events as his cousin's engagement ball.

"Did you hear, Your Grace?" A familiar feminine voice whispered in his ear.

"You know I avoid gossip, Lady Drake." He wanted to avoid her. She was becoming downright irritating with her pursuit this evening.

"But this tidbit will interest you."

Nash seriously doubted it. Lady Drake had been attempting to corner him since his arrival, and the last thing he wanted was to entangle himself in an affair. He wasn't in the mood. He wanted to offer his felicitations and be gone.

The day had ended with another failure. The thirteenth Bow Street runner he'd hired in the past eight years had delivered a devastating blow, and now he had to figure out what he was going to do next. Should he give up the hunt and accept that he had committed a heinous wrong against six innocent girls? Or should he continue this losing quest which had consumed his life for far too long?

Lady Drake moved closer and he glanced down from his perusal of the ballroom to eye the woman rubbing her breasts against his arm. He had never engaged in a dalliance with the enchanting widow before, if she weren't Nithesdale's mistress ... he would find the coy curve of her lips intoxicating. The tip of her tongue wetting her full pink lips mesmerizing. He would definitely see the amount of flesh she exposed at her neckline as more than a soft place to rest his weary head.

But she was Nithesdale's mistress, the man who had mentored him into manhood and the dukedom the way a father should have. Their bond was more special than any other in Nash's life. No, Lady Drake's twin pillows did nothing but make him want to take a nap. He needed sleep, not a fickle widow in his bed. According to his mother, he also needed to find himself a wife—God help him.

He shouldn't be here. He should go to his club, toss back a few drinks, and find his bed.

Alone.

His search for the Blair girls had run its course. His latest runner had given him so much hope to finally right the wrong of his past, not to mention his father's evil deeds. The lead to their locations had blossomed into hope, then certainty and then poof. Nothing. The leads had proven as false as his congratulatory remarks to his cousin on his upcoming nuptials.

Damnation. The runner had been reporting for months that he was close, only to report this evening that he had been following the wrong family. How many bloody Scottish families had six girls with no boys?

Nash ignored Lady Drake's flirtation as she continued to run her gloved hand down his bicep. "Nithesdale married his whore."

Despite his lack of interest, Nash found himself the slightest bit intrigued. Nithesdale was married? After all these years of bachelorhood, Nithesdale had married without a word of warning? A duke shocking society with such a blatant lack of concern for propriety was unheard of, but then it was Nithesdale's actual mistress telling him Nithesdale married a whore. Scandal meet scandal.

The Duke of Nithesdale made a habit of raising eyebrows throughout society. For years the Ton had gossiped about his two unidentified bastards whom they claimed Nithesdale planned to introduce to the Ton one at a time. Even Nash didn't know their identities, but now to marry some ladybird and not Lady Drake, it was as if Nithesdale was telling society he was opening the gates of hell for all the single bachelors to follow him into the den of iniquity. What Lady Drake suggested wasn't done by anyone—not even Nithesdale.

He shouldn't encourage her gossip, yet he had to ask. "Why would Nithesdale marry a whore?"

"Oh, it's not any whore. It's his ward. Imagine ..." She fluttered her eyelashes in invitation. "A former ward—now a duchess. He's kept her hidden at one of his country estates for the past eight years."

The hairs at the back of his neck stood on end at the depravity of the statement, yet he still found himself defending the old scoundrel. "I've never known Nithesdale to care for anything but the most *experienced* bed partners." Nash had, after all, lost his virginity at one of Nithesdale's infamous house parties. Nithesdale's parties were not for the faint of heart, nor were the ladies of the Ton who attended them. That had all been before Lady Drake. Since then, Nithesdale had been a veritable saint.

Lady Drake chuckled and swatted him with her fan. "This one comes from good stock," she purred, as her hand glided down his hip and progressed to his thigh.

Good Lord, the woman was becoming more brazen by the moment. Nash took a step to his left to put some distance between them, and let his gaze return to the room at hand. He should probably call it a night and head for his townhome. Alone.

But Lady Drake wasn't finished. "I'm sure her mother is rolling over in her grave. Her father," she shrugged. "Well, if he were alive, he would probably cheer his darling daughter on for her expertise at climbing. She's a chip off the old block, with a bit of blue blood to entice any lord."

It wasn't just the hairs on his neck that stood on end with that declaration. His entire body stiffened with apprehension. The story sounded all too familiar, and his gut lurched as if he'd consumed an entire bottle of whisky.

"Nithesdale wouldn't." Would he? Especially not after Nash had asked for the older man's assistance in locating the girls who had disappeared from Urquhart Castle without a trace. He'd tried and failed to put these particular sins of his father's, and his, to rights. It'd been eight years since he'd returned to London determined to find a way out of the mess with Urquhart Castle. The last thing he'd wanted to be involved with was the eviction of six orphaned girls. Their father's passing had exposed them to the harsh realities of life, thanks to his former solicitor stepping in and taking absolutely everything they owned, on top of their good names.

And Nash knew what it was like to be bastard-born. He may have enjoyed the riches his own *father* had bestowed upon him, but he'd never felt the loving touch of a doting parent. His mother blamed him for her banishment to the country. His father wanted nothing to do with the child that reminded him of the way his duchess had cuckolded him.

Yet his father's best friend, Edward Hancock, Duke of Nithesdale, knew the truth, and had always treated him as if he was his father's true heir. Stepping in with advice when a father should have, but hadn't. It had been Nithesdale to whom he'd turned in his formative years—the same man he'd sought out to assist in the Urquhart debacle. From puberty to Parliament, he had always turned to Nithesdale for advice. Unlike his father, Nithesdale cared about people. He was a man of his word. A man Nash could trust.

Yet Nithesdale had been best friends with his father, who had been an odious human being. Could the two men have had more in common than Nash had realized?

"Who is the chit?"

Nithesdale's former lover nearly cooed as she grabbed Nash's arm and pulled him down to whisper in his ear, her warm breath chilling his blood. "His country home has been his playground with Iseabail Blair, or would it be Isabel Sinclair? I'm not certain, since her parents' marriage may as well have been a performance in Covent Garden. Would she have her mother's surname, or her father's?"

Now he knew it wasn't true. It couldn't be true. He had been to Nithesdale's country home at the end of last season for a hunting party. There had been a few women present, but none had been in residence upon his arrival, and Nithesdale had not engaged in any relations. Nor had Nash.

Before calling out the lie for what it was, he decided to bait Lady Drake a bit further to irrefutably disprove her unseemly gossip and put it to bed—where most lies of the Ton started. He took a sip of his drink not tasting a bit of the expensive champagne being served. "His country home in Wales?" he asked.

Phoebe's hands began to roam on his person. "Oh, no. Nithesdale's kept this one to himself in Scotland."

He frowned. This rumor would be a bit harder to dispel. "Caerlaverock?"

"Yes, have you been there?"

He gave a noncommittal, "Mmmm," as he downed the remainder of his drink.

Eight years? A young girl on the cusp of adulthood. It couldn't be true, could it? Had he incorrectly read the character of the only man he'd viewed as a father figure? And if he had, that meant he'd committed a more grievous act against Iseabail Blair than what he'd previously believed. This error had led a depraved Nithesdale right to her doorstep.

He remembered the young girl like it was yesterday. Her flaming hair curled around her face, while hatred burned in her eyes. In his nightmares, he imagined her as she walked the streets of Edinburgh in filthy, tattered clothing hanging on her scrawny, starved body as she promised to do every manner of disgusting act in order to feed her sisters. Though he had no idea where the Blair sisters were, the reoccurring dream shredded his slumber night after night.

Lady Drake had to be wrong. Nithesdale wasn't virtuous, but he wasn't a cad, either. Granted he never married, and although Nash had thought it odd for a Duke not to desire an heir, he'd never questioned Nithesdale's reasons.

He should have questioned it, dammit, but it had been Nithesdale who'd taught him to ride, hunt, box, and drink. Nithesdale who'd introduced him to his club. Nithesdale who'd assisted Nash in righting too many wrongs his father had meted out onto others.

Countless heirs, who had gambled and lost to his father, had been given back their hope for a future, all thanks to Nithesdale's philanthropic endeavors to get them back on their feet financially. Nithesdale's actions hadn't been for personal profit, but rather for the betterment of England and the people who depended on those estates for their livelihoods. Together, he and Nithesdale had taught countless men of the Ton how to manage their estates wisely. In turn, those men had helped their families, their servants, and the tradesmen who worked for them.

Lady Drake continued her attempts to shock him. Her retelling of the story of the ward's *training* nearly gutted him. "On her twentieth birthday, he introduced her to a life of sin." She looked around the room and then pulled him into an alcove for more privacy. He knew how it would look, but at this point, he didn't care.

"I actually took part in her downfall." She waited for this bit of news to sink in.

"You did what?" He couldn't stop the incredulity from seeping into his voice.

Lady Drake rolled her eyes. "As you well know, we widows have needs." Her hand reached for his cock, but he side-stepped the maneuver. Her smile returned as if she thought she could persuade him to change his mind. Not a chance in hell after that last confession.

"Nithesdale asked me to touch her in a manner no woman should touch another."

He scowled and put distance between them when Lady Drake ran her hand across his chest and brushed the tip of his nipple, but she was not to be put off. "I pleasured her and taught her how to pleasure another. We became lovers, and then I allowed the Duke to watch us together in the bath, on the bed, even on the lawn of his estate."

Her voice became breathy as if she were there at this moment. It was unseemly, yet he couldn't walk away.

"She was seduced into our den of pleasure, but it didn't end there, because the Duke is a man who not only enjoys watching, but wanted more, as all men do. I became the tutor once more and showed young Iseabail the ways of seducing a man." She moved in closer. Leaning forward to whisper a juicy bit of gossip in his ear. "The Duke found her to be a very good pupil, and the innocent became the whore ... for no one but the Duke ... and me, of course."

God, the way Lady Drake related the tale made the whisky in his gut ignite in a fierce firestorm ready to explode. It couldn't be. Guilt and anger amassed and he wasn't sure he could suppress it. *I'll kill the bastard.*

Lady Drake laughed. "Kill who, darling?"

He had no idea he had spoken aloud.

"Nithesdale? Now wouldn't that be the biggest scandal to hit the Ton in a decade. A duke dueling a duke over a whore. Come, I will ease your jealousy with something special. Perhaps you would like one of my maids to join us tonight? Will that make you feel better? To *train* your own little whore?"

The disgust he felt for himself and Nithesdale compounded with Lady Drake's suggestion. Only a wicked woman would subject another in her service to such treatment in the name of her own pleasure. He wasn't quite sure how he'd ever thought this woman appealing.

"You are mistaken, Lady Drake. I don't wish any unwilling miss, compelled or otherwise, in my bed. If you'll excuse me." He attempted to pull away, but Lady Drake would have none of it.

"Darling," she simpered. "You should have said you'd like a ruined duchess in your bed. Why don't we visit the newlyweds together. It will make for a very entertaining and cozy house party."

Nash froze. His gaze returning to the woman attached to his arm. "What did you say?"

"You and I could take my carriage to Caerlaverock. I'm certain Nithesdale would share his young bride with *you*."

Despite his efforts to find and protect her, Iseabail Blair was now the Duchess of Nithesdale ... he scrubbed his hand up and down his face trying to erase the images Lady Drake described. Iseabail Blair should have been protected—saved from the likes of men of Nithesdale's ilk, but Nash had been a blind fool and his stupidity had been her downfall.

"Nithesdale's cousin is quite furious," Lady Drake imparted with a smirk.

"Is Nithesdale's hatred of his cousin the reason he abused a child?" He asked, uncertain if he should trust anything coming out of her mouth.

Lady Drake pulled back as if he'd said something vile, and he had. Yet she had been involved in a heinous act. She laughed and swatted his arm as if she thought he was teasing her. He wasn't.

"She is three years older than I was when I married my late husband. I was a widow at her age. She is hardly a child now at two-and-twenty."

Nash pulled his arm loose. "What about her sisters?"

"What about them?" Lady Drake's hand rose to her décolletage.

"What type of unsavory men do you think will pursue them?" He didn't wait for her to respond. They both knew exactly who would pursue the Blair sisters. Nash made his way through the throng of people on the dance floor without a backward glance at the glares being hurled in his direction. Iseabail may not have been a child when her '*training*' started, but she had been an innocent, and Nithesdale was going to pay for his actions.

Two couples collided as they dodged his path. Nash didn't care if he caused the revelers to miss their turn, lose their place or fall on their blasted faces. If anything had mattered to him but his determination not to let another minute go by without getting to the bottom of this nightmare, he may have witnessed Lady Drake's collapse into a nearby settee and her seductive mask drop as an embarrassed flush crept up her neck.

Instead, his gaze blazed forward as he walked out of the ball-room. He only had his youth and fatuity to blame for his mistakes which led to the girls being evicted from their home. He'd fired the weasel Bremble, but it had been too late. The Blair girls were gone without a trace. No one had been able to locate them. The servants had been as unhelpful as the idiot solicitor his father had hired and Nash had fired.

The years stacked up in his head like a pile of bodies in war. Eight. Eight years, and to now finally hear that the only man he'd ever admired was the one man who'd betrayed his trust ... it was inconceivable.

Nash was going to kill him.

He walked out of Tempest Manor without a word to his hosts. He wasn't sure he would be able to speak without cursing, and the newly betrothed Viscount Weldon and his viscountess-to-be deserved better than his foul mood.

A footman hailed his coach and Nash was inside muttering to all that was holy before he even realized they were on the road. He would have the answers he sought. He'd spent too many years searching, agonizing, seeking redemption for his own sins of complicity in the Blair sisters' fate. He would demand answers from Nithesdale—that damned, despicable bastard.

Nash glared out at dark night sky. The sound of the wheels groaning, hoofbeats pounding, and the horses snorting would normally lull him to sleep. Tonight, they broke the peace, all because of his naïveté toward a depraved duke. Nithesdale had turned that young girl into his whore, thanks to Nash pointing him in her direction. Her title would open doors, but many would see her as a climbing bastard whore, who would undoubtedly be the gossip rags' favorite caricature for debauchery. Even if Iseabail Blair had become a duchess, what type of woman would she be now? What type of mother would she make to the next Duke of Nithesdale?

Could Nithesdale have such little care for his own child? His own flesh and blood?

Nash closed his eyes and sighed as he rubbed the stress from the bridge of his nose. He needed to sleep. He would finish the contracts he had to sign in the morning and then head to Caerlaverock.

And damn all the dukes of the Ton to hell—including himself.

Four

Lord Duke,

The trap has been set. The poor man was nearly gaunt with fury. I am afraid he is most displeased with your duplicity involving the Blair girls. I hope you know what you are about and that our young Iseabail does not suffer for our actions. If Nash has not arrived prior to my missive, I would expect him to arrive shortly after.

Despite your wicked scheme, you truly are the best of men. I am eternally grateful for your care of the children, since I am hardly a suitable guardian. I will not deny how difficult this role was for me to play, but to my shock and possibly his, I was rather scandalous.

I hope and pray your health improves and that I may see you again with a young and vibrant duchess at your side.

Yours,
Phoebe

—*A letter from Lady Phoebe Drake to Edward Hancock,
Duke of Nithesdale, December 1810*

Paddington stood at the doorway to the grand parlor she'd acquired upon her marriage two weeks earlier, with a stoicism she couldn't fathom. Before her marriage ceremony, the butler had treated her like a grandchild. Now it was as if she were a stranger in this giant house that had somehow become hers—for the next nine months. What happened after that, she hadn't begun to figure out.

"A carriage approaches, Your Grace."

Your Grace. She would never get used to hearing that title, nor did she know how she would carry out His Grace's ridiculous scheme to get with child. No one, let alone an eligible man, would visit her or give her the time of day.

"Is it Mr. Forrester?" she asked, focusing on tying off the thread to her needlework.

"No, Your Grace. He has been with the Duke most of the morning. The coach appears to have a seal on the door."

"A seal?" She set her needlework down and looked out the window. "Were we expecting anyone?"

"No, Your Grace."

In a matter of days her entire world had been turned upside down. Iseabail had a parlor in a part of the castle she'd rarely visited prior to her marriage. Her rooms now adjoined the Duke's bedchamber, not the nursery, so when she did sleep, she could actually hear her husband snore.

Her *husband* ... who was old enough to be her parent.

"Your Grace?"

She looked up at Paddington and his features softened. The faint hint of sympathy evident in his gaze.

"Whoever it may be, they have undoubtedly traveled for several days. Take them to the drawing room and I will greet them shortly ... and if you could have Mrs. Hagerty prepare tea?"

Paddington nodded in approval then winked, thoroughly warming her heart. There was still affection between them after all. She returned the gesture and put down her embroidery, a sense of confidence she hadn't felt moments ago now restored.

It was little over a sennight since Lady Drake had departed and the house had seemed empty ever since. She and Lady Drake hadn't conversed much during their time together, but she knew Lady Drake could be trusted despite how uncomfortable Iseabail made the widow. Perhaps it was her inexperience or the fact that they were ... were ... well, their relationship would distress most of the Ton.

Mr. Forrester strode into the parlor wearing his ever-present smile. "Your Grace, you look lovely today." Despite being the person who took her away from her sisters, Mr. Forrester was the one person with whom she found herself most at ease. On that initial trip to Caerlaverock, as today, he had a calming demeanor. For years she'd dreamed of him taking her away from this strange place. He hadn't, yet he had returned every month to apprise the Duke of his many financial endeavors, and each visit he made time to update her on her sisters and pick up packages she wanted to send them.

"Thank you, Mr. Forrester. How was your conversation with the Duke this morning?"

"Your husband's mind is alert and well. It is his body that concerns me. His breathing is quite labored this morning." His smile was sad, but accepting of his employer's fate.

She nodded because she knew it was true. His night had been plagued with fitful coughing spells. "Did you have much to discuss?"

"Yes, he wanted to make sure all his affairs were in order. He is determined for his estates and business ventures to remain healthy for his son—" he paused, as if realizing just whom exactly he was speaking to, and cleared his throat. "Or daughter ... well past adolescence, and of course, he wants to ensure you are well cared for as well."

She fidgeted in her seat. "I would like to speak to you about that as well. I need to know his plans for my sisters and me ..." Her face heated at the topic. "If I do not ... do not ..."

A commotion in the great hall prevented her from continuing. Voices rose and glass shattered. Mr. Forrester immediately turned toward the disturbance. In her youth, Iseabail would have fancied the castle under attack. Now, she suspected a drunken old crony of the Duke's had come to pay his respects to a dying friend.

"Where is she?" A man bellowed throughout the hall. "I don't give a bloody damn if Nithesdale is dying at this very moment, I want to see Iseabail Blair. Now!"

Dear Lord. Who could possibly be seeking her, and by her father's name? No one had used that name in the past eight years. Iseabail jumped to her feet, letting her needlepoint drop to the floor in her haste and approached the disturbance just as Mr. Forrester took matters into hand.

"My good sir. Please calm yourself, and we may discuss what seems to be the problem in the privacy of—" Mr. Forrester's breath caught.

Iseabail couldn't see the man's face, but he was broader and taller than Mr. Forrester, and his hair was as unkempt as a beggar in the village. He must have been well into his cups when he'd decided to travel to Caerlaverock, since it wasn't even midday, and the attire he was wearing appeared to have been worn for several days straight. She had no desire to approach the man who took no pride in his appearance and barked at Paddington as if it was his given right to order about the servants in the Hancock keep. It wasn't as if he was the King Regent himself. It was best she let Mr. Forrester see what this particular madman was about.

No sooner had the thought crossed her mind than the man pushed past Forrester, only to come to a complete stop when his gaze landed on her. Mr. Forrester recovered from the affront when he realized she had followed him from the drawing room.

"Your Grace, I must apologize for the disruption. Are you acquainted with—"

If Mr. Forrester identified the stranger in front of her, she didn't hear his name because his presence assaulted her soul. He did not belong in middle of the great hall with her broken vase of lilies.

Her hands balled into fists. Her breathing went from mildly affected, to nothing passing through her lungs at all. He was older, but just as coldly handsome as she remembered. Black hair glistening like the dark abyss, with eyes the color of a stormy sea. He appeared much larger than he had, which was an oddity in and of itself. Most things she'd remembered as being large in childhood, were smaller as an adult. It was definitely not the case with the man responsible for having evicted her and her sisters from their home. The same man who'd named her and her sisters bastards.

Her temper flared like it had not in years. Not since she was forcibly removed from her home like a sack of rotten potatoes that smelled too foul to serve to the pigs. This man dared to enter her home and demand to see her?

He must be mad.

Her lip curled and her eyes narrowed as her balled fists clenched and unclenched at her sides. "You dare to come into *my* home and *demand* to see me," she seethed. Her chest rose as if she had just run down the hill, through the gates, across the bridge, and over the moat to defend her castle.

"So, it's true." He looked at her with what appeared to be pity.

She would not be pitied by the likes of him. "What's true?" She demanded.

"He made you his whore."

The words slapped her face as hard as any strike, and she took a step back. Mr. Forrester growled. The footmen stepped forward to stop the violence ready to explode. Paddington was opening the door as if to allow the Duke of Ross to be thrown out on his arse. It would serve him right to receive the same treatment he'd dealt six young orphans. The man could rot if he thought she would stop the servants from dumping him in the moat. "Get—"

"Your Grace, pardon our intrusion. We have come to see Nithesdale. Is he well?" Everyone froze. Lady Drake stepped out from behind the Duke of Ross, her gown rumpled from travel, her features as beautiful as ever. They may look like sisters, but Lady Drake carried herself with a born assurance Iseabail did not. Lady Drake commanded the room as if she were the lady of the castle, dressed in an elegant confection of claret red silk, hugging her form in all the right places. Her skirts swished, and every man in the room stared at her as if she were the Madonna herself.

Well, if not the Madonna, perhaps Aphrodite was a better comparison. Both images would cause men to drop at her feet, one in reverence, the other in lust.

Ross was the first to recover. He shrugged the tight muscles of his shoulders and held his arm out for Lady Drake to take. "Lady Drake, please forgive my rude remarks."

Lady Drake laid her fingertips on his forearm, their manner as formal as if they had arrived at a ball, and Iseabail couldn't help but wonder why he would afford Nithesdale's mistress such respect while he called her a whore.

Iseabail stiffened her spine. "I am the Duchess of Nithesdale. Not Lady Drake, and this is my castle."

"Actually, it belongs to Nithesdale." His voice held the smug tone of a born duke.

She wanted to scratch his eyes out. "Your Grace, since you seem unable to address me as my station dictates, perhaps you should take your leave."

"On the contrary, I came to see your husband." He began leading Lady Drake into her drawing room.

Iseabail looked to Mr. Forrester for guidance, but for once the man looked as lost as she was, and she asked the one question that had plagued her for years. "Did my father do something to you that would cause you to judge me so harshly?"

Her question stopped Ross in his tracks, but he didn't turn to address her. Instead, he looked down at Lady Drake as if he were explaining himself to her. "He owed a debt."

Iseabail snorted. Actually *snorted* in the presence of a duke and countless others. Lady Drake flinched, but Iseabail refused to let the matter drop. "A debt of one hundred pounds?" She walked in front of him and forced him to look at her, not Lady Drake. "Surely the hundred pound note you held of my father's was not the reason you evicted six children. I could pay the debt today, if you'll allow me to buy back my home."

"Urquhart Castle?" He searched her eyes as if he was looking for signs of madness.

Perhaps she was mad, but she couldn't forget all the things he'd said about her home. He found the rugs, the walls, and the roof to be lacking—and they had been, but to her, they reflected the better times of her youth. The stains of crushed berries on the marble floors from little Robina's attempts to make the perfect wine were priceless, yet he didn't even remember the Scottish castle that belonged to six young girls.

"Are we talking about the estate where children painted on the walls?" He asked.

He wasn't even certain of which estate she spoke of. "The painting on the wall was done by my sister Ailsa. It is her interpretation of *The Falls of Clyde* by Scottish artist Jacob More." She was proud of the way she controlled her speech while her heart pounded to the rhythm of his death march.

He looked perplexed. "Really? I remember scribbles."

"Ailsa's version is through the artistic vision of a *child*. My parents loved that painting." She would never admit to her own criticism years earlier. All that mattered was that their parents had praised her sister's talent as if she were a prodigy of the artist himself, and the servants had been forbidden from cleaning it off the walls.

"Sorry, I did not." His apology held no sincerity, but perhaps the slightest bit of guilt?

She gasped. "You didn't." His continued gaze gave nothing away, yet she knew what he had done without him saying it. "You destroyed it, didn't you?"

For the first time Lady Drake looked at him as if he had done something inconceivable, and it was her reaction, not Iseabail's, that forced his defensive confession.

"I haven't been back to Urquhart Castle since that day."

"You haven't been back?" Lady Drake's voice sounded as incredulous as Iseabail's was. The two of them asked the same question in unison.

Every tear in the carpet, every mark on the furniture spoke of her childhood. It had been the only home she'd ever known. She loved Urquhart Castle ... and it had gone untouched for eight years.

She strangled the snarl rising in her throat. If he had no use for her family home, he'd probably allowed it to go into more disrepair in the years hence. She could live there once again. She could have Mr. Forrester bring her sisters home, and perhaps he would want to join them ...

She gazed at the solicitor, who didn't seem to know if he should throw the Duke out or pour him a drink. If it was left up to Lady Drake, they would be sitting down for dinner.

Dear Lord, she wouldn't—

Iseabail bit out a command. "I want him gone."

Lady Drake laughed, her hips swaying as they turned for the drawing room. "She jests, of course. Nithesdale would be furious if she were to close the doors on you like rubble. Please, Your Grace, won't you send for tea?"

"Tea? You want me to serve this ... this *miscreant* tea?" She was dumbfounded. Granted she wasn't necessarily acting like a duchess, but nor had the Duke of Ross acted like one of the highest peers of the realm when he'd stormed her castle and called her a whore.

"Of course, darling. We have traveled a great distance. Tea is the least you can offer while the maids prepare our rooms."

Iseabail stood in shock as Lady Drake and the Duke of Ross walked into the drawing room where she had originally planned to serve her guests.

Except he was not a guest! He was a beast who didn't deserve her time, or her tea. Her knees began to tremble and she found she could hardly stand. She was grateful when Mr. Forrester approached her and held out his arm for her to take.

"Why would she bring that man here and allow him to get away with saying that to me?"

"I cannot speak for Lady Drake. I can say that your husband is quite fond of him." Mr. Forrester's expression showed his concern and his sympathy. "However, I must tell you that I plan on demanding an apology as soon as we enter the drawing room."

"No," she blurted before she could even consider what Mr. Forrester was suggesting. "If he is a friend to my husband, then I must determine what he has heard and why he is here demanding to see me. How did he even know I was here?"

Mr. Forrester shook his head. "I do not know."

Iseabail took a deep, steadying breath. "Then I guess it is time to find out exactly what Ross thinks he knows and what he has heard."

"That would be the wisest course of action." He smiled down upon her. "I would ask one small favor."

The request took her aback. "Of course."

"If he utters one more disparaging word, do I have your permission to throw him out the window?"

She grinned. "I will open the window above the moat myself."

Five

Mr. Joshua Forrester,

Please escort the eldest daughter of Lady Blair to my country estate in Dumfriesshire. The five younger children are to remain with their nanny. Compensate the nanny for her services with a monthly allowance to ensure the children have adequate living arrangements and tutoring. Once the oldest chit arrives at Caerlaverock, she shall be prepared for a proper marriage.

Nithesdale

—A letter from Edward Hancock, Duke of Nithesdale to his solicitor, Mr. Joshua Forrester, February 1803

H e made you his whore.

Why the blazes had he said that? There was no excuse for his utter lack of decorum.

Nash made his way down the grand staircase to have tea in the drawing room with the ladies for the third day in a row. Caerlaverock Castle was the perfect quiet sanctuary—if one wanted to ruminate day after day over one's stupidity. Which he did not.

Yet he didn't know how to erase that awful label he'd put on her when he should have been congratulating her on her recent nuptials. She was a duchess, for God's sake, and he'd addressed her as if she were a common trollop in Covent Gardens.

Three days of this torture. Three days of being denied an audience with Nithesdale. Three days of his initial incivility constantly forming a wall, regardless of how humble he'd tried to be.

When he met the Duchess as she broke her fast, they may as well have been talking through stone. She wouldn't look at him. When she took him riding across the moors, she on a stunning golden-brown mare, he swore she wore blinders. Her regal form had been breathtaking, and when he'd attempted to do the gentlemanly thing and apologize for his unconscionable behavior, she'd galloped away. Her head never turning to see if he followed. Nor did she garner to look in his direction when he'd caught up to her and openly watched the ease in which she rode the mare. It had made him think of other ways she would ride with ease, his mind going where it shouldn't. Yet he couldn't stop the thoughts from forming.

At dinner, the Duchess and that blasted Mr. Forrester conversed around him. Lady Drake was included, of course, but he was not. If it weren't for Lady Drake, he suspected he'd be out on his arse. It was maddening. Had there ever been a lady who ate meals with her husband's man of affaires and his mistress while she ignored a duke sitting at the same damned table? Of course, his own mother and father had never dined together, but he was quite certain if they had, a few barbs would have at least been exchanged.

He welcomed a set-down from those lips.

He didn't want the Duchess of Nithesdale as *his* duchess. She was Nithesdale's, and she was nothing like the child he'd encountered eight years ago. As a duchess she was beautiful, imposing, and cold—no that wasn't true. She was cold toward him. Not toward Forrester, Lady Drake, or the servants. However, the only time he'd witnessed a spark of flame in her eyes in the past three days had been when he'd called her a whore.

Damnation.

Since his initial blunder, conversation between them was polite, but unrevealing. He still had no idea why Nithesdale had brought her into his home. Three days of seeing her in gown after gown, her firm creamy bosom put on display for everyone to observe. Three days of him being unable to ferret out the location of her sisters so that he might at least keep the other girls from having their virtue destroyed because of his being a first-class ass when he'd gained his title.

Not that being a duchess was a bad thing, but he and the last Duke of Ross had made her acceptance as a young lady entering the marriage mart impossible, and after Nithesdale's passing—the circumstances of her birth would be unchanged, and she could quite possibly still be a pariah as well. Yet she still had her title and the ability to eviscerate an opponent with the heat of a glare—if she would let her spirit ignite into flames.

Once again, as with every other afternoon, Nash found himself outside the drawing room door holding out his arm for Lady Drake to escort her to tea.

"Good afternoon, Lady Drake."

"Your Grace. I hope you had a delightful ride this morning."

He glanced at her as they walked toward the library. Had he heard an innuendo in her comment? He hadn't wanted to believe the rumors about her, either. Yet by her own torrid account, and the manner in which she touched the Duchess ever so familiarly, Lady Drake was the whore, not Iseabail. So why hadn't he judged her or condemned her in front of the servants? Instead, he treated her with the reverence of her station as a member of the Ton.

There must be something seriously wrong with him. From the moment he laid eyes on the Duchess, every last fear he'd had in the years since she'd been a child staring down upon him with so much hatred, had come to fruition. She may look more vibrant and beautiful than even he'd imagined she would become, but the fire he'd experienced blazing in his direction eight years ago had been tempered. He mourned the loss of the spark that had leapt from her mercurial gaze. It seemed to be lost forever ... and he couldn't stomach the very idea of that loss.

The Duchess of Nithesdale led the way into the drawing room on the arm of Forrester, who'd wanted to tear him limb from limb just a few days earlier. From his manner, Nash suspected Forrester held himself in check every moment they were together.

"I suppose an occasion such as this may call for something stronger than tea," Lady Drake suggested, as she rubbed up against him. "May I pour you a brandy, Your Grace?"

Nash wanted to recoil, until he looked down and saw the uncomfortable grimace Lady Drake quickly hid with a flirtatious smile as she looked up at him through her lashes. The room shifted. He looked down at the graceful widow on his arm, and for the first time he realized her flirtatious manner wasn't real—it was a facade. An act better than any play he had seen in the past decade.

But why? The revelation made him wonder about every other person in the room. Lady Drake had been terribly shy as a young woman. Her first season had seen her married off for her dowry to an old goat. Despite that, Nash had always believed her late husband loved her, just not enough to save her from his disastrous gambling habit. If the man hadn't died in a drunken duel, Nash had no doubt Lady Drake's husband would have gambled through her money in no time.

"What is the occasion?" he asked, while trying to gain his footing in this uncertain game he'd been caught up in.

"The doctor says Nithesdale is doing much better today. He thinks he may be on the mend."

His gaze landed on Nithesdale's wife. Her expression revealed neither relief nor regret at this turn of events, and it made him want to throttle Nithesdale even more. So far, he'd been denied an audience with the Duke, something he would have never expected before now.

He smiled at Lady Drake. "By all means, I believe the occasion does call for brandy, my lady. Thank you."

"Allow me to pour. Would you like one as well, Duchess?" Forrester interjected.

Nash looked at the man in question, who led the Duchess to the settee where she sat down and pulled at the rather scandalous blue silk of her bodice. The long slim turn of her neck made a man want to bury his face in the delicate curve as he pulled out every last pin in her hair.

"Of course she does," Lady Drake responded. She acted as if she were the lady of Caerlaverock, and Iseabail a mere visitor. And it was Lady Drake, not the Duchess, who reported the doctor's news about Nithesdale feeling better than he had in weeks.

He watched the three other people in the room and tried to make sense of it all, but nothing had made a lick of sense since the moment he'd encountered Lady Drake at the ball in London.

"Yes," the Duchess responded in a soft, almost dead tone.

Suddenly aware he stood stock-still in the middle of the room, Nash took the seat opposite the Duchess. There were several vacant seats he could have taken near Lady Drake, but the one directly opposite the Duchess was from where he hoped to read her emotions.

"I'm sorry Nithesdale has not been able to receive visitors, Duke. When he heard you had arrived, he wanted me to send for you right away. I declined, of course, at the doctor's insistence." Mr. Forrester proffered a glass to Lady Drake and then to the Duchess as he spoke.

Nash nodded as if his extended stay was inconsequential. "I understand your dedication to Nithesdale's recovery and I am glad he's feeling better." It might still give him the opportunity to kill

Nithesdale and then turn his sights on his over-handed man of affairs.

The Duchess let out an inelegant snort, and Lady Drake sent her a quelling look. The Duchess of Nithesdale, however, chose to ignore the rebuke, and he felt the corners of his mouth rise in the first hint of amusement he'd felt in days.

He addressed the Duchess. "Will Nithesdale be able to receive visitors tomorrow?" he asked.

"He actually asked that you be sent to his room now, but I advised the staff you will wait until after the Duke's dinner," Mr. Forrester interjected. Again, someone speaking for the Duchess, who shouldn't. Mr. Forrester gave a slight bow of his head as he extended a tumbler of brandy.

"That is very good news. Thank you."

"The honour is mine, Your Grace."

In any other situation, Nash would have immediately put the man at ease and offered his hand in thanks. Mr. Forrester, however, made him want to embrace his title and tell the man where he could shove his over-protectiveness for the Duchess and the barriers erected around Nithesdale. He suspected the disdain was mutual. Mr. Forrester took a seat to the right of the Duchess, and he had the distinct impression it was a show—these three against the world—or rather, against him.

As if he were the one hiding something, and not the other way around.

"Is there anything I can do to assist you during this difficult time, Duchess?" His tone was that of a concerned peer, as he purposely ignored the two flanking her and addressed the Duke of Nithesdale's wife.

"As a matter of—"

"It is enough that you have come to visit during this trying time." Lady Drake interjected before the Duchess could deliver the set-down he had coming.

"Damnation, he would have admired it. The question

remained, however, how could Nash turn the tables on what he and his father had done to the beautiful, corrupt, graceful, improper, extraordinary, immoral creature—the Duchess of Nithesdale?

"Tell me Your Grace, what really brings you to Caerlaverock?" the Duchess asked without a trace of subterfuge.

Ahhh, but he could see the embers attempting to burn. "Nithesdale was present when my ... my father passed."

Nithesdale had been at the same house of ill repute Nash's father was visiting when his heart failed. Nithesdale had not been married, and there was nothing wrong with an unattached lord visiting such an establishment—but a brothel was last thing he was going to discuss in mixed company.

Her delicate eyebrows rose as if waiting for Nash to continue. He downed the contents of his glass. "He was there for us, and I merely want to return the favor." He cleared his throat and gave her the one honest response she deserved. "Nithesdale gave me more fatherly advice than my own ... sire."

It was Lady Drake who seemed more touched by his confession than the Duchess. At present, the Duchess was more interested in her nails. "You may not know this, Ross, but I benefitted from Nithesdale's advice as well when my husband passed. The Duke has taken on many an orphan throughout the years." She reached over and squeezed the Duchess's hand as if the Duchess could also relate to the generosity the Duke bestowed.

A growl escaped his throat, and he quickly turned into a cough. He wanted to throttle the old rake.

"I'll get you some more brandy, Your Grace." The Duchess rose with such swiftness he was caught off guard. It was only when Mr. Forrester glared down upon him that he realized he was still seated and immediately jumped to his feet and handed her his glass.

"Thank you."

Lady Drake took Mr. Forrester's glass, which was still half-full, and followed the Duchess to the other side of the room while he watched, unsure of what he should do next.

"Hurt her, and you'll be seeing me at dawn." Forrester's voice deepened with the threat.

"I beg your pardon?" Nash wasn't certain he'd ever been challenged by another lord in such a manner, let alone a man of service.

"You heard me, Your Grace. I will not stand by and let you hurt her."

He pulled his head back and looked at the man in a new light then scoffed in disbelief. "You love her."

Mr. Forrester ground his teeth together. "The Duchess's husband is my employer. I look out for Her Grace's best interests."

"That doesn't discount for the fact that you care for her."

"As I do for all of my clients."

"So, you would challenge *a duke* to a duel for all of your client's wives?"

"If need be."

It was another lie, and Nash couldn't help but wonder about the lies stacking up at Caerlaverock. He refused to study his own feelings toward Iseabail Blair—*Hancock. Iseabail Hancock.*

Mr. Forrester turned and met his steady gaze. "The Duke has asked me to care for her welfare. I will do just that."

"Does that include in her bed as well?"

He shouldn't have asked, but he couldn't stop the question that was burning the tip of his tongue.

Through clenched teeth and an inflexible jaw, Forrester said, loud enough for only Nash to hear, "It means, whenever and *wherever* Her Grace requires."

It was the last thing Nash wanted to hear, yet he'd asked for it, hadn't he?

~

He was in her library. *Her* library. No one came into her library. Not one person had entered this room since her arrival at Caerlaverock eight years ago, when Paddington had shown her the magnificent room filled with shelves so tall, a ladder was necessary to reach the literary treasures on the top shelf. The ladder alone was a bit of joy. Attached to rungs near the ceiling, the bottom step was flanked by wheels which allowed it to transverse from one end of the room to the other. On her first day, Paddington had shown her how to brace herself between the rungs and push off. She'd laughed for the first time since her father's death, as she'd trailed her fingers lovingly across the spines of the books for the entire length of the wall.

A bit of joy in her somber path to adulthood.

Whom was she kidding ... she'd done the exact same thing the very morning *he'd* arrived and turned her world upside down. But that was exactly the point. In here, she was free to act as childish as she liked. She'd come to the library this evening to escape his intrusion. It was supposed to be her sanctuary, her home ... and he invaded it like he had Urquhart Castle. Now he was staring at her as if she were an oddity he thought to never encounter.

When he finally spoke, he said the exact opposite of what she'd expected. "Duchess, I apologize for trespassing upon your sanctuary. I was told I might find you here."

His voice was deeper than she remembered from her childhood. Richer, like malt Scotch whisky aged to perfection. It was all the more delicious because of his acknowledgment of his intrusion.

Where in the devil had that thought come from? She loathed this man. If he was skillful in any manner, it was in the art of deception. He didn't have a caring or polite bone in his body. She closed the book she'd been trying, and failing, to read and laid it upon her lap.

"How was your meeting with my husband?" She asked.

"He slept through it." Frustration tinged his statement, and

Iseabail found herself feeling a bit sorry for this man who obviously held Nithesdale in high esteem. It may have been years since her parents died, but she knew exactly how a goodbye could be a blessing and a curse.

"He does that frequently. How may I be of service, Your Grace?" The fictitious smile on her face was as artificial as his, and yet he seemed to be able to read what she hid underneath the falsity much better than she could. Drat.

He stepped into the room and closed the door before turning back to stare at her once more. She arched a brow in question as he made his way over to the settee next to her. Thank goodness she hadn't lounged on it as she was wont to, but had instead chosen to sit closer to the fire.

"I don't know if you remember our first meeting at—"

She laughed, a hideous noise escaping her lips that sounded more like a cackle than the light-hearted flirtation she had intended. "Your Grace, I seriously doubt I could forget meeting you." She paused, and let her compliment sink into his arrogance before continuing her attack. "I'm not surprised, however, that you have confused me with one of your many conquests." There. Let the man believe she had no recollection of his cold-hearted regard for six orphaned girls.

His smile wavered as he searched her face. "You really don't recall it?"

"I've never been to a ball, I've never been to London, or out of Scotland for that matter. Where in the world would a woman like me meet a duke like you?" She brought her hand to her chest in mock innocence. She'd read the scandal rags and their judgement of her character. Her innocence was forever tarnished, regardless of what the truth may be.

"We met at your family home," he said, in a rather strangled voice.

This time her laughter sounded almost real. "I hardly think

Nithesdale would have introduced us ... here." Saying it felt like the biggest betrayal of her life.

Especially to this man. Nithesdale was her guardian angel compared to the Duke of Ross. Even cloaked in the deepest of black, her husband was the purest color on the palette. His innocence was found in the absence of light. This duke's guilt, however, was luminescent.

Ross shook his head, and she had to admire his ability to feign sorrow. The added touch of running his hand through his dark locks as if he were loath to continue, was brilliant. Yet he refused to drop his gaze. "No. We weren't formally introduced, but I saw you at Urquhart, before you came here. You were standing at the top of the staircase to the great hall ..."

Her heart stuttered in her chest. She'd never expected him to be so forthright. "Oh?" she said, because really, what else could be said without cursing him to hell? Damn the man.

"Yes, it was the week you were forced to leave your home." He searched her face, looking for what, she had no idea. Hatred? She had plenty of that.

"I ... I ..." Her tongue was completely worthless. Her brain a jungle of what she'd been schooled to say and what she so desperately wanted to rage.

"I'm sorry to be the reason for your eviction," he admitted, in a soft tone that almost sounded contrite.

She knew better. She stood and walked to the other end of the room and returned her book to the shelf as she gained her composure. "The past is incurable, Your Grace. I've never been prone to look back and wish it undone. Just as I would never wish I hadn't finished reading a book. Regardless of how unpleasant an event or story may be, there are future chapters to experience and knowledge to gain. That is where my focus rests." It was a lie, of course. Her heart would forever cling to happier times at Urquhart.

"What about your sisters?" He sounded confused, yet she

couldn't turn to decipher his meaning without exposing her true emotions. All she could do was stare at the volumes of texts on the shelves in front of her and get a grip on her anger. How dare this man come here and feign concern for her and her sisters! He was the reason they were in this predicament. If it hadn't been for his greed, she would be with her sisters now—living on the loch in the Highlands.

She twirled around faster than she should have, the skirts of her gown swirling between her legs like angry waves of silk in a storm. "No need to concern yourself, Your Grace. We landed on our feet. Climbers always do." She nodded in the direction of the bookshelves. "Please help yourself to my library while you're here. We wouldn't want our *guest* to be lacking entertainment." The smile on her lips felt tight and brittle. If she didn't escape this room this very minute, she feared she would shatter into a million deadly pieces.

"Will we see you at supper?" She sensed rather than saw him nod, and continued. "If you will excuse me, I must attend my husband," she said, as she floated past him. There was something about this man that unnerved her. She'd envisioned him as a cold, calculating duke of the realm, and yet during this exchanged he seemed to genuinely care.

Which was utterly preposterous. A man who'd done what the Duke of Ross had done did not care one whit about anyone but himself.

Nash had never dreamed Iseabail Blair could grow into the woman before him. He'd known she would be a fiery beauty, but this? No, the passion in her eyes was enough to undo any man. Her lips were plump, a smile slightly larger than what the Ton thought of as classically beautiful ... but a man? A man could only envision the ecstasy her mouth could wring from his cock. And the glimpse of the trim turn of her ankles as the frothy swirl of her skirts fought with the speed of her movements—holy hell, if he let his imagination run wild, he'd find himself getting hard while he was attempting to come clean.

In two steps he grabbed the delicate form of her wrist and pulled her back before she could escape. "Iseabail, I …"

She whirled around as if to strike him, a move that caught him, and her, off guard. Her arm froze the moment he grasped it, her forward motion stopping of her own volition, not his and he found his hand crossed over his body gripping her other wrist. For a moment they stood there, both of them breathing heavier than what the situation warranted. He suspected the causes of their erratic gasps, however, to be entirely different. His was from the arousal he fought, hers from the anger she was attempting to control.

"Unhand me, Ross." Her demand was breathy and her chest heaved, drawing his attention to her modest décolletage.

He released her immediately. The last thing he needed to experience was a growing attraction for a woman to whom he owed so much. He cleared his throat. "I'd like to offer my sincere apologies."

"Done. The incident is all but forgotten." She turned to leave, but he stopped her once more.

"I meant for what happened eight years ago."

Her mouth fell open in pure astonishment.

He continued. "I can't possibly make amends."

"You could give me back my home."

"Our Regent has entailed it to the duchy."

A derisive snort escaped her. "Then it seems we are back to where we were. Good day, Your Grace."

He felt the insult in the honorific title as strongly as if the palm of her hand had encountered his cheek. "I'd like to sponsor your sisters."

If she'd been angry before, now she was inflamed. Her eyes lit brighter than the embers of the fire in the hearth, and her face flushed with her attempt to control her passion. He had no doubt her nails were digging into her palms as she clenched her fists at her side.

"An unmarried duke does not sponsor young *ladies*."

Bullocks. He knew that. He'd meant to say he would have a friend sponsor her sisters. "I beg your pardon. I did not mean to insult—"

"And yet you did. I believe we are both better off pretending this conversation never occurred. Don't you?" She didn't wait for his response. She quit the room like a goddess wrapped in sky-blue silk. The way her gown moved with the sway of her hips was like the caress of a lover, and this time he didn't attempt to stop her retreat. It was too glorious and magnificent to stop Iseabail Hancock, Duchess of Nithesdale, from putting a true bastard in his place.

"Bravo, Duchess," he whispered. "Bravo."

Six

My Lord Duke,

As you requested in your last correspondence, Miss Blair's appointment with the modiste, Madame Vionnet, has been postponed until a more eligible class of suitors has come of age for her hand in marriage. If circumstances change, Madame Vionnet has assured me of her availability to travel to Caerlaverock at a moment's notice.

Respectfully yours,
Mr. Joshua Forrester, Esquire

—A letter from Mr. Joshua Forrester, Barrister to Edward Charles Hancock, Duke of Nithesdale, February 1807, the month Iseabail Blair turned eighteen

"He's perfect."

"He's a rat." Doubt crowded her thoughts. Over the past several days she had observed Ross interact with the house servants and the stable hands. He acknowledged them in a manner even her husband wouldn't. As if ... they served him, but they weren't beneath him. The few members of the peerage she'd met over the years at Caerlaverock had reinforced her thoughts of the Ton believing they were above the rest of society. Yet with Ross, she couldn't say the same.

Which was utterly absurd. He evicted six girls from their home.

Lady Drake shrugged. "All the better."

Iseabail's hand shook as she reached for the decanter. "All the better for what?"

Lady Drake leaned in, her décolletage revealing entirely too much flesh as she took the decanter from Iseabail. "All the better for you to seduce."

"I won't."

"You must."

"I can't." The Duke of Ross and Lady Drake had been at Caerlaverock for almost a week, and Iseabail found dinner to be the worst part of her day. His presence tied her in knots.

"Why not?"

"We have history," she hissed.

Lady Drake looked at her as if seeing her in an entirely new light. "Then as I said, he's perfect."

"Not *that* kind of history."

"History is history my dear. It matters not what kind."

She took the glass Lady Drake offered as her maid added the finishing touches to her hair and left the room. Iseabail needed fortification to get through this disaster without throttling one or both Lady Drake and Ross. Lady Drake arched a brow without a word.

"I wouldn't be here if he hadn't *stolen* my family home when my father died." She downed the contents of her glass. Thank goodness Lady Drake hadn't filled it. The amber liquid burned all the way down, and Iseabail had to cover her mouth with the back of her hand in order not to sputter the vile drink.

Lady Drake rested her hand on Iseabail's arm. "As I said, he's perfect. There's no better way to exact revenge on a member of the Ton who did you such a disservice than to have their bastard be raised as one of the highest members of society. Even Nithesdale approves."

Nithesdale approved? What mad world was this?

"Accept what fate has determined," Lady Drake continued. "No one else will visit Caerlaverock while the Duke is in his sickbed. It isn't done. Nor will they come pay respects after his death ... they'll send their regards through the post. Ross is the only man who will step into this house, other than a servant. This is your one chance to get with child, and Ross is the perfect man for the job."

If Lady Drake said 'perfect' one more time, Iseabail might hit her. Her father had taught her how to throw a punch—how hard could it be to use that skill on the porcelain features of a lady?

She shook her head and desperately suggested an alternative. "Mr. Forrester."

Lady Drake's wane smile invited attack. "No, my dear. Mr. Forrester has too much honour. He will not bed you while your estate pays his salary."

"I don't even—I wouldn't know how to begin?"

"Take him for a stroll in the garden. Given the opportunity, any man will take the reins and do the rest."

This could not be happening. She was plotting her ruination with her husband's mistress to have a bastard child with the one man she despised with every part of her soul.

"When?" Surely that wasn't her voice asking that scandalous question.

Lady Drake grinned triumphantly. Iseabail's fist clenched. "After he finishes his brandy. I've found two glasses are enough to loosen a man's starch without affecting the stiffness of his shaft."

Good Lord. Iseabail was certain she couldn't repeat *that* in polite company—if polite company actually existed in the world of peers. She suspected it did not. She understood why men disappeared into their studies to drink brandy. It had taken one-and-a-half glasses of the vile liquor to gain the courage to do what she must to save her sisters. Brandy made one brave, because without it, she would crumple into a heap on the floor.

Anything to save Caillen, Máira, Ailsa, Edeen, and Robina.

She repeated the mantra over and over as she looked out the window. Dressed in another gown by the famous modiste, Madame Vionnet, it was part of the daring ensemble Nithesdale and Lady Drake had insisted she obtain after her wedding. Iseabail glanced down at her décolletage. It was plumped and exposed in the manner Madame Vionnet demanded of her creations.

Iseabail moved to the full-length mirror and gazed at the woman she no longer recognized. The fine-spun muslin clung in ways it shouldn't, due to wearing it without the layer of petticoats beneath. A layer Madame Vionnet had insisted Iseabail omit from her wardrobe when she wore one of her creations. Iseabail cringed as Lady Drake began to dampen her gown to ensure Iseabail's nipples were desperately hard and flaunting her femininity. It was like standing naked in the middle of a stage. It was humiliating.

"Chin up, Your Grace. You are a seductress. You must carry yourself as though every man in the house is unworthy of your affection—all except one."

She couldn't agree more, although she imagined the gentleman in question to be a mister, and not a duke. Sadly, Mr. Forrester was off limits. It seemed she was doomed to choose between two dukes —one on his deathbed, and the other—a rake of the worst sort.

Perhaps she could seduce a stable hand ...

No, of course she couldn't.

There was that one footman, Louis ... who still stared at her with lechery in his eyes, but she couldn't possibly approach him, the man scared her half to death. She was truly stuck with the Duke of Ross, because despite having spent part of every night since her wedding in her husband's bedchamber, there was no child in her womb, of that she was certain.

"We do what we must for our families," Lady Drake whispered.

Iseabail took a fortifying breath. "Yes, anything and everything is worth giving my sisters a true chance at love."

Her lack of hope for that kind of relationship for herself went unspoken. Her future was stacked in the somber stones of the great hall. Lonely, cold, silent. In reality, the hall, like her heart, was a complete waste of space. Only the thought of all her sisters laughing and dancing around the grand space made a smile form on her lips. They would have adored a ball at Caerlaverock. Granted, the nude statue in the center of the space would have to be draped with a gown, but she could imagine what a treasure it would be to raise her own children at Caerlaverock. The laughter and joy would echo through the castle, just as it had at Urquhart.

Instead, she would have to settle for one child and pray her sisters would bring their children to visit them. It was the only hope she had to fill the gloomy castle with the joyous sounds of children at play.

She and Lady Drake descended the stairs, and as luck would have it, Louis was the footman standing at the entrance to the drawing room. Despite not meeting his gaze, she knew his eyes roved where they shouldn't, and for once she accepted his insolence as a blessing. He was the perfect person to practice giving a haughty glare. It was time to take command of her own future.

She turned, tilted her chin upward and delivered a scathing look, with as much distain as the most seasoned dowager. The bobble of his pronounced Adam's apple as he gulped down his discomfort was the victory she needed to fortify her courage. Louis swung open the door and she entered with Lady Drake on her heels.

Her gaze traveled across the room to where the Duke of Ross stood with one arm leaning against the fireplace mantel as he stared down at the tawny liquor in his crystal tumbler. The firelight glistened off his ebony hair, and she had to remind herself to breathe. He lifted his glass to his mouth and froze when he caught sight of her. Something flickered in the depths of his eyes that she couldn't quite identify until his scrutiny traveled the length of her. It was the same perusal the footman Louis had given her, but with the Duke's lusty examination, heat traveled through her body as if it were his touch, not his gaze, to caress her.

His mere presence had always made her nerves jump. His attention at that moment, however, made her body tingle in places she never thought possible from a mere look. Especially when his admiration snagged on her nipples making them ache almost painfully. She wasn't sure what he'd aroused in her, but she didn't like it, and she refused to display such a weakness to this man who had stolen her future out from underneath her. She lifted her chin a notch higher.

"Remember, you have to seduce him, not give him the cut direct," Lady Drake whispered in her ear. "Walk over and take his drink from his hand and take a sip while gazing at him over the rim of the glass … and don't forget to sway your hips."

Iseabail nearly tripped over her own feet with the reminder of just how corrupted she had become. She recovered in time to do her duty and put one foot directly in front of the other, the way Madame Vionnet had shown her, to display her figure and gown in the most advantageous fashion. She was rewarded when his regard roamed every curve and jointure of her body. He slowly took in her form like a hungry beast.

He bowed deeply as she approached and she returned the polite gesture with a curtsey. A curtsey which gave him an even more daring view of her décolletage.

"You look ravishing, Duchess."

"Thank you, Your Grace."

The Duke began to look past her toward Lady Drake and she took the opportunity to relieve him of his glass. Her bold action had the desired effect of bringing his attention back to her, and she reveled in her small victory. The intensity that smoldered in his eyes ignited the heat coursing through her body, as she ran her finger around the rim before dipping it into the glass. The amber liquor was colder than she expected, the exact opposite of the liquid fire heating her core.

Bolstered by the way his gaze followed her index finger, she brought it to her mouth and slowly, luxuriously wrapped her lips around it. Taking it all the way into her mouth, she let her tongue caress the length of it. His eyes darkened like a gale-force storm crashing into the shores as she pulled it back out and let her lips pop over the tip.

He froze. His body tight and tense as if he would pounce on her any moment.

She sipped the rich, bold Scotch, suffering none of the earlier effects from her first two drinks. Licking her lips, she was once again rewarded by the way her actions seemed to mesmerize her prey, because he was her prey whether he realized it or not. Were all men this easy to lure into an illicit affair?

"Your Grace, dinner won't be served for another hour, would you care for a tour of our gardens?" Her voice sounded full and raspy to her ears, as if she were hearing someone else offer the invitation.

"I would be honoured, Duchess."

Iseabail rang for Paddington who immediately brought their cloaks, and she couldn't help but wonder if he had been aware of the plan to lure the Duke into the garden.

"I hope you don't mind if I stay behind and wait for Mr. Forrester. I find the chilly winter air more than I can bear in my advanced years," Lady Drake smiled the grin of a demure lady of the Ton well past her prime.

Her advanced years? Surely, Phoebe could make up a better excuse than that. She couldn't be more than thirty. "Of course, Lady Drake."

The Duke bowed his head in deference to Lady Drake and held out his arm for Iseabail. A moment later, she found herself walking on the arm of her biggest foe in a winter wonderland, as snowflakes swirled around them and her heart galloped across an icy landscape.

Although, in all honesty, she wasn't sure if her heart was frozen, or it was her dampened breasts radiating the cold. Why hadn't she asked him to take her for a turn around the great hall, where her dress could do the seduction for her? At the moment, all Madame Vionnet's wet handy work was doing was causing a chill to course through her body.

He turned her direction when she shivered. "Is it too cold, Duchess?"

"No." Despite her clipped response, the whole-body shudder that traveled through her form caused him to stop at the entrance of her favorite place in the garden, a maze trimmed and sculpted to challenge the beauty of any of the royal gardens with its lush shrubbery. The copse of trees on the opposite side of the moat served as a contrast in its unadulterated wild abandon.

"Do you see the forest on the other side of the moat?" she asked, to keep him from turning back toward the castle.

"Yes, it's quite thick. I used to play there as a boy."

She glanced up and was caught off guard by her attraction to the darkly handsome man at her side. He was taller and much broader than most men of the Ton. He reminded her of the tales her father told of the fierce Gallowglass warriors from western Scotland. She supposed the comparison came to mind because she knew of his ruthlessness better than most. "I find it hard to picture you as a boy running carefree through these woods. I think suited in armor would be more appropriate, with your dark hair curled around the edge of a helmet that protected your Romanesque nose from your enemies." She felt the muscles of his forearm tighten under her fingers. "I have no doubt you could swing a heavy sword, a battle ax, or claymore with ease to dominate any field of battle ..." She turned to see him studying her lips as she spoke before he laughed in mocking self-deprecation.

"I wasn't big enough to storm a room, let alone a castle the size of Caerlaverock."

"I have no doubt you've learned to conquer much more as a man." The coy smile on her lips almost felt genuine as she thought of him overthrowing the castle and subjugating a woman's body with his steel form. The thought shouldn't enthrall her—except it did. She blinked up at him, as he studied her face before choosing to laugh at her flirtation.

He escaped her flirtation by looking up at the snowflakes beginning to fall. "A boy fantasizes about playing the hero on a daily basis."

"Let me guess—you fancied yourself as quite the huntsman," she teased, and batted her eyelashes.

"The innocent creatures of the forests were safe from me."

"What about the innocent creatures in the garden?" she asked. He searched her face looking for the true meaning behind her question, and she had to bite the inside of her cheek to keep from blurting out, *Yes, the young debutantes who have no idea what kind of devil lies beneath your armor of civility.*

"I do not see an innocent creature in the vicinity." His tone was hard and brash.

Blast it. She had provoked his ire, not his desire, and her own temper stirred at the rebuke she was forced to ignore. She had to do something to entice the rumble back into his voice, the masculine growl that had the ability to make her quiver. It was either that, or their mutual disdain would burn the garden to the ground.

"No, you don't." *You tossed all six of them to the wind.* "Yet there is still game to hunt, and according to the scandal sheets, you like the pursuit."

The rags had reported story after story of different widows Ross had chosen as his latest lover. He was a paragon of the type of rakes society adored. He didn't ruin the virginal—he quenched his thirst for women in the beds of lonely widows. A veritable man among men who provided services to needy women.

And she was a needy woman. *Save Caillen, Máira, Ailsa, Edeen, and Robina.*

She donned her own armor and smiled coquettishly up into his deep blue eyes. On any other man those eyes would be intoxicating, and the fact that she thought that sent fear skittering through her veins. They entered the maze and she paused, her back to shrubbery taller than the Duke by at least a head.

"Are my affaires of particular interest to you, Duchess?" There was a tick in his jaw and she suddenly realized he didn't like calling her Duchess. Perhaps he viewed her as a climber like her father, and if that were the case, she was more determined than ever to get what she came for.

Oh, but she would enjoy bringing this man to his knees. "As I'm sure you are aware, I have not had the pleasure of knowing a man like you—so young, strong, and virile." She forced her hand to his chest and despite her gloves and his coat, she could feel the heat radiating off him. She stepped forward, unable to stop her gaze from dropping to his lips. They were plump but strong, commanding. The type of lips a woman would like on her body.

That, however, was neither here nor there. She had need of this man, and as much as the idea of bedding him made her skin tingle in a manner she was unaccustomed to, she needed to regain what he had taken. The act between them would merely be her exacting revenge: An eye for an eye.

~

She was every bit the hellfire he knew she'd grow into, and more. The melancholy he'd seen in the depths of her eyes over the past several days was absent when she'd appeared wearing a gown that could have been worn by the best Parisian courtesans. It was as if the young woman full of misery and despair never existed. The lace across her breasts allowed the hint of her dusty pink areolas to show, while her nipples pebbled delectably underneath. It'd taken every bit of his control not to get a cockstand, yet still he wasn't sure a swim in one of the two moats surrounding the castle would calm his desire—perhaps a break to take himself in hand would work.

As if his struggle hadn't been hard enough by the vision of her in that gown, witnessing the sway of her hips, and the way her lips wrapped around her finger had sent his imagination to a scene that would scandalize most ladies of the Ton. Her lips were made to be wrapped around a man's cock—his cock.

This seductress was no innocent—any man with a pulse would end up ensnared in the promise of pleasure her jade green eyes delivered. Gone was the anger, the fuel to her fire, only to be replaced by passion that simmered to a boil. It was there in her manner, her dress, the fluid movements of her body. How Nithesdale had seen *this* in the girl she had been, he did not know, and just thinking of the way Nithesdale had corrupted his young ward made his own temper churn—

Until they'd strolled in the garden and her hand touched his chest. At that moment all his resolve to ignore the attraction he'd felt towards Nithesdale's duchess disappeared. He was powerless to resist her allure. All thought disappeared as he looked down at her now with her mantle gaping open to expose the delectable flesh of her body. But it was when her lithe form pressed into his and he felt the tremor of her desire run flush against him that all decorum was lost. It was almost as if she stumbled, or perhaps threw herself at him and he raised his hands to her waist to steady her.

It was the opposite of what he should have done. He should

have push her away. Even now he should step back, but he found himself as trapped as a fox surrounded by hounds—unable to climb the shrubbery at his back, incapable of disappearing into its midst, and thoroughly frozen in place. It wasn't fear of the hunter, but something else just as unacceptable blocking his escape—lust. He was stuck in time—waiting, anticipating. Wanting it to be over, yet frantic for it to begin.

When her lips touched his. It wasn't the practiced kiss of a whore, but rather the fresh, vibrant, new dawning of a yearning he'd never experienced ... and God help him, but he succumbed to the allure. Her body molded to his and when his tongue slipped through her lips, it was pure ecstasy. She tasted of whisky and mint and feminine temptation that made him crave her even more. Never had he tasted anything like her as their tongues entwined erotically like that of the dancers he'd seen in India—rhythmic and free, with her hips perfectly molding into his. The control he'd held in check since the moment he'd first seen her at Caerlaverock disappeared on the wind.

He pulled her tighter, loving the way his cock reached for her belly. Never had he felt so instantly aroused, so alive as he was with this woman in his arms. Every part of him wanted to claim her, own her. Something feral came alive inside him the moment they touched, and he couldn't stop it if he wanted to. His hands slid down her backside and his fingers sank into the round, soft globes.

Iseabail gasped as he lifted her against him, forcing her gown up her legs and onto her thighs. "Wrap your legs around me," he ordered, the need in him too great as his lips crashed down upon hers once more.

Yet still, it wasn't enough. He pulled her closer, grinding his cock into her soft womanly center while extracting a deep moan from her throat. It was a sexual call to arms no man could ignore. He moved his lips down her jaw to her neck and nuzzled her cloak to the side in search of those breasts she'd displayed so enticingly. The soft silk of her skin tasted like pure sin. He was thoroughly lost in the moment—until he reached her décolletage and felt the chill of the crisp winter air saturating her body. The wet lace of her gown, dampened as a temptation no man could ignore, was like a slap in the face, and he nearly dropped her right there.

He pulled back and looked at the sensual creature in his arms. Her head thrown back exposing the evidence of his whiskers on her neck and delicate collarbone. Her neatly coifed mahogany curls falling from their carefully placed pins, her swollen lips parted in rapture. His fingers clasped her legs above her stockings and his thumb found a ridged imperfection of a scar across the backside of her bare thigh. A scar he had no right to explore, no right to know existed.

What had he done? He was in the gardens of the man who had shown him more fatherly guidance than the man who'd been responsible for his upbringing. Iseabail was a married woman, and since the day his own father had told him he was his mother's bastard, he had vowed to never put his seed in a married woman. He would not sire a child to be raised by any man, and he certainly would not place his own son in the ducal seat of another.

Her body stiffened in his arms and her eyes opened to reveal just how lost she had been in the moment. He lowered her to the ground as she watched him carefully, a shroud dousing out the flame of desire in her eyes. He pulled her mantle closed and stepped away.

"You are better than this," he said, and bowed before her. "I know I am." Then he turned and walked away, leaving behind the fiery ice queen who would now haunt his dreams more than ever before, but in a very different manner.

$\mathcal{S}$even

Dear Lady Drake,

 I find myself in need of your assistance with my young ward. I must ask you to travel to Caerlaverock several times throughout the year. I regret the further damage to your reputation this may cause, but I see no other way without exposing the girls to more scandal.

 Yours, Nithesdale

 —A letter from Edward Charles Hancock, Duke of Nithesdale, to Lady Phoebe Drake, March 1808

$\mathcal{S}$omething vile and foreign had taken over her body, and if she did not leave this room, she would heave the contents of her stomach onto the vast table where her three guests sat. She'd heard stories of men and women deep in their cups acting as though the boundaries of society did not apply to them, only to become violently ill for all to see. She was suffering those effects. Her stomach churned and her pulse beat erratically. She had to leave this farce of a dinner before she embarrassed herself further.

The polite conversation between Mr. Forrester, a man she admired, and Ross, a man who'd lowered her to a new level, was more than she could bear. The topics had ranged from a bill in the House of Lords, to shipping and last year's crops. She kept waiting for the Duke to ruin Mr. Forrester's kind regard of her, yet nothing about what had occurred between the two of them came up in conversation. In fact, the discussion was rather boring, which frayed her nerves even more.

How could he speak as if nothing had occurred between them? The way his mouth had burned a trail of lust across her flesh. The way her body betrayed her heart and had been willing to do anything the man desired. She still couldn't believe that had been her in his arms.

Dear God in Heaven, she had sunk beneath anything she could recognize in herself.

She brought her napkin to her mouth and pressed the despicable words threatening to spew forth from her lips back down where they belonged. Her parents had raised her better. She should follow their path and escape to the Highlands, except she had no haven to escape to. Her father had purchased Urquhart and eloped with his bride when her grandparents attempted to marry her mother to a nobleman twice her age. The Ton had turned their backs on her parents. Her father was a mere man of trade, and yet her mother hadn't cared. She'd found a man who loved her as much as she'd loved him, and unlike the peerage, who only celebrated the birth of an heir, her parents gloried in the birth of each of their six daughters. Their castle truly was their home. They had everything that made them happy.

And *he'd* destroyed it all when he'd stolen their home.

"My dear, is everything all right?" Lady Drake asked discretely.

"I ... I seem to be suffering from the effects of a megrim." She was, wasn't she? Nothing else could explain the pounding in her temple, or the way her mind traveled back in time and out of her body to peer down at herself at the moment in the gardens when she'd wrapped her legs around his waist as she shamelessly reveled in the feel of his manhood against her center. She was married, and she had attempted to seduce another man.

She was a scandal neither her mother nor father would recognize, nor would they condone her actions—no matter what the cause.

"My mother suffered from megrims." Mr. Forrester looked at her with such concern she wanted to cry. He was a true gentleman. "She found a dark room and a cold compress on her forehead were the only remedies to give her relief."

Forrester was the man she should have married, not the Duke of Nithesdale, and yet if Mr. Forrester knew how far she'd lowered herself, she would be ruined in his eyes as well.

"My grandmother had her lady's maid mix a poultice that was spread on a cloth then bound to her forehead." Lady Drake tapped her lip with her spoon in a most unladylike fashion as she appeared to sift through her memories. The action caught Ross's attention and his eyebrow quirked, but he did not comment as he continued to eat his soup. "I believe it consisted of leeks, flour, and ..." She pondered for a moment. "... earthworms!" The last word burst through her lips with an exuberance that would have made Iseabail laugh, if she wasn't so miserable.

"It is a true sign of a duchess, to suffer from megrims," the Duke interjected. "Although some physicians are inclined to say only martyrs suffer from the ailment." He casually brought another spoonful of soup to his mouth as if he hadn't just insulted her.

Iseabail wasn't certain if it was the volume of Lady Drake's voice, the thought of earthworms on her head, or the way Ross stared at her with neither concern nor disdain that drove her to her feet. "If you'll excuse me," she said, and quit the room without a backward glance.

She heard two chairs slide across the stone floor and was certain it was Mr. Forrester and the Duke attempting to be polite, but she found she didn't care. She could not have casual dinner conversation after what had happened less than an hour earlier. Instead, she ran across the great hall and up the stairs to her bedchamber. Once she was behind her closed door with the only sound being that of the fire crackling in the hearth, she finally felt like she could breathe. The pretense of being a duchess, and a true wanton, while hosting a dinner was too much to bear.

A faint tap on the adjoining door to her husband's bedchamber made her jump. She stared at it for a moment, reluctant to give up her seclusion.

"My dear, it's your husband," a weak masculine voice said from the other side of the ornately carved panel.

Her husband? What was he doing out of bed? *How* was he out of bed?

She ran to the door and opened it. Nithesdale was leaning against the door jamb as if he visited her room every evening in his night shirt. This, however, was the very first time their roles were reversed, and she couldn't help but notice the quiver in his legs.

"Your Grace, please come in and have a seat." With his feet bare, she had no doubt her husband would want to raise his chilled limbs to the fire for warmth. She hoped her suggestion kept him from her bed, this room had become her only place of refuge away from the prying eyes of the servants ... and the rest of the household.

"The ravishing will come later, my dear." The Duke winked as he took her arm and she assisted him across the room. Once he was seated, she grabbed the extra blanket from the foot of her bed and laid it over his lap and tucked it under his legs. He smiled at her nursemaid tendencies.

There was a day when his comment would have sent a blush to her cheeks, those days seemed to have been a lifetime ago. "You look very well, Your Grace." He did. Her husband hadn't left his room in weeks and today he was seated in her room.

"After the intimacies we've shared, my dear Iseabail, I would hope you would feel comfortable with me by now."

She stared at him, his words making little sense to her muddled brain. "I ... I ..."

He smiled. "Nithesdale, my dear. Call me Nithesdale."

His smile faded, however, as his gaze fell on the only painting in her pastel blue room. A deep, unending pain crossed his face. When she'd first walked into the room a month earlier, she'd been shocked by the seductive painting of a nude woman looking over her shoulder as her raven-black curls gracefully fell to the sheet around her waist. There was no escaping the love burning in her blue eyes. Whoever this woman was, she had loved with all her heart the man she was peering at.

"Who was she?" she asked, because despite her inquiries to the staff, not one person had been able to answer her question. She suspected the Duke was the only one in the household to know the mystery woman's identity.

He didn't turn away from the portrait as he gazed at the face with a longing she'd never witnessed before. It was as if the woman had captured her husband's heart and taken it into the painting with her, never to release it again. For the first time, Iseabail felt as if she was the one intruding on *his* privacy, not the other way around.

"She was to be my duchess," he whispered, his unshed tears making her even more uncomfortable. His grief made her want to change the subject, but the Duke seemed to need this moment. "Emmaline was the toast of the Ton from the moment she descended the stairs at her very first ball. Every toff in London wanted her hand. She was intoxicating. When she walked into a room, men were instantly mesmerized. She had more grace on the dance floor than all the other debutantes combined, and her smile ..." The memory brought a sad expression to his face. "It truly was glorious. The brightest chandeliers in the Palace of Holyroodhouse couldn't hold a candle to her spark."

Iseabail had never been inside the royal palace, but she'd seen it from the window of her family's carriage on the one trip they'd taken to Edinburgh, before her parents had died. The grand home of the royal family had been so much more imposing than Caerlaverock or Urquhart.

"Somehow, I became the lucky one out of all of the gentlemen vying for Emmaline's attention ... and we fell in love." The reverence in his voice was nearly heartbreaking. Her husband, a man with a reputation vaster than all of Scotland and Britain for his wild spirit and countless paramours, had loved and lost.

She sat down at his feet and laid her head upon his lap. Listening to him speak of his love while it was obvious that his heart had been broken beyond repair, brought out a tenderness for him she'd never felt before. She couldn't stop the question from spilling from her lips. "What happened?" It was rude and possibly cruel, but she had to know how a love like that could die an early death. She'd seen how her mother's premature death had destroyed her father, and she couldn't help but wonder if love was worth the risk of the destruction it wrought.

"She didn't have a shilling to her name."

She looked up then and watched as a tear spilled down Nithesdale's cheek, his gaze never leaving the portrait of his affection. He swiped the tear away and cleared his throat. "My father threatened to disown me if I didn't choose a woman with a sizable dowry. He had run the estate into the ground with bad investment after bad investment."

His voice grew wistful. "I didn't care. We were in love, and Emmaline was going to be my bride." Nithesdale cleared his throat. "I was in London for the Season when I received word that my father had been injured in a carriage accident and I should return to Caerlaverock at once. I came home, and while I was away, a rogue who had just returned from a tour of the Continent compromised Emmaline in the eyes of the Ton. I wasn't there to protect her."

"Compromised her?" If anything, Iseabail thought sitting for a nude portrait would ruin a young lady in the eyes of the Ton. Fearful that her skepticism would show, she laid her head back on her husband's lap and took comfort in the way his hand brushed through her hair. It wasn't erotic or vulgar, but rather the most loving thing he'd ever done, and she suspected he was thinking of another woman.

"He kissed her at the annual charity ball at Buckingham Palace. I suspect he planned it with Prince George himself. It was our Regent who found them and made the spectacle."

"She betrayed you." Her voice was full of indignation for her husband.

"No, she did not. It was I who betrayed her."

She met his gaze and instead of pain in his shadowed blue eyes, she saw a deep shame.

"I wasn't there when the scandal unfurled, but I believed the story I was told. The commotion caused a stir in the ballroom, and most of our acquaintances witnessed the fallout. What was relayed to me nearly tore my heart from my chest. Emmaline's dress was in disarray, her attacker was beaming like the champion of a pugilist match when he announced to all who were present that my Emmaline had accepted his suit and they would be wed within the fortnight."

She gasped on his behalf. To have lost the love of his life in such a manner was unconscionable. Nithesdale smiled and shook his head.

"Don't feel sorry for me, my dear. Emmaline tried to tell me the truth of the matter, but I turned my back on her. I was too proud to listen to the woman I claimed to love. I didn't know her betrothed all that well, but what I did know was that he was vastly wealthy. I let my feelings of inadequacy rule my thoughts. No one was aware of our relationship, and when the opportunity presented itself for the scoundrel to steal society's darling, the man took it. He forced his kisses upon her when an audience was imminent. Her gown was in a shambles, not because of her wanton behavior, but because of how hard she fought him from kissing her.

"After their marriage, I learned the truth of the matter, but she would no longer accept my correspondence, nor would she grant me an audience."

Iseabail began to protest in his defense, but Nithesdale soothed her and continued. "I tried again after her husband died, and she was a widow. I wanted to make amends. After all those years, Emmaline still held my heart. My betrayal, however, was too grave. Emmaline had long ago closed her heart to forgiving me, and him."

Tears fell down her face at the thought of such a tragedy ... it was unbearable. Pride and vanity had kept them apart, and for what? So that they could both be miserable in their own little corner of the world? What was wrong with the people of the Ton when pride stopped them from having the only thing that mattered in life—an undying love shared between two people that could blossom into so much more?

He smiled down at her and she realized she was probably the only person alive who knew the story of their lost love in the name of pride and honour. "Where is she now?" She asked.

"London. Living out her days alone."

"She has no children?"

"She bore him an heir, but he refused to let her take part in the child's up-bringing, and by the time he died, his heir believed she deserted him."

Iseabail gasped and looked up at the portrait of the happy woman whose entire life had been manipulated by a man who hadn't a care for her heart or her soul. In many ways she was walking in the same footsteps as Emmaline, yet Iseabail's husband was trying to do right by her, despite his unconventional tactics.

"Why did you marry me instead of setting me up with a dowry?"

His smile was kind, and in some way, it made her feel the same way she had the first time he'd invited her to play chess as a young girl. "Do you know what happens to young women with large dowries?"

"They receive many offers of marriage."

"True," he said, "But not all of the men making offers would be worthy of you or your sisters." Nithesdale pointed toward the chess board she'd set up in her room in the hopes that he would want a match in the near future. It seemed her wish was about to come true. She smiled and felt the warmth she always did when they met over a game filled with cunning and strategy. It was the only time when she could be herself in front of another human being.

"I hardly think a mere Miss, especially one labeled a bastard, can be choosey." She picked up the game board and moved it onto the ottoman.

They set up the board, the loser of their previous match receiving the lucky color for their current match. Nithesdale moved his black pawn to the D5 position.

"I see you choose to expose your queen."

Nithesdale waggled his eyebrows. "An exposed Queen always gets lucky."

She laughed at his debauchery and the sudden marital warmth that was developing between them. "You should have invited me to play more often."

His smile dimmed. "You were too young, and I had no desire to corrupt a child, but there are men who would take advantage of any girl or young woman who possesses the least bit of vulnerability."

She refused his bait and moved her knight to F3. "And you think I would be vulnerable because of my parentage if I had been granted a large dowry?"

"I do." He moved his pawn to C5, and she countered with her pawn to E3.

"But as your duchess, no one will take advantage of me?"

"They will attempt to take advantage of the duchy, but Mr. Forrester will prevent it." He moved his knight to C6.

"Why didn't you just marry me off to Mr. Forrester?" She played it safe with her pawn going head-to-head with his at D4. He shook his head and grinned at her perceived error, then took her pawn with his from C5 to D4. She frowned at the move, but refused to show any weakness, and in turn took his pawn with her own.

"Are you fond of Mr. Forrester?" He moved his bishop to her side of the board.

She countered with her pawn up one at C3 and looked at him through her lashes wondering if she heard a hint of jealousy in Nithesdale's tone. "He's kind, intelligent, and has good manners."

"You're describing a mount." He quickly moved his queen diagonally one space.

She grinned. "Isn't that the point, husband?" She made a play he wouldn't expect, and moved her knight along the edge to A3 and put his queen in jeopardy.

Nithesdale looked up with such warmth in his deep blue eyes that for a moment she could see the virility of the man he was when he was half his age. Strong, passionate, caring. Nithesdale cared for her, of that she had no doubt. In the years she had lived at Caerlaverock, she had always been uncertain of her standing in the household. At this moment, however, she knew she was his duchess through and through.

"A mount is not someone you want in your bed for years, but rather for a quick romp in the hay." He challenged with his pawn and exposed his king even further. She had forced his hand with her knight and had his queen on the retreat, then she moved her pawn on the opposite side of the board at G3 one slot, to face off with his bishop.

"Isn't that what you enjoy most?" She asked.

He glanced at the painting on the wall. "No, but I'm afraid

you will have to endure a few romps to inherit my kingdom and secure your future, and that of your sisters as well." Her husband countered with a move she hadn't expected with a pawn, and she matched it with one of her own.

"Most women expect that out of marriage." She could hear the jaded tone of her voice and shrugged when her husband eyed her.

"I suppose you're right, but if I had given you the dowry you deserve, there are men who would use force to compromise you for such funds." Her eyes widened and she thought of the way the footman, Louis, followed her from room to room. "By the look in your eyes, I suspect I have not protected you as well as I should have over the years."

She shook her head. "No, that's not true. It's just that I ... I know what it is like to have men think poorly of me—as if despite their lower station, I am beneath them."

Nithesdale frowned. "Someone in my household?"

She shook her head and reached over to pat his hand. "It's nothing, Nithesdale, really. Just the insecurities of a young girl coming out."

"Tell me, Iseabail. If a man of lower station looks upon a duchess poorly, what do you think he might do to a scullery maid?"

For a moment she couldn't breathe, because she had seen a few members of the female staff walk quickly in the opposite direction of Louis, the footman who sent shivers up her spine. Had he behaved in such a manner that would cause them harm? Had her silence hurt other women in the household? "I ... I can't imagine."

"Unfortunately, I can." Nithesdale growled. "On the morrow, I want you to give his name to Mr. Forrester. He will see the man gone."

"But I don't know if he's guilty of anything—"

"He's guilty of treating my duchess as if she were a common whore, and if he is comfortable doing that, he is guilty of far worse,

I am sure. On the morrow, Iseabail. I want him gone so that I know you are safe."

She smiled at that because the man was a dear. If only she had known how precious he was before now. "Of course, Nithesdale. I will speak with Mr. Forrester."

He grinned and looked down at the board and retreated one position with his bishop to H5, opening the door to the opportunity she sought. With a few sacrificial moves she put him into a position where he could not move without giving up his king and queen altogether.

"Are you admitting defeat, Your Grace?" she asked with a coy smile on her face. She couldn't remember a match she'd enjoyed more.

"You have improved your game tremendously, and my king bows to yours in defeat." He tipped over his king. "What I would like for you to take from this, however, is more than the joy of victory."

Her brow furrowed. "What else is there?"

"The knowledge that if a king leaves his queen vulnerable, he leaves himself vulnerable as well. I refuse to leave my queen with her back against the wall. She will have the power of my kingdom behind her when I am gone." With his strategy exposed, Nithesdale pushed from his chair with more power than she had seen in over a month. He bent down, kissed her on the forehead, and turned toward his bedchamber.

"I hope to see you and Lady Drake in a few hours, my dear."

"Of course, Nithesdale." She stared at the carved wooden door well after her husband closed it. She hadn't dominated the game after all ... but she had won something far greater when she married her husband, because her victory on the board was nothing compared to being championed by a king.

Eight

My Lord Duke Nithesdale,

You will find a most unkind caricature in the gossip rags this week of my latest visit to your home, and for that I am truly sorry. I cannot erase the disgraceful image of my widow's weeds thrown up over my shoulders while seated upon your lap in the midst of your great hall. The fact that I can write about it suggests a certain depravity on my part as well.

I do hope my cousin is not harmed by our actions. An unmarried miss of ten-and-nine is at a very impressionable age, and I fear my visits to your home may have an adverse effect upon her reputation. I will await your reply before I return to Caerlaverock.

Yours,
Lady Drake

—A letter from Lady Phoebe Drake to Edward Charles Hancock, Duke of Nithesdale, January 1808

"She's a rare beauty."

Nash looked up from the book he was attempting to read in Nithesdale's study. "I beg your pardon?"

Lady Drake strode into the room, once again as if she were the duchess of this castle and not Miss Blair. Blast it. He had to stop thinking of Iseabail as a young miss. She was a duchess, and not just any duchess, she was Nithesdale's duchess. No matter how many times he told himself otherwise.

"Her Grace. She is nothing like the other ladies of the Ton."

He nearly scoffed. She was like every other lady of the Ton who was married to a man her father's age. She wanted excitement she couldn't have. She wanted to enjoy the touch of a man who wasn't hers. Plain and simply put, she wanted to live a life she never would. Yet somehow her plight meant more to him than the circumstances of all the other ladies of his acquaintance.

"No, she isn't," he replied. She wouldn't be here, if it weren't for him. "And what of you, Lady Drake?"

"Me?"

"Yes, you. Are you like other ladies of the Ton ... bitter about your lot in life? Determined to see other women as miserable as you?"

She sucked in a harsh breath. "Iseabail is a duchess. I hardly think that to be a hardship."

"Yet she is married to a man who is old enough to be her father. I'm not sure she would have accepted Nithesdale's suit without your assistance with her ruination. Has life been so unpleasant you'd wish this life on a young woman, or were you driven by your own attraction toward Iseabail?"

Blotches stained her cheeks red. "How dare you, sir!"

"It's *Your Grace* to you."

She laughed and her demeanor changed. Instead of being insulted, she appeared to actually enjoy his ire. "Yet here you sit using the Duchess's Christian name as if you were intimately acquainted."

He scowled and took a drink of his Scotch before he said something he'd regret.

"Nithesdale said you would come riding in on your white horse. Is it your intent to rescue her?" Lady Drake eyed him in a manner that led him to believe she truly did hope he'd run off with the young duchess.

Yet neither he nor Iseabail were in a position to seek the other out, regardless of what had occurred between them in the garden. No, Iseabail was forever off-limits, and that was the reason behind this obsession.

"You must help her." Lady Drake implored.

"I beg your pardon?"

"The Duchess. She will be in need of your assistance when she goes to London." Lady Drake poured a cup of tea, and Nash put up his hand in refusal when she offered it to him.

"What makes you think she will head for London?" He asked.

"Nithesdale wants her there."

He muttered a curse under his breath before asking, "Does she do everything Nithesdale wants?" His mind went to places it shouldn't.

"Yes. She is an ever-dutiful wife."

Dutiful. The images coursing through his mind were of a dutiful mistress, not a wife. Damnation. "Many wives in the Ton are dutiful. That does not mean they do everything their husbands want them to do."

"Your Grace, the Duchess of Nithesdale will carry out her husband's requests, no matter what they are—of that you can be assured." Her gaze met his straight on, and then she blushed before she turned away.

Had he imagined her embarrassment?

"I don't think you give her enough credit. Her Grace is stronger than you believe." The woman who had kissed him in the garden was bold beyond his wildest dreams. Hell, before that moment he hadn't been aware of his wildest dreams. Now he didn't seem to be able to get them out of his head.

Before she could respond, Mr. Forrester entered the room and then paused. "I hope I'm not interrupt—"

"Not at all," Lady Drake replied, before the man even finished his sentence.

An awkward silence befell the room, and it seemed the perfect time for him to escape. This hell was more than he could swallow. If Nithesdale didn't see him soon …

"I believe I will go for a ride." Nash stood up and bowed toward the woman he'd thought he'd known up until ten days ago. This creature, however, was entirely different from the demur widow to make his acquaintance in London years ago.

Lady Drake smiled. "The weather is exceptionally nice for this time of year. In fact, I believe Paddington told the stables to have your mount readied for you."

Nash's foot caught on the edge of the rug. "Excuse me?"

"The stable boy is getting your mount ready as we speak," Forrester added.

Nash went to the window. "I found that poor creature tied up in the woods and under attack by a pack of wild dogs. For the past three years, my groom and I have been the only two people on earth who could approach the beast."

That was the very last thing he wanted to hear. His horse had finally made it from the posting inn the previous afternoon, with strict instructions for his groom to be the only one to handle the stallion. Týr was not a common horse. Like his namesake, the Germanic god of war, Týr could be brutal, and the sight in front of him was the last thing he wanted to see.

"Dash it all." Nash ran for the stables. Death was knocking on more than one of the Duke's doors.

~

Gazing out across the gardens from her bedroom window was the best part of being a duchess. It was here, when her maid wasn't present, she could open the glass and absorb the tranquility of Caerlaverock. From her first day at the estate, she'd adored the landscape that was so different from the blustery winds on the Highland lochs. The salt brine of the sea was evident on the breeze. From her old room on the second level, the dense, dark-green forest had blocked her view. From the Duchess's chamber on the third floor, however, she had a view of the deep azure sea.

Her breath hitched as she caught sight of Ross racing through the garden and taking off his clothes. He was taking off his clothes.

What the devil was the man up to?

His jacket landed on a bush, his waist coat—the garden path, and his cravat—well she wasn't sure where it landed. She was too busy watching the muscles of his body tighten and flex with every long stride he took. The only items of clothing he wore were his trousers, a white lawn shirt, and boots.

The wind whipped at his shirt, making it mold to the rippling muscles across his abdomen. His defined chest put the *Farnese Hercules* to shame, and she imagined him posing in the same manner as the famous nude statue. Nithesdale had commissioned a replica to be sculpted in the garden when she was fifteen, but she'd been forbidden to enter until she was nearly eighteen, only to be disappointed by the artfully designed topiary hiding everything below Heracles's waist. She had admired the Greek god's musculature, but to date, she had never gained the nerve to peek behind the bushes. Partly out of fear that he would be vastly disappointing, but mostly because she had never seen a man of that particular form and didn't want to feed her girlhood fantasies further. At least she had not seen a torso like Heracles ... until now. She bit her lip in anticipation of the Duke exposing what the garden had not, and found herself a bit disappointed when his shirt didn't join the rest of his clothing.

The thought made her cheeks heat until the sound of an

angered horse drew her attention away from the Duke. A large black horse she'd never seen before jerked at the reins held by the youngest stablehand. Bundled in a coat too large for his small frame, Benjamin pulled on the reins as the horse tried to take control of his head. Tightening his grip, Benjamin strained and dug his heels into the ground. The Duke began to run faster toward the bold and violent horse.

Unlike her husband, most members of the Ton had no use for children getting in their way, and Iseabail knew how callously this particular Duke had treated six young orphans. Would he abuse the stablemaster's son as well?

He yelled something unintelligible from where she stood at the window, and her breath hitched. He was going to punish the boy, and she could do nothing but watch in horror.

The more Benjamin struggled, the more the horse resisted, its sable mane and tail flashing in the wind. The beast raised on his hind legs and froze, posing for anyone and everyone to admire his great beauty, strength, and devilish temper. Raven-colored hooves pawed at the air as if the hounds of hell pulled on its reins, and not the scrawny, young Benjamin. The boy lurched forward and stumbled again, before falling to the ground, directly beneath the angry hooves.

Iseabail gasped. "No!"

She watched in horror as Ross ran for the horse—she was too far away to do anything to protect the boy, too invested in his welfare to look away. Benjamin scrambled backward on his hands and feet like a petrified crab in the sand. His large brown eyes mirrored the terror in his soul. At the last moment, he raised his hands to cover his face, accepting the inevitable.

But then *he* was there. Covering Benjamin's body with his own. Ross threw his body over the top of the boy just in time to take the brutal onslaught. His arms braced on the ground as his body shook from each blow of a hoof. The horse calmed almost instantly. If she hadn't seen it, she wouldn't have believed such a change could occur in the animal. She watched as the Duke rolled off to the side and sat with his elbows hung over his knees, his head bent low between his legs. Finally, he turned his head toward Benjamin and ruffled the boy's hair, a smile breaking out on both their faces.

The Duke of Ross had ruffled the boy's hair—

—With genuine affection and a smile on his lips. Then he turned toward the horse, who'd sauntered up to him in a gesture of contrition, and the Duke rubbed the animal's nose from where he sat in the dirt. Not a breath of anger toward boy or beast.

Benjamin was the first to stand, the Duke's movements a bit slower. It was only then that she saw how badly he'd been hurt. The back of his shirt was torn and covered with streaks of mud and blood. The bare bronzed skin peeking through the shredded fabric was splashed with red, the stains growing in size on the tattered shirt.

The Duke's groom came running from the stable, and a serious conversation ensued between the three of them before Ross turned toward the house and looked up directly into her window. Their gazes held. Something tense and charged passed through her. Her body tingling in a manner it had never done before—until he tripped—over nothing. Her breath hitched as he fell to his knees and slowly got up again. He was hiding much more than Benjamin or the groom had known. Seeing that put her feet into motion.

Iseabail ran for her door and threw it open nearly barreling into her new maid. "Mary! Hurry there's been an accident near the stables. Have Mrs. Hagerty prepare her salve and get me clean water and cloths. Meet me in the drawing room and then tell the doctor the Duke of Ross needs him at once. Hurry!"

Mary didn't hesitate. She scurried down the servants' stairs, moving as fast as she could, as Iseabail hiked up her skirts and took the main stairway to the front door. "Paddington open the doors!" The butler scurried toward the door and just as she was about to run through, a large frame blocked the doorway. Iseabail slid across the floor attempting to avoid a collision, her satin slippers failing to gain purchase as Ross entered the house. She collided with his rock-hard chest. Her body pressed to his in a manner more intimate than any waltz, her heart pounding to the rhythm of a drum only a woman would understand.

Yet *she* didn't understand her reaction to this man at all. Her visceral response was undeniable as her gaze snagged on the open collar of his shirt. The dark hairs curled in a fashion she had never seen before, peeking out where the buttons lay undone. The strong sinew of masculine power evident in his clavicle that was only made more prominent by the corded muscles traveling down the column of his neck. Perhaps it was his large, strong hands gripping her biceps, pinning her body close to his.

"Your Grace, I ... I'm sorry." Her voice was soft and breathless, as if she had been the one to save a child and tame a beast while sustaining serious injury.

She stumbled backward. Brushing at her skirts and turning toward Paddington and the two footmen who looked on as if they didn't know what she could possibly do next to make this moment more awkward. It was the slight nod and knowing look from Paddington that reminded her of her station. This was her house. Her servants. Her guest.

She cleared her throat. "Your Grace, are you all right?"

His gaze bore into hers before he took a deep breath and bowed over her hand. "I must apologize for my appearance." His eyes never left hers as his lips brushed bare knuckles she'd forgotten to cover. The touch was too much. Soft and gentle, everything Ross was not. She could almost get lost in the connection between them and forget the past ...

Beyond his dark, wind-blown curls, she caught sight of the dirtied frayed shirt marred with blood as he bowed in front of her. One of the footmen gasped, his eyes glued to the Duke's back as he stepped forward. "Your Grace ... would you like the doctor?"

It was her turn to be horrified. Ross was adhering to social etiquette while standing before her needing a doctor. She gripped his hand, pulling him forward. "Please, Your Grace, you must rest. I saw ... what happened." Her gaze traveled to the smudges of dirt on broad, squared shoulders, the wrinkles spreading across the front of his shirt telling the story. He'd clutched Benjamin close to protect him from pounding hooves.

Her mind replayed the violent attack and the protective nature of the man in front of her. It was as if two different men stood before her—the villain of her childhood, and the hero who'd put his life on the line to save a young servant. "If you'll come into the drawing room, the doctor will be here shortly."

"That's not necessary. My valet can attend me."

"Is your valet a physician?" She refused to let go of his hand, but instead of allowing her to pull him into her drawing room, he guided her toward the steps she'd recently descended.

"Better."

"I doubt that."

"You doubt my word?" His brows furrowed as he took her hand and wrapped it around his forearm, the heat radiating off his muscled arm as if the dense appendage she was gripping was a heated brick. Had she ever noticed a forearm such as his? Her husband certainly didn't sport an arm of near solid proportions, and she couldn't say she'd noticed Mr. Forrester radiating such a fierce masculinity either.

"I doubt your valet has the same level of expertise as Dr. Wakefield," she said, now walking up the stairs side by side with the demon from her childhood. Could a person's character change so drastically?

She heard Mary in the entry way below. "This way, Mary." They ascended to the floor of her own bedchamber and was shocked to find Ross had been placed in the bedroom next to her own.

He stopped in front of the door. "I think Daniel can take it from here," he stated.

Something in her demanded she meet this Daniel, valet extraordinaire. "Nonsense. You are our guest. I will ensure you receive the proper care after you so valiantly saved our young Benjamin." She twisted the door handle and entered his room as if it were her own. A man with red hair the color of the sunset in fall was sitting in front of the window polishing a pair of the Duke's boots and jumped to his feet. Deep-blue eyes looked from her to the Duke.

"His Grace has been injured. The doctor is on his way."

The valet looked to the Duke for instructions, but the stubborn man only rolled his eyes before admitting, "I will need assistance removing my shirt and cleaning the wounds on my back." Then Ross took her by the arm and guided her back to the hall. He released her arm and stepped back into his room, and his valet closed the door in her face.

She should have been affronted by the move ... instead, she returned to her own room and closed the door on her tumultuous thoughts that perhaps her young self had misinterpreted. The Duke of Ross was a more complicated man than she could have dreamed.

Nine

Dearest Sisters,

I have met the most elegant lady to ever walk the earth. (Excluding Mama, of course.) Lady Drake, the Duke of Nithesdale's friend, has been the only visitor at Caerlaverock to acknowledgment my existence, other than the Duke's man of affaires, Mr. Forrester, who could hardly be called a visitor. Although I believe her to only be a handful of years older than myself, she is all that I hope to be when I have my Season. Her gowns are of the most exquisite colors you could possibly imagine, with intricate beading and lace that is simply divine—I can only compare her dresses to some of the gowns Mama held onto from her Season in Town. (How I wish we still had her trunk of mementos!)

I long to meet a man of means who will allow me to have a house full of children.

I suppose we witnessed other women of elegance during our travels to Edinburgh, but again, none of those ladies seemed to share the vibrant air Lady Drake displays. I overheard the servants telling the story of her husband leaving her in dire *straits upon his death. It seems she is yet another lady rescued by our dear benefactor, the Duke of Nithesdale.*

Truly, there must be more men of the Ton who have such warm and open hearts that the mere hint of our illegitimacy won't scare them away. Once I marry, I promise to send for you. I simply cannot wait until the day when the six of us can be together once more.

Your Loving Sister,
Iseabail

—A letter from Iseabail Blair to her Sisters Caillen, Máira, Ailsa, Edeen, and Robina Blair, May 1808

The time had finally come. Nash had been ready to challenge Nithesdale to a duel for weeks when Nithesdale sent word for him that very morning. His back was healing, but every moment he spent in Iseabail's presence was utter torture. He wanted her, and he damn well couldn't have her.

He knocked on the bedroom door that belonged to a man he'd once admired. The oversized doors hewn of alder wood opened immediately to the vast bedroom that smelled of death. His rage disappeared. The footman on the other side of the door allowed him entry then exited the room to leave them alone. Despite everything Nithesdale had done, Nash felt a pang of loss for the only father-figure he'd known.

It shouldn't end like this.

"I can see you are torn between throttling me and toasting a life well-lived," the bundle on the bed rasped. It was nothing like the strong, booming voice he'd known.

Nithesdale waved toward the empty chair next to the bed and Nash made his way across the room. "You have always been perceptive."

Nithesdale chuckled. "A blind man could read your face."

"Or maybe you would feel the same, if you were in my shoes."

"Mmmm, you have me there. I would probably call you out despite your inability to rise from this bed."

"Do you deserve it?"

"Doesn't every man deserve it at least once in his life?"

Nash thought of the kiss he'd shared with Nithesdale's wife. "Probably," he admitted.

"I suppose you want answers," Nithesdale coughed, the fluid in his lungs evident with the raspy noise that seemed to never end. The deep breaths he took after the cough proved how hard he was working to have this conversation.

When his racking breaths calmed, Nash gave him a simple reply. "Yes."

Nithesdale smiled faintly, his color more ghastly than it had been upon Nash entering the room. "I located her as you asked—"

He could not stop his temper from spiking. "I did not ask you to take advantage of her!"

Nithesdale waved off his anger as if it was inconsequential. "Nor have I."

"What of the rumors being bandied about in regard to you and Lady Drake *with* the Duchess?"

"Iseabail is my duchess. I had her brought here with the promise of a Season and found I could not give her up."

It did not pass his notice that his friend did not answer his question. "You are her father's age." He argued.

"I don't see where that is any concern of yours." Nithesdale bit back.

"I have been looking for Iseabail and her sisters for years. Why didn't you tell me you found them?"

"Blame it on the actions of a besotted old fool."

A growl rumbled in his chest. "That's not good enough."

"Maybe not, but right now, I have to do what I think is best for the woman I love and my son."

His son. Dear heavens, Iseabail was pregnant? "How do you know she's with child, or that it's a boy if she is?"

"A father knows the love in his heart. One day my son will know it as well."

Nash snorted. "My father didn't."

Nithesdale's eyes bore into his. "He did. He just couldn't show it."

Nash wasn't sure if it was his words, or the sorrow filling Nithesdale's eyes that gave him pause. "You know my real father's identity?" It was the first time Nithesdale hinted at the knowledge. After all these years, the old bastard knew, and kept it from him. What kind of game was he playing?

Nithesdale slowly shook his head, a sad smile spreading across his lips. "If your father knew of your existence, he wouldn't have been able to stay away. You've grown into a fine man. Whoever your sire, he would be lucky to know you." He patted Nash's hand as if he was the one who needed comforting at the time of his death. "Go. I find I can barely keep my eyes open."

It was true. Nithesdale's gaze was growing heavy, yet Nash paused when an unexpected tear rolled down the old man's cheek. It was as if Nithesdale knew this would be the last time they spoke. He turned his hand over and squeezed his old friend's hand. A lump forming in his throat.

"Promise me you will take care of my duchess. She will need a champion, and I need to know the woman I love and my son are well."

Nash nodded. His own emotion threatening to bubble to the surface. Regardless of what had transpired with Iseabail, Nash had a hard time reconciling it with the man he loved beyond measure.

Nithesdale's withered hand grasped his. "Promise me."

"I promise," he said, although he wasn't certain he would be able to keep that promise.

Nithesdale smiled before his eyes closed and Nash sat there and stared. He was still holding Nithesdale's hand the same way he had as a boy. The blind worship of him gone, but the love and admiration for the man still present.

And Nash wondered if he could ever live up to Nithesdale's expectations.

～

A rapid pounding on the door to her library door interrupted the letter she struggled to write. She'd found the circumstances of her wedding unbearably difficult to explain in terms her young sisters would understand without destroying their romantic views of marriage.

She turned around on the damask cushioned chair and away from her elaborately carved desk. "Come in."

The door nearly flew open as Paddington and Mrs. Hagerty stepped into the room as one. The housekeeper's eyes were filled with tears, and the stodgy butler seemed inordinately stiff, his expression pained. It was a look she'd never registered on the man's face the entire time she'd been at Caerlaverock.

Two previous times in her life, however, had prepared her for the awkwardness of this moment. They expected her to break. To wail. To let her emotions dictate her actions. She would not.

"I'm sorry Your Grace. I went to wake the Duke for his evening meal, but he apparently ..." A sob passed Mrs. Hagerty's lips and Paddington finished the sentence for her.

"His Grace passed in his sleep. The Duke of Ross was with him."

She swallowed the lump in her throat. Her husband was gone. The man who had risked society's disdain to save her ... was gone.

She should have been there when he passed, not Ross. A real duchess would have been by his side. Shock took over her world and utter panic gripped at what this meant for the future. How would she save her sisters? She was not with child, she knew that with a certainty that chilled her bones.

The happiness of her sisters was at stake. Yes, she could live in the dowager house when no babe arrived in nine months and the new Duke of Nithesdale was named. She could even be content with the lonely existence her future held in the country, with no further prospects of friendships, marriage, or children. Yet still, her hands went to her empty womb as she prayed that one day, a babe would grow inside her. How that would happen now, however, was a mystery.

She was truly a ruined duchess.

Her future would be written in stone in the family plot behind Caerlaverock with the Duke, yet somehow, she still had to secure proper marriages for her sisters. Her own scandalous marriage had hit the gossip rags, Nithesdale had made sure of that. It was the only reason the Ross had called upon them. Yet not one other person of the Ton had called upon her to express congratulations for her marriage, and she suspected their sympathy over her husband's death would be withheld as well. "Your Grace?"

She startled, so lost in her thoughts that the sight of the two servants standing in front of her waiting for a response from her caught her off guard. She stared back at them, knowing she should say—do—something.

"Y-yes?" Her voice sounded as if she had just crawled from her bed.

Paddington stepped toward her as if he might take her in his arms. Something she truly wished he'd do. Instead, a pinched look creased his lips. "Lady Drake and Mr. Forrester are waiting to see you, Your Grace."

"Of course. Do they know what my husband would expect to be done?" she asked, unsure if she wanted the gossip columns to know of Lady Drake's attendance at the time of Nithesdale's death.

"Yes, Your Grace." Paddington's expression was locked down as tight as the grate she'd found to the ancient dungeon below the castle.

Iseabail wrung her gloved hands together but lifted her chin. "And the Duke of Ross?"

"His carriage departs as we speak."

Of course it did. He was leaving without a word to her, and for that she only had herself to blame. She had failed to become pregnant by her husband or the only man available to her, and with that failure, she'd sealed her sisters' fates. Yet the loss of Nithesdale suddenly made her heart want to split in two.

She steeled herself against the overwhelming thoughts of abandonment by both men. "Very well. If you could serve Mr. Forrester and Lady Drake tea in the blue salon, I will be there shortly." Then she turned to the housekeeper and embraced the strength Nithesdale had instructed her to display. "Mrs. Hagerty, if you could have Mary dye a couple of my day dresses and one evening gown, I would be very grateful. I will also need you to send for Madame Vionnet to have mourning dresses made."

Mrs. Hagerty sniffed and dabbed at her nose as she nodded in response. "Of course, Your Grace."

That strength failed as she tried to think of what would come next. "Sh-should we call for ... for ..." Who the devil did one call at the time of death? Her father had handled her mother's arrangements, and her father had been away from home when he'd died. She had no idea who handled anything.

"The Duke's doctor is on his way, and the undertaker has been sent notice. Mr. Forrester is seeing to everything," Paddington added in a gentle tone.

She nodded as a tear began to work its way down her cheek. A sob broke free from Mrs. Hagerty as if the housekeeper could no longer hold her grief at bay, and the butler put a protective arm around her as they left the room.

Iseabail nodded as if they were still waiting for her response. Her library seemed entirely too vast at that moment, the space large enough to house an army. Once again, she stood alone. The chasm between her and the rest of the world felt enormous and uncrossable. Death had taken everything from her. Her mother. Her father. Her husband. By now she should be used to the cruelty life offered, yet once again she was alone with her grief. Alone with her sense of responsibility to her sisters' future.

She left the room and walked up the stairs to her bedroom, then stopped in front of the door to her husband's bedchamber before pushing it open. Two maids were busy brushing her husband's hair and straightening out the bedclothes where he lay. They looked up and froze.

"Leave us, please," she said, as if she was there to have a chess match with Nithesdale, not say a final goodbye. They curtsied and left the room, the only noise in the room was the quiet snick of the door closing behind them.

Gone was the rasp in his chest as her husband breathed. It was a silence she thought she would welcome, but she did not. For with the silence came the realization that Nithesdale was no longer in the room with her.

In the short time she had been duchess, she had become quite familiar with the masculine elegance of his room that now seemed like a tomb. Nithesdale lay on the bed, his hands neatly clasped across his belly. He looked almost as if he were sleeping. She knew better. Not a night had gone by without the unrhythmic sound of his snoring. She missed that sound immensely.

She approached him slowly and took in the pallor of his skin. The slackness of his jaw. The vigor and vitality no longer present on his person.

"For better or worse. In sickness and in health. Til death do us part ..."

Tears spilled down her cheeks unchecked. She'd been wrong. She felt many things for this man, but until that very moment, she couldn't have put it into words. "I love you," she whispered. Their marriage may not be what her parents had wanted for her. For that matter, it was never what she had wanted for herself, but she was one of the lucky ones. Her husband had given her hope for the future. Now she just needed to seize the opportunity and give her sisters the best chance at the happiness life had to offer—the freedom to make their own choices.

Iseabail pressed out the imaginary wrinkles in her gown with her palms, pinched her cheeks to give them color, and attempted to ascertain if the mass of russet curls stacked upon her head were still under control or not. On most days they refused to be tamed. She was certain today was no exception.

Taking a deep breath, she opened the door and made her way toward the blue salon. Her heart raced and her hands grew damp inside her gloves. Lord. She was supposed to be carrying the Duke's heir. How was she supposed to act? Should she faint? Run from the room feigning illness? How did one pretend to be pregnant when she hadn't the faintest idea how it felt to carry a child in her womb?

She stood in front of the door to the blue salon, experiencing the same sense of dread she'd felt when she stood outside the Duke's chamber the day he'd announced they would be wed. She had once dreamed of a fast-paced life that caused her heart to pound as she went from ball to ball, but now ...

How did one endure such repeated exposure to ruination? How did a fallen woman face the gossips?

Louis, the footman she despised, was staring at her. Waiting for a signal. If she met his gaze, like she had once or twice since her wedding, his eyes would be scanning her form. His lips would be moist, and he would make that noise ...

The same foulness she had been subjected to upon her arrival at Caerlaverock. He had ever *dared* to stare at the Duke? Yet she knew why Louis didn't hold her in the same regard as the other women of the Ton. Nithesdale's actions had put her on the same level as a whore in the eyes of many. Even if she was one of the highest paid whores of the nation, to some, Iseabail was damaged goods.

She lifted her chin and nodded without meeting his gaze. The horrible noise he always greeted her with filled the silence, but she refused to meet his leer. When he finally opened the doors, Mr. Forrester rose to his feet and came to her side, just as he had on every other occasion.

"At your service, Your Grace," he said with a gentle smile as he bowed.

Hearing Mr. Forrester address her as *Your Grace* made the nightmare sound so very real. "Thank you, Mr. Forrester. I must admit, I welcome a friendly face."

His smile disappeared. "Has someone treated you poorly?"

"No, no. They have been wonderful." She lied. Mrs. Hagerty and Paddington had worked tirelessly. The rest of the staff hadn't been wonderful at all. Some looked at her with disdain, while others acted as if she wasn't present. A few treated her like waste.

Mr. Forrester lowered his voice. "Do not cover for them. This is your castle now. We will replace any who do not recognize your station." He glared at the footman in the doorway.

Iseabail could imagine she heard the man gulp before the door closed and she looked up to catch that fierce expression on Mr. Forrester's face. His grey eyes were stormy, which looked very appealing with his dark features. Yet something had changed. Somehow, this man she had dreamed of saving her seemed quite incapable of rescuing her heart.

"Lady Drake and I wish to convey our deepest sympathy."

She wanted to laugh. Even now, Lady Drake was everything she once wanted to be, as she dabbed at her nose with a delicate lace-edged handkerchief, her eyes filled with sympathy and unshed tears. She was beautiful.

But somehow, knowing the ugly truth of her friend's life, she wanted to recoil from the emptiness, the hollowness that surrounded her, and the utter desolation of a widow with no purpose. Instead, she accepted the tearful embrace Lady Drake offered. She counted Lady Drake as her dear friend. How could she not, after spending her wedding night with her and Nithesdale locked behind closed doors?

She stepped back as shame began to wash over her. With their scandalous behavior known throughout the castle and town, she shouldn't fault the footman for his disdain. Members of the Ton would be even more critical of their behavior. The gentlemen would make the same noises as Louis, and she wasn't certain how would she ever endure it. Lady Drake's presence at Caerlaverock had made all the gossip rags, and would no doubt start tongues wagging once again now that Nithesdale was gone.

She confessed her fear. "I no longer have the protection of Nithesdale behind me. Even from his sickbed, his presence was an embrace no one could conquer. Yet that armor disintegrated within moments of his death." She had a sense of falling off a cliff once more. Her heart was in her throat and her legs no longer wanted to hold her.

Mr. Forrester grabbed her arm as if he thought she was going to faint. She wanted to say she wasn't a ninny, except recently she seemed to define the term. She gave him a weak smile of gratitude as he guided her to the settee, and Lady Drake began to pour tea and serve cakes as if she were the hostess. She had served for the Duke on numerous occasions in this very room. Who was Iseabail to stop her from doing it today?

Mr. Forrester seated himself in his normal seat opposite the Duke's chair. "What I'm about to say is completely inappropriate, but the Duke gave me strict orders to follow upon his death." Mr. Forrester's cheeks pinkened ever so slightly. "Is there a chance you are with child, Your Grace?"

"No." Her voice sounded like a whisper and she prayed he heard her response. The last thing she wanted to do was repeat it.

He nodded. "Then tomorrow, we will proceed as the Duke planned."

She was going to be ill.

"How do you propose we do that?" Iseabail asked. "Ross left."

Mr. Forrester rubbed his chin. "Yes, things have taken a twist for the worst."

"That's an understatement. My husband is dead and there's no babe in my womb. How do I save my sisters now?" She looked to Mr. Forrester for guidance.

Kind, considerate Mr. Forrester. He was just the sort of man she had always dreamed of marrying ... somehow, she could no longer see him in the role of husband. Why was that? Regardless, she had to push forward. "What about you, Mr. Forrester?"

Lady Drake's cup jingled on the saucer as the man in question choked on his tea and nearly sputtered in Iseabail's direction. "M-me?"

She steeled her pride. "Yes, you."

He set down his cup. "I'm afraid that's not possible."

"Why? If someone must get me with child, why can't it be someone I'm fond of?"

"I-I appreciate the offer, but I can't, Your Grace."

Iseabail threw her hands in the air. "Why not? Men do it all the time."

"Yes, Mr. Forrester, whyever not?" Lady Drake chimed in, as she nibbled on a biscuit like it was the most delicious thing she'd ever tasted.

"Because the Duke forbade it."

Iseabail blinked long and hard. "Excuse me?"

He pulled on his cravat. "The Duke did not want his heir to be of lower birth."

That didn't sound like the Nithesdale she knew. She was a bastard and he'd made her his duchess, yet what did she know of her late husband? Up until a little over a month ago, he'd been her guardian who lived in one wing of the castle while she inhabited another. He could have been as snobbish as her father said all the members of the Ton were. Only her mother had passed muster in her father's eyes when it came to the members of the peerage.

Hadn't the Duke of Ross proven to her that he saw himself as superior? He was an untouchable Duke to women like her.

"That hardly sounds like Nithesdale," Lady Drake added. "He was very fond of you." There was something in Lady Drake's gaze that made Iseabail think she was also very fond of Mr. Forrester. "However, we must honour his wishes."

Iseabail stood up to pace the room. "How do you propose we do that, considering I am to be in mourning for the next year and the only gentleman who will call upon me will be Mr. Forrester?"

Again Mr. Forrester shifted uncomfortably.

"I don't mean to distress you, Mr. Forrester, but I need to get to the heart of the matter now, rather than later. My sisters' futures are at stake."

Lady Drake took great care to ponder the solution. "I will return to Town and announce a house party at my country estate." She sipped her tea as if everything was settled, despite the shroud of sadness in the room.

"How on earth will you hosting a house party solve my problem?" Iseabail asked.

"Nithesdale always said you and I could have been sisters. In the dim lighting of a bedchamber most men would believe you are me."

"I don't understand." It seemed she wasn't the only one who couldn't make sense of Lady Drake's statement. Mr. Forrester was eyeing her with a furrowed brow.

"It's quite simple. I will seduce a man at the party ..."

Was that a growl from Mr. Forrester?

"... and you will be waiting in his chamber to finish the act. With a low firelight, he will assume it is me waiting to be ravished."

Iseabail blinked long and hard, her face scrunched in pain as if she'd been gutted by a sword. *This was not her life. This was not her life* ... and yet it was exactly what she must do.

Ten

The Comfort Ball and House Party
"Let us enjoy the pleasurable diversion of life"

Lady Phoebe Drake requests the honour of the company of
Nashford Xavier Harding, 8th Duke of Ross,
at the Comfort Ball and House Party to be held at Drake
Manor,
on the seventh of February 1811

Dearest Ross,

After our latest meeting, I have found myself thinking of you often— it is a predilection I find myself powerless to deny. With bated breath I await your response.

Phoebe

—A most personal invitation from Lady Phoebe Drake to Nashford Xavier Harding, Duke of Ross, January 1810

There was only one reason he was here ... to find her sisters. With his glass to his lips, Nash watched Lady Drake glide across the room, the sway of her hips entrancing the men in her wake. The cut of her gown a pure invitation to any man ... or woman ... or both who wanted to indulge in her curvaceous body. It was as if she were telling the entire world she was back on the market. That market, however, did not appear to be the marriage mart. No, by the coy smile she tossed at several gentleman, Lady Drake was ready to take a lucky person, or persons, to her bed.

There was a time he would have jumped at the chance. This evening, he found himself comparing her to another. A woman with very similar features who captivated him more, and if he believed Lady Drake's story, a cousin she knew rather intimately.

Lady Drake's gaze fell upon him, and for a moment he could have sworn she froze, despite her still moving in his direction. It was something about the way her eyes glistened, yet lost their light. The way her demeanor softened, yet her body stiffened. But mostly, how responsive she became to his attention, while her own desire appeared tempered. She was nervous, not excited.

She looked like a woman headed to the guillotine with the decorum of a queen in heeled slippers that were hurting her feet. How very interesting.

She stopped in front of him and he bowed, reached for her gloved hand, and brushed his lips across her knuckles. He should have been flattered by the tremor his touch inspired, except he suspected it was due more to apprehension than arousal, and he couldn't help but test his theory.

His eyes traveled up her body and held on her breasts longer than what was acceptable. "Lady Drake, you look absolutely delectable in that gown."

A blush started at her cheeks and reached the mounds of her breast he'd openly admired. Yet despite her embarrassment, she pushed through her nervous state and leaned in closer, requiring him to bend over for her to whisper in his ear. "I have found that I very much like to be a man's dessert."

Something in her gaze flickered, almost as if guilt lay behind her guileless smile.

Lady Drake was the person he needed to find the five remaining Blair sisters. He wasn't deflowering her. Corrupting her. Or taking away her innocence.

The back of his hand grazed down Lady Drake's arm, his brazen act causing her to flinch and a couple of the ladies next to them to gasp. He may as well have branded her a whore.

She took a step back and smacked his hand with her fan. "You grow too bold, Your Grace."

For a moment, he thought he'd misjudged her, then she winked and licked her lips in a practice as old as time. One she was very good at, but not quite comfortable performing. Was the gesture a newly acquired talent?

"Meet me in the garden at half past the hour," she purred. With her invitation delivered in a soft husky voice, he watched as she glided across the room to a group of ladies standing by the fire.

So that was how she wanted to approach their liaison. He would keep her at bay—for now. When he was through, however, he would have the Blair girls' location in hand.

He watched as the ladies turned in unison to gaze in his direction, their expressions full of an array of fascinating expressions. Scorn. Disdain. Ridicule ... and interest. Leave it to the ladies of the Ton to regard him with censure, at the same time relishing the diversion he could offer to their otherwise dull marriages. Nash raised his glass to let them know he deserved their disparagement, and their favor.

A rake was a rake after all.

He walked out onto the balcony and into the garden. Each step feeling as if he was sealing his fate. He ignored his lack of interest in the sexual liaison he was about to experience. He had a way of life to return to, past sins to forget, and a beautiful lady willing to be used.

What more could he ask for?

~

"I can't do it," Iseabail said to the woman who'd become her best and only friend in a matter of months.

"You must." Phoebe insisted.

"It's one thing to talk about switching places or even plan it. It's quite another to go through with it."

Phoebe shook her head in a manner that looked very much like pity. "You don't have a choice."

She didn't want pity. Iseabail held her head high. "Of course I do. I'm a duchess."

"For the next eight months, and then without an heir, all you'll have is the title and pin money."

"That will keep me in the dowager cottage with enough left over to afford a Season for my sisters."

"The amount of pin money you receive will be determined by the next Duke of Nithesdale. Mr. Jarvis does not strike me as the generous sort. It may not be enough to feed and clothe you, let alone your sisters."

Iseabail closed her eyes. She couldn't look at her image in the mirror any longer. The gown was stunning and completely unacceptable in society. How Phoebe had been able to act in that manner was ... well it was beyond Iseabail's ability to fathom, let alone carry out.

"I can't act the harlot. I can't."

Phoebe's voice softened. "We've practiced this over and over. Mr. Forrester believes you're ready. Is he the reason you can't?"

"No!"

"Are you certain?"

Iseabail smoothed down the front of her gown as she stood in

front the mirror. For the past fortnight she'd practiced her flirta-
tions with Mr. Forester and found it very easy. They'd laughed and
made sport of her trips and bobbles. With Mr. Forester it was easy,
whereas to the Duke of Ross she'd been painfully inadequate. She
caught Phoebe's gaze in the looking glass as she patiently waited for
an answer.

She shook her head, unable to voice what she had hoped would
occur. Mr. Forrester had been the most wonderful man she had
ever met. His attention had been comfortable. His touch had not
caused her body to stir, but her heart had longed for something
more from him. She didn't need to be a duchess. She could be Mrs.
Forrester and make a good life for herself and her sisters—but Mr.
Forrester deserved more.

Phoebe sensed her thoughts. "The Ton would destroy him."

Phoebe's argument was strong, and true. Iseabail paled at the
thought. She wouldn't inflict her father's fate on Mr. Forrester.

"You're right, of course. I'm just being a ninny again."

Phoebe laughed. "You are being cautious. A better duchess
could not have been born." She fluffed the curls to Iseabail's coiffure and peeked around Iseabail's shoulder to meet her gaze in the
mirror. "It truly is amazing how similar our features are."

"Uncanny, really."

"Remind me to never wear my hair the way you have for the
past fortnight." Phoebe shuddered. "I could not bear to wear my
hair pulled tightly against my scalp in such a hideous manner."

Iseabail laughed. "Did you just tell me I looked hideous?"

Phoebe tucked her chin and shook her head in denial. "That
would be like saying *I* looked dreadful with my hair pulled back
and no ringlets around my face." They laughed together and tossed
their ringlets back and forth as they gazed in the mirror.

"These curls give me a sense of freedom I do not have." Iseabail
smiled wistfully at the image looking back at her.

"They give every woman a sense of freedom we do not have.
Do you want to know my definition of liberty?" Phoebe asked.

"What?"

"Not wearing those blasted heels I've been forced to wear all evening until Ross finally arrived. It is a crime to make my feet suffer in such a manner in order for us to look similar in height." Phoebe plopped down on the settee and wiggled her bare feet. "I will be happy to stay in this room all night long resting these poor things."

"Lady Drake, I'm scandalized by your vulgar language and actions," Iseabail scolded in her best impression of a matron.

"Then I will not tell you what I plan to do with the wrappings around my chest when you leave. They are worse than any corset. I cannot breathe!"

Iseabail couldn't help but laugh once more. The entire scheme was ridiculous. "Do not tell me about the pain you are experiencing. My chest was not meant to look so ... so ..." She waved her hand in front of her breasts, unable to come up with a word that would describe the rather obscene display.

"Sensual?" Phoebe asked.

Iseabail blushed. She supposed she would look sensual in the right circumstances.

"I still think you should wear padding on your derriere."

Iseabail's eyes widened. "Absolutely not. That is something I refuse to do."

"You must have the same sway as I do, darling."

"If the Duke reached under my gown and got a handful of nothing but pads, he'd probably be so repulsed, he'd call the whole thing off. Which would leave my womb empty while he marched over to White's for a couple drinks and spilled every last tidbit about my boyish figure." Iseabail lowered her voice to imitate the Duke of Ross. "'I expected a handful of lush flesh and ended up with my fingers embedded in a seat cushion from a settee.'"

Phoebe giggled. "Yet it would be *my* figure they would be discussing."

Iseabail found herself giggling along with Phoebe once more, despite the entire situation being one of the least humorous experiences of her entire life. Her tone sobered. "I can't do it."

Phoebe stood up and moved next to her so Iseabail could see their similarities in the mirror. "You must see this through. If not for your own future, then for mine and your sisters'."

"I don't see how labeling yourself a whore has helped you find a future husband."

"You let me worry about my future after this is done. Right now, I need you to make certain this tryst is carried out. The Duke of Ross must believe he and I had a passionate rendezvous in my gardens."

"What if I don't get pregnant?"

"That's why you must make him want you again."

Her gowns swished as she swirled around toward Phoebe. "What? You said nothing of this occurring again. You said one night. One odious night with that wretch."

Phoebe laughed, pure amusement shining in her eyes as she grasped Iseabail's hands in hers. "I don't think I would ever describe a night with the Duke of Ross as *odious*. Dreamy, passionate, or even magical, but never odious."

"Believe what you may. I do not expect anything but a painful nightmare I want to forget."

Phoebe frowned. "And if his seed produces a child, will you blame the babe? Resent its very existence when its black hair shimmers blue in the moonlight?"

"Don't be absurd. A child isn't at fault for poor parentage. Look at my mother and father. They were in such an awful rush to get away from my grandparents they didn't even know they weren't legally wed. Then they had six children out of wedlock. They were the most loving parents any child could have, but in the end, they were as irresponsible with their children's future as the Duke of Ross will be with his.

"No. I will make certain my child is raised in a loving home, with a parent who is very aware of how precarious wealth and position can be."

"Then I suggest you make your way to the garden, or you won't have the opportunity for wealth or position."

Iseabail nodded slowly, kissed Phoebe on the cheek and whispered. "Thank you." When she pulled away, she thought she caught a glimpse of tears in Phoebe's eyes, but she didn't dare examine them further lest she break down and sob. Instead, she stiffened her spine and slipped into the darkened hallway leading to the stairwell used by the servants. She had a future to secure, a night to endure, and all of it involved an assignation with a man she loathed.

What more could she ask for?

Eleven

Lady Drake,

I look forward to the pleasure of your company.

Ross

—An acceptance from Nashford Xavier Harding, Duke of Ross, to Lady Phoebe Drake's Comfort Ball and House Party, January 1811

He wasn't there to woo anyone. He wasn't there for conversation. He'd been invited for a tryst, and that was exactly what he planned to do ... that, and discover the location of the Blair sisters. If he purged a certain duchess from his thoughts at the same time, he would count his blessings.

Nash walked through the garden with a purpose to his gait. He didn't care if one of the other guests observed the direction of his travel, nor did he care if they found him in the middle of the garden with a bared arse and his cock buried deep within her mouth. He was here to bring Lady Drake to her knees.

He nodded to a young married couple he'd briefly exchanged pleasantries with earlier in the evening. Although a full moon filled the garden with light, at that particular juncture the ancient trees created shadows and hid the young bride's blush as she turned her cheek into her husband's chest. The state of her coiffure, however, told the story of their stroll more than mere words could. Something in his gut longed for the type of intimacy the couple shared —the type of relationship he'd never know. He was a duke bound by his responsibilities and duty. Something the previous duke didn't think him capable of.

A bastard having the fortitude to run the ducal seat is like a whore stepping in to be queen. It can't be done. Your blood is too weak.

He'd proven his *father* wrong. It was too bad the man had died before seeing how a ducal seat could be run profitably and honourably—without corrupt petitions to the Crown to collect debts that were not owed. Yet he still felt the sting of one fraudulent payment collected under his watch—Urquhart castle.

It was the last estate any of his solicitors would ever petition the Crown to acquire. The last family destroyed because of the Harding family crest, and certainly the last dishonourable debt collected in the Harding family name. Even if Harding blood did not run through his veins, he bore the name, and he was making damn sure its legacy was held with esteem and deference. He was determined the Ross duchy, one of the most prestigious dukedoms in the kingdom, would also be known as the most honourable by the common man.

The peerage be damned. He didn't care for their opinion.

He walked past the greenhouse and made his way to the garden, where delicate plants and statuary were covered with cloth to protect them from the cold winter temperatures. For February, however, the air was warmer than expected and perfect for an *al fresco* rendezvous.

Nash paused when the scent of a cheroot carried through the

shrubbery and he spied a gentleman leaving through the gate of the walled garden—the very garden where he was supposed to meet Lady Drake.

There was something familiar about the man, and the aroma, that tugged at his memory. Something he had been introduced to ... as a young man ...

By Nithesdale.

Damnation. Nithesdale had offered the same island brand of cheroot to him on his first holiday, when he'd learned his father was not his father. It was also the same brand Nithesdale's man of affaires had been smoking at Caerlaverock. Was Mr. Forrester here at Lady Drake's house party, and if so, what kind of game was this?

Anger coursed through his body as he stalked through the gate and made his way to the arbor. He caught the faint scent of a lady's perfume, lavender infused with a hint of mint. It was the first time he noticed that particular fragrance associated with Lady Drake. Before tonight, only one woman had stirred his senses with her fresh innocence and spice. Could it be her?

No. His desire for another was leading his mind astray. Lady Drake was leading him on the hunt with a trail for him to follow in a game of hide-and-seek through a garden. He couldn't deny that despite everything, there was something very alluring about catching his prey by moonlight, even if she wasn't the woman he truly desired. Silently he stalked through a maze, listening for her movement. He would have her this night, he'd already made up his mind of that, and if it took thoughts of a green-eyed spitfire to lead to his release, so be it.

A scrap of white lying in the middle of the path gave him pause. He bent down and picked up her kid glove, delicate and small, representing everything he wanted to devour. He smiled and looked around for her from the vantage point of a predator hunting prey.

He picked up speed and rounded the tall hedge that hid the lady from the view of the ballroom's balcony. There on the path lay a second kid glove, as soft to the touch as the first. A growl formed low in his chest and then he heard her, a small gasp deeper in the garden. Silk rustled and pebbles skidded across the walkway as if she were trying to elude him, and he broke into a run. She would not escape her destiny, or his. Tonight he would obtain the information he needed from Lady Drake, and then depart this godforsaken estate and never return.

She was there in front of him, sprinting to a corner in the shrubbery. Her skirts held high to expose her long glorious legs leaping like a gazelle over a fallen branch. She glanced over her shoulder, and silken strands of her amber tresses burnished in the moonlight. In that moment, the resemblance between Lady Drake and Iseabail was uncanny. The incandescent midnight blue of her gown accentuated her curves in the darkness, and the pale glow of her flawless skin glistened in the moonlight. She was a vision to stir any man's blood, but it was the auburn curls tumbling down her back that gave him pause. He'd known only one woman to possess the type of hair that made him want to wrap her silken strands around his fist and pull her head back to expose her erotic pulse point until it thundered out of control.

It seemed he was wrong. When Lady Drake stopped, he could think of nothing else he'd rather do than take her up against the stone wall and drive savagely into her. Her breathing was heavy as she gazed at him like a frightened animal waiting to be devoured. It only made him crave her more.

It seemed his anger had fueled his hunger. He calmed his raging desire. "I didn't think you could look more lovely," he said, as he slowly approached. The deep timbre of his voice roughened with arousal. He had planned to be in control—he was not.

Her expression, shrouded in shadows from the trees, gave nothing away. It was as if she chose the one spot in the garden where the full moon couldn't illuminate her face. "Thank you," she whispered, her voice soft and timid.

That would not do. He could not think of her as innocent. This woman was a consummate actress.

"Turn around."

"Wh-what?" Her voice shook and it was the last thing he wanted to hear.

"Turn around. I want to take a good long look at you in that gown before I tear it from your body."

If anything, her rapid breathing increased, instead of calmed. His own pulse galloped as she took on a seductive pose only a woman who knew what she wanted from him would be capable of pulling off. Her chin dipped as she looked up through her lashes. He couldn't make out the sexy glint in her eyes, but he felt it on his person as if she reached out and touched him. One of her bared hands raised to her mouth, her fingers tracing the edges of her full lips as she slowly turned in a circle giving him a view of every delectable inch of her body. When she finished, her hips swayed as she stalked toward him and that was all it took. Gone was the skittish, shy act some men craved—he did not. In front of him, stood a woman who knew exactly what she wanted—what *he* wanted.

He lifted one of her delicate hands to his lips and took her finger into his mouth. It was the most succulent bit of flesh he'd had since ...

No. They both knew what they were here for. There was to be no courtship, no wooing, or games. Just desire. Base and raw—and then answers. He kissed his way up her hand, to her wrist and forearm. Her breath hitched, and he knew she wasn't unaffected by his touch.

"Was that Mr. Forrester I saw leaving the garden?" Tempted to pull her into the moonlight, he watched for any sign of deception, but the only sign of her shock, was the widening of her eyes before she answered.

"Yes."

Amazed by her candor, he pushed for more information as his

lips grazed the curve of the inside of her elbow. "What is Nithes-dale's man of affaires doing at your house party?"

"He ... he services me, as well."

His lips paused at the meaning of what she had just confessed, and he stood up straight. "Services?"

She gasped and attempted to pull away, but he used her unsteady balance to his advantage and pulled her closer, her body aligning with his perfectly as he peered down at lush, full lips. He didn't remember her features being quite so intoxicating or her body being quite so trim. What had changed?

"He serves as my solicitor. He has assisted me with the financial holdings of the estate ... nothing more."

He didn't know why, but he was glad of that. Thinking of being with her after him ... it didn't sit right. It wasn't because he cared. He didn't. He pulled her arm around to his backside and put her bare palm against his buttocks. A groan escaped his lips as her fingers flexed and he buried his head in the crook of her neck, the flutter of her excitement teasing his senses. He laved and sucked at the delicate skin of her throat, not caring if he marked her for the whole world to see. What he'd been dreading had suddenly turned into something he couldn't wait to consume. Her.

"Wait ..."

He pulled back, every fiber of his being demanding he do the opposite. "Have you had a change of heart?" he asked, praying he wasn't the only one caught up in this mad moment of desire. He was amazed at the calm, matter-of-fact tone of his voice. How he pulled it off was nothing short of a miracle.

"I ... I ... well, don't you want to talk first?"

He should, but his body was hard pressed to hers and he suddenly couldn't think of a single question he wanted to ask about the Blair sisters. "With your fingers massaging my backside, I find it very hard to come up with a topic of conversation."

Her fingers stopped their caress but stayed firmly planted

where they were, and he could have sworn her cheeks darkened in a blush.

"I never dreamed a man could be that muscular," she confessed.

"I like to ride—long, hard, and often." He pushed his stiffened cock against her to ensure she understood his meaning. Sex hadn't been a regular outlet for him in a very long time. He planned to remedy that this evening.

"I see."

"I hope you feel."

Her fingers tentatively moved to the lower curve of his ass as if she'd never explored a man's body so openly. Perhaps it was the difference in the age of her lovers. Her late husband and Nithesdale had been much older than Lady Drake, and although she looked quite young in the dim moonlight, he suspected her to be well past her prime, perhaps eight-and-twenty.

The corner of her lip turned up. "Oh, I definitely feel."

"Then let us not delay."

Her free hand raised up to pull on his cravat. "Kiss me."

"As the lady wishes ..." He lowered his lips to hers, savoring the soft velvety touch. She tasted like berries and wine, and he wondered if she had imbibed in a bit too much spirits. But when her tongue ran across his bottom lip, he needed no further invitation.

Let the seduction begin.

❦

She had planned to be in control—she was not.

The moment their lips met, he commanded her trembling body. He lifted her with ease and wrapped her legs around his waist. The act mirrored their first kiss in the gardens of Caerlaverock, but this time, he seemed determined to see it through—with Phoebe. Her gasp was lost in a sexual battle of the forbidden, as his tongue plunged through her lips in a kiss more passionate than their last. Her gown rose even higher, exposing not only her calves, but her knees and thighs as well.

She should be scandalized—she was not. She should care that he thought he was kissing Phoebe—she did not.

She was lost in the assault of his kiss. The mesmerizing sweep of his tongue tempted her to dance an erotic waltz she'd only experienced once before ... with him. Her hands went to his dark tousled curls that advertised his roguish behavior almost as much as his sardonic smile. Soft strands flowed through her fingertips. Whereas she felt almost wild with abandon, she sensed his restraint. She was nearly lost in the passion, unable to think beyond the way his tongue stroked, his lips moved, and his hands reigned over her senses ... yet he held himself back.

She didn't want him to hold back. A moan escaped her as his hand came to cup her breast. His long, strong fingers kneading her flesh in a manner so erotic, she couldn't stop the wild thrust of her hips. The sensations too irresistible to ignore. She wanted everything with this man. He may be her enemy in every sense of the word, but her body craved what only he could give.

She whimpered when his hand left to cup the back of her head, but then he gently laid her down on a garden bench and the cold stone made her body come more alive. A mere second later, he was on top of her, his large warm body harder than cliffs of Dover would ever be. A shiver ran through her, but she couldn't be certain it was from the cold stone, or the hard length of his arousal prodding her core. She arched into him, rocking against his manhood in an attempt to feed her body's hunger. His strong, masculine hand moved to her shoulder, slowly pulling down the edge of her gown, inch by inch. She wanted him to move faster, and when his mouth left hers to trail kisses across her jaw to her ear, she nearly screamed with frustration. Yet still, she marveled in the way her body responded to his touch. The way he claimed her. Branded her *his*.

He was a rake through and through, and for tonight, he was her rake. Or rather, he was Phoebe's rake. Whatever the circumstances, Iseabail had never felt so alive as she did in his arms. He sucked at her runaway pulse and she gasped. She could no longer stop her hands from exploring his broad shoulders and powerful arms. Even through his coat she could feel his muscular build that was unlike most gentlemen of the Ton. He was by far the largest man of her acquaintance, in height and stature. Nithesdale employed strong young footmen, but they were nothing like Nash. He was as immoveable, as strongly sculpted as any marble statue, and for some reason, that made her crave him more.

His talented tongue traced down her neck and across her collarbone as his hands proceeded to bare her breasts to the cold night air. Her slippers dug into his lower back as he unleashed something primitive inside her. She looked down at the most enticing, carnal image she had ever seen. Nash ravaging her breasts. Never would she have thought her breasts could look so tempting ... so erotic ... but with his mouth plumping her meager mound, the view from above was thoroughly titillating. If his rousing display of masculine desire was to be believed, he found her utterly desirable as well. A man couldn't fake that.

But then, he didn't know they'd shared another kiss before this moment. He didn't know the woman he'd turned away was in his arms right now. Would he want her this much if he knew her true identity? Yet he caressed every inch of her body with a reverence that could not be false.

His hands, his tongue ... God, his tongue. That wicked, tantalizing tongue was doing things to her body she had no idea were possible. Heat curled in her chest and raced to her lower belly where it turned into something more. His hand trailed down the back of her thigh and stopped to run circles around her scar.

He all but turned to stone in that moment—leaving her sex demanding more of the agonizing pleasure only he could give her. "Don't stop," she demanded.

He lifted his head and looked at her, examining her face in a manner she neither understood, nor wanted to.

"Please," she begged. Her voice sounded as if it belonged to someone else. He reached back and unclenched her ankles, and she nearly cried out in anguish. He couldn't stop. Not now.

Not. Now.

To her utter amazement, he didn't. He repositioned himself and her, gently untangling her legs from his back. Just when she thought he was going to leave her, he kissed the back side of her thigh before gently placing her foot over the back of the bench. "Don't move. I want to look at you."

He pushed the layers of her gown up further, exposing her drawers, and she couldn't help the thrill that passed through her as he gazed upon her. Her breasts were bare to the night air and to anyone who happened along this part of the garden, yet she somehow didn't care. The heat of his gaze warmed her when the temperatures should have made her shiver. Then he pulled off his jacket and folded it.

"Lift your hips for me."

She did as he instructed and he placed his jacket under her backside. Then he slowly removed her drawers, lifting her core to the moonlight and his gaze. Her body was exposed to nature and this man like it had never been before. She wished her entire body was exposed—to him. Wished he would tear her gown from her body and leave her utterly naked for his eyes to devour. She could see how her body affected him. Yet he held himself back, as if the animal inside him was caged.

She wanted to open his jail and release the wild beast from within. Unleash the savagery he held at bay, because if the straining of his breeches was any indication, his restraint was weakening and she wanted the barriers destroyed.

"Are you wet for me?"

Wet for him? How could she answer that?

"Touch yourself."

Iseabail raised her hand to her breast and stroked it as he had done. Plumping and pinching. How fascinating to be watched, not touched. Heat and desire pooled in her belly.

"Now your quim. Stroke your quim."

She did and gave a throaty moan. "I'm wet, so very wet." She ached for more.

He was there in an instant. His face between her legs and she moaned as his mouth consumed her. She should be shocked, but she was lost to the sensation. Her back bowed and she couldn't imagine anything feeling better than this. The act wicked and wild. Noises escaped her lips that couldn't possibly be her—she was utterly lost on the precipice of something so magnificent she begged for more.

"Please."

He devoured her. His tongue and lips creating a wave of pleasure that swept away the reality of the night. She was lost in the moment. His finger entered her body, testing her, taunting her teetering nerves beyond anything she had ever experienced. She panted and pleaded, needing a release from the sensation, yet at the same time never wanting it to end. His finger stroked her inner walls as his tongue flicked the center of her pleasure in a carnal demand that drove her over the edge of ecstasy. She shattered into a million pieces, keening and shaking. Wave after rippling wave of pleasure made her legs quiver uncontrollably with her release.

"I've never heard a more enticing invitation on a lady's lips."

She froze. The Duke's head lifted.

The owner of the deep masculine voice on top of the garden wall continued. "You were supposed to wait, but I completely understand your inability to keep your hands off such a decadent piece. Although given the choice, I'm certain the lady would have preferred more."

The way the man emphasized "*more*" dripped with innuendo. The Duke stood up to his full height and placed his body between her and the other man as she scrambled to her feet, pushing down her skirts and pulling up her bodice. The fantasy of being exposed had been naughty and deliciously wicked. The reality of being caught—was not.

"I believe she voiced her pleasure perfectly," the Duke said, his tone mockingly arrogant. She flashed him a look, but realized the shadows that hid her identity also masked her scorn.

Dead leaves shook and the snap of a branch was followed by a hollow thud. A low groan came from where the gentleman had obviously fallen.

She could not be found out by another guest at the house party.

For his part, Nash didn't look the slightest bit concerned or annoyed at the interruption. He adjusted the large bulge in his trousers, making her blush as he reached into his pocket and took out a handkerchief to wipe the evidence of her arousal from his face.

At least the shadows were hiding the color of her cheeks.

"Simon, you are late, and now you are undoubtably filthy after climbing that wall."

"The fairer sex likes me dirty, that's why you invited me."

He had *planned* this? While she had been planning a private assignation, he had planned to meet her—Phoebe, with another man—Simon.

She thought of the long list of the scandal rag articles she'd read about Ross, his friends, acquaintances, lovers, and the scandals that surrounded every last one of them. Only one man's name had been linked to the stories of most lurid debauchery with Ross —Simon Clark, Earl of Astley—a scandalous rogue who held no shame and sported the worst moral turpitude the Ton had ever known. To some, that placed him on the fringes of polite society, despite his rank of earl.

And here he was, with an invitation from Nash to join them. What had Phoebe gotten her into?

"I must go," she whispered as she picked up her skirts.

Ross's hand gripped her bicep in gentle but firm hold. "Is— Lady Drake, the night has just begun."

She looked down at the long fingers wrapped completely around her arm. He may not have been able to see her face, but her message was clear. This was not her idea of an affair. Before she could finish the words, "Unhand me," his fingers dropped, releasing her from his hold. She left without a backward glance.

Once out of sight, she paused on the other side of the ever-green shrubs.

The Duke swore at his partner. "Why the hell didn't you use the damned gate?"

"There happened to be a gentleman camped outside it smoking a cheroot."

Her stomach churned, and Iseabail knew she didn't want to hear the rest. She ran for the exit as fast as she could. Breathing heavily, she paused at the gate, afraid someone would see her. She peeked through the opening and was relieved by a familiar face.

Mr. Forrester stood outside waiting for her as he smoked the cheroot Astley spoke of. She burst through the gate, thankful, yet embarrassed that he would take one look at her and know what she had done.

Twelve

Astley—

Lady Phoebe Drake has requested our presence at her Comfort Ball and House Party to be held at Drake Manor, on the 7th of February, 1811. She promises pleasure beyond our imagination—apparently, she is unaware of the extent of your creativity. The endeavor does come with a price for Lady Drake. She has information I need.

I look forward to sharing the lady's company with you and extracting the Blair sisters' location from her pliant lips.

Ross

—A letter from Nashford Xavier Harding, Duke of Ross, to Simon Benjamin Clark, Earl of Astley, after the Duke accepted Lady Phoebe Drake's invitation to her Comfort Ball and House Party, January 1810

"I'm not certain I care for your brand of a good time." Simon rubbed the back of his head and Nash crossed the study and handed him a brandy.

"You've suffered worse."

"Yes, but I always had a rather interesting story to go with it. A brawl with half the King's navy, a cargo hold full of hard-won loot, or battle scars from being ravaged by a few feisty wenches." He raised his brows and then winced.

Perhaps his friend had been hit on the head a bit harder than he thought. Simon never spoke of business, legitimate or otherwise, in the same sentence as pleasure.

"What can I say about tonight's entertainment?" Simon continued. "I sat on a wall while the Duke of Ross pleasured a woman until she screamed, and then I fell and got hit on the head with a branch?"

Nash grinned. "You could say you learned something from the best."

Simon scoffed. "The day you teach me a thing or two about pleasuring a woman is the day I set sail and never return."

"That's not something a sailor is supposed to joke about." Nash took a thoughtful breath as he sat across from the only man he trusted. One upon a time, he would have included Nithesdale in that category. He and Simon had met at Eaton, both of questionable birth, one hiding it and the other unable to conceal the obvious. But Simon had adored his mother and fought with his siblings. He'd grown up in the perfect household, at least in Nash's opinion, albeit not the Ton's idea of perfection.

Simon shrugged. "What are we doing in Lady Drake's private study with no women on our laps? I thought this party was meant to show off my prowess."

"You failed miserably."

Simon looked affronted. "I have never left a woman wanting."

Nash tossed back the remainder of his drink. "You just sent one running in the opposite direction."

"I'm not responsible for Lady Drake's escape." Simon grumbled and swung his leg over the edge of the feminine floral settee.

Nash refilled his glass at the sideboard, then raked a hand through his hair.

"Regrets?"

Yes. "No." He couldn't explain his feelings to himself, how could he possibly broach the subject with his best friend. "Although I'm not sure my plan will work."

"Then I suppose I will have to enchant the lady with my charms." Simon's smile was self-assured and cocky. His white teeth gleaming against his unfashionably dark skin. His friend may travel the high seas, but the unrelenting sun aboard ship was not the only source of his complexion. After Simon's birth, his father had born children from England to India to the Caribbean, and his countess had taken in his bastards with the love and warmth most mothers of the Ton didn't afflict on their own children. Whereas Simon's father had sewn oats far and wide, Simon's mother had earned the status of sainthood.

Their less-than-stellar parentage had created the bond between them. It was that bond that had led Nash to enlist Simon's assistance with this scheme as well. Simon understood his desire to vindicate the Blair sisters' plight.

"Then at least one of us will obtain the whereabouts of five younger Blair sisters and get them placed in society."

"That may not work since I'm not certain Isea—the Duchess knows where her younger sisters are."

The door to the room quickly opened and closed in a flourish of midnight-blue silk skirts. Nash looked at the woman with her forehead resting on the wood panel, her shoulders slumped as if she couldn't bear to face what was waiting for her on the other side. Simon cocked an eyebrow and lifted his leg off the arm of the settee. The rustle of his clothing caused her back to stiffen and she slowly turned around to gaze at the two of them.

Lady Drake stood before them, her cheeks flushed, hair

perfectly coiffed without a tendril out of place, her skirts flowed smoothly to the tips of her heeled slippers, and her bodice appeared neatly pressed.

Simon rose to his feet and her eyes darted in his direction as if trying to place his identity. "Your Grace, sir," she curtsied, and both gentlemen bowed in return.

"My lady. Please forgive us," he said.

Her chest rose and fell rapidly, but her face remained carefully masked. "What should I forgive you for?"

"We didn't want to join the rest of the party and we sought the privacy of your study."

A smile spread across her face as she swept into the room with all the refinement of the lady she was. "You are my guests. The entire house is at your disposal."

"The entire house?" Simon grinned, his voice laced with innuendo.

Lady Drake's cheek quirked but she did not smile as she looked Nash in the eye. There was no hint of recrimination or embarrassment.

"Are you going to introduce me to this gentleman, Your Grace?"

He stared at the woman in front of them.

"It appears Ross is lost in your beauty. Allow me to introduce myself. I am Astley, at your service." Simon reached for her gloved hand, and ran his lips across her knuckles, his eyes never leaving Lady Drake's as he held her hand, and her gaze, longer than acceptable in polite society.

"Ahh, Lord Astley. My lord, you are as naughty as you are rumored to be."

"Would life be worth living without a bit of sin to make it interesting?"

She smiled and slipped her hand from Simon's as she turned toward the sideboard and poured herself a glass of brandy. "I hope you are enjoying my brandy, my lord. May I offer you a refill?"

"Are you attempting to get me deep in my cups, my lady?"

"And if I were?"

"Then I would say I perform best when not too inebriated."

"Am I to surmise you don't allow yourself to become too deep ... in your cups?"

The grin Simon gave her was purely wicked, and Nash had a moment when he thought he should allow Simon to handle this sinking ship. After all, what better man to be at the helm than Simon? But no. He had vowed to find Iseabail's sisters and make things right.

He stepped forward, putting on a mask of charm he didn't feel. "I can handle going deep, my lady. Please, allow me to show you."

The corner of her mouth definitely quirked with the tug of a grin as he held out his glass for more of the brandy he needed to get through this affair.

The tremble in her hands as she poured his drink was real. Once again, he sensed that she was uncomfortable with the coyness she displayed. "Would you like to pick up where we left off in the garden?" he whispered.

Her gaze met his and then strayed to his friend who had returned to his seat, his leg comfortably hooked over the arm once more. Simon grinned, and he saw the flair of panic in her eyes. Her hand rose to her throat, more an attempt to breathe than to accentuate the creaminess of her skin. Only belatedly did she catch her action and run her finger down her décolletage in a practiced manner of a coquette. The pulse point at her throat fluttered like the wings of a hummingbird, a rapid beat he rather thought he should be able to hear.

"Don't you think it would be best to continue in ... in your bed chamber?" Her voice was breathy as if she was finding it hard to breathe, and Nash stepped back, allowing her space. The last thing he wanted was to have the woman crumple at his feet. His priority was to obtain the location of the Blair sisters.

"I will meet you there at half past the hour," he agreed.

"I take it I'm not invited to watch this time?"

Her eyes widened, darting from his to Simon's and back.

"You are not invited, Astley," he clarified, nor did he miss the thankful whoosh of air that expelled from her lungs.

"If you'll excuse me. I must ... I must ..." Her hand vibrated with nerves down the length of her body.

"Slip into something more comfortable?" he asked, a seductive smile spreading across his face.

Her cheeks regained their color in spades, but she recovered and gave him a coy smile. "Your Grace." She curtseyed to him. "My lord." She nodded in Simon's direction, who didn't even bother to stand up as she left the room.

"A fine piece," Simon said, as he took a drink of his brandy and stared at the fire. "I don't suppose you could introduce me to a sister or perhaps a cousin?"

"Lady Drake has no sibling that I'm aware of."

"You won't hurt her, will you?" Simon was looking at him now, as if he didn't quite know the man behind the ducal facade.

"I won't hurt her," he said matter-of-factly. "While I'm busy, I need you to make some inquiries among the servants."

"What exactly am I looking for?" Simon finally sat up and straightened his cravat, his dark, unruly hair a lost cause.

"I want to know if there is any information about the other Blair sisters, and find out everything you can about the lady."

Simon nodded and threw back the rest of his brandy. Returning his glass to the sideboard, he turned and said, "At your service, Your Grace." He conducted a ridiculous bow with his arms waving in the air like a peacock in heat. "I hope you don't mind if I find my own diversion while you're bedding the lady. Wandering the hallowed halls of Drake Manor alone holds little appeal."

Nash rolled his eyes. "I promised you a tryst, and if it's a tryst you seek, then by all means, indulge yourself."

Simon grinned. "I knew you were a reasonable man."

"I hope you won't spread such a nasty rumor."

Simon's hands went to his chest in mock indignation. "I would never dream of such a thing." He left the room and closed the door behind him.

Nash looked at the clock on the mantel. Eleven o'clock. He still had time to prepare himself for the deed ahead of him and then at half past the hour he would find out exactly what kind of game Lady Drake was playing.

∿

"I can't do it."

Phoebe sighed. "You've said that before."

"And I'm saying it again. I will find another way."

"This is the path Nithesdale suggested."

"And where is he now? He is gone." Her voice sounded shrill to her own ears. No doubt the stable cats were yowling in response. She paced back and forth across the carpet in the lavish room where she'd been hiding since the house party began. She couldn't fault Phoebe for her lodgings ... she'd given Iseabail the best room, one that adjoined her own. Decorated in pastel blues, the room held an air of serenity Iseabail didn't feel.

Phoebe wore a soft expression of understanding, but she couldn't possibly comprehend what Iseabail had been exposed to in the garden. "Have a drink to soothe your nerves," Phoebe suggested.

"It will take more than a glass of madeira to calm me." At this rate she would wear a path in the carpet like the ruts in the road. "I just can't go to his room."

"If you don't, I'm afraid he will show up at my door this evening."

Iseabail's fear made her stumble. She caught herself on one of the massive four poster supports. "You don't understand. The Earl of Astley was *there*."

Phoebe's brow furrowed. "In the garden?"

"Yes, in the garden."

"Did he say something to upset you?"

"Yes." Of course that wasn't exactly right. "Well, no, he did not, but he was there while ... while ..." She waved her hand in exasperation as her face heated with color. "You know."

"While the Duke kissed you?"

"Yes."

"In front of the Astley?" Phoebe whispered.

"Yes." Where was her fan? She needed something to cool the heat scorching her body.

"Darling, that shouldn't bother you."

"It wasn't that sort of kiss," Iseabail muttered. If it had only been that sort of kiss.

"Oh." Phoebe responded automatically, but Iseabail couldn't look at her face. Couldn't watch as understanding sank in. "Ohhh-hhhh," Phoebe exhaled, and Iseabail wanted to hide behind the curtains. Her tone said it all.

"Yes, ohhhh."

"Am I to understand he had his face buried in your décolletage?"

She snorted. Anything else was beyond her capacity to verbalize. She'd found that experience to be pure bliss, but what had followed had been sinfully wicked, and there was absolutely no way she would share that moment with anyone.

Well, apparently that wasn't completely true—she'd shared the experience with the Earl. She plopped down on the bed and covered her eyes. "I was ..." How did she say this? "I was exposed when the Earl entered the garden."

"Iseabail. The garden is dark. That is why we chose it. The Earl could not possibly see."

"He was directly above me on the wall, looking down."

"Oh."

Only a blind fool would not be able to see every exposed part of her body. The man had seen and heard her reaction to the Duke's attention. When she thought of the throes of wild abandon she had experienced, she wanted to crawl into the coffin with her husband. Let it be done. Over.

"That isn't the worst of it," she confessed.

"It isn't?" The shock in Phoebe's voice would have been comical if they were discussing someone else's experience.

"No. The Duke *invited* Astley to join us in the garden."

Phoebe's eyes widened and her breath hitched, then it was her turn to jump to her feet and pace the floor in the exact pattern Iseabail had taken. The rug would be threadbare by the end of the night.

"I see."

"Yes, I believe you finally do."

"That doesn't change our plans."

"I beg your pardon?" Surely her ears were playing tricks on her. She wasn't certain she could handle one commanding man, let alone two like the Duke and the Earl. Bloody hell—what had she gotten herself into?

Phoebe turned to her and squared her shoulders. "We stick to the plan. If ever a man deserved to be tricked into siring another man's heir, I believe Ross is the one."

Iseabail shook her head in disbelief. "But I can't. Not with two young and very virile men."

Phoebe was at her side in an instant, grabbing her shoulders and forcing Iseabail to look her in the eyes. "Iseabail, darling. I would never subject you to such abuse. I understand now the unique conversation I had with Ross and the Earl in my study. I made it abundantly clear that it would only be myself and the Duke in his room this evening—"

Iseabail bit her lip. "They are rogues. I've read the stories ..."

"I am well aware of their reputations. I promise you, Astley will be preoccupied while you are with your Duke."

"He's not my Duke."

"Of course not." Phoebe smiled. "But tonight, he will be your lover. So, for this night, you must think of him as your own." When she started to argue, Phoebe held a finger up to her lips and passed Iseabail a glass of brandy, not wine. "It is the only way that you will experience the pleasure you deserve."

Iseabail doubted she would feel anything but hatred for the man.

"Think of your sisters," Phoebe added, and Iseabail knew her fate was sealed. Her friend was right. She could not let a new duke take over Caerlaverock. Nithesdale's cousin would not inherit her new home. This path, no matter how objectionable, was the only way she could secure her future and procure honourable partners for her siblings.

It was their only hope. She downed the brandy, then held the back of her hand to her mouth and allowed the burn to travel through her entire body. In order to succeed, she had to sleep with an ogre—a very dangerous and sexy ogre who had shown her the meaning of true passion ... yet he was a monster just the same.

Thirteen

Ross,

I have missed our joint ventures involving the widows of the Ton. I confess, I would have never expected Lady Drake to be among the ladies of our particular set, and I find the notion of a debauched Lady Drake beyond my ability to refuse.

With much anticipation,
Astley

—A response from Simon Benjamin Clark, Earl of Astley, to Nashford Xavier Harding, Duke of Ross, accepting his invitation to join him at Lady Phoebe Drake's Comfort Ball and House Party, January 1811

Nash stood in front of his bedroom door, his hand resting on the cool handle. Music played and laughter rang up the staircase. It wasn't a large house party, but the guests were the type to sink well into their cups and enjoy the evening's entertainment.

He gazed down at his hand firmly wrapped around the handle now, his knuckles white. If he entered, there was no going back.

Lady Drake held the key to protecting the Blair girls' future respectability or potential path to ruination. If the Duchess of Nithesdale bore the dukedom's heir, doors would open to her sisters despite their parents' nullified marriage, and the unscrupulous men of the Ton would swamp Caerlaverock for a taste of the financial pie.

The voice of his own father rang through his thoughts. *You will never be accepted in the House of Lords or society once I denounce you.* The old Duke had held those words over Nash's head the last few years of his life. Making Nash jump to his every whim to save his mother's reputation.

He rolled his neck, loosening the tension. He let out a breath before he turned the handle and walked through the door. The room was darkened except for the light emanating from the embers in the fireplace. A chill mingled with the tension in the air, and he could have sworn he heard a slight intake of breath coming from his bed. He closed the door and turned the key, locking them inside—together—before he placed the key in the pocket of his waistcoat.

"I wasn't certain you would be here," he admitted.

"I wasn't certain I would come."

"And now that you're here, do you wish to stay?" This would be by her hand, not his. He stared at her, lounging on his bed. Her gown was gone, but her corset tempted him to undo the laces with his teeth. The bounds of his desire knew no end as her scent reached him, lavender and mint—what a deliciously erotic fragrance to stir his need. His cock twitched and he marveled how much he ached for her.

"Do you?" Her voice shook with uncertainty.

"A man could never say *no* to a night with you in his arms." He found that statement disturbingly true. He wanted this woman like no other. He seemed to come alive in her presence, at least when they were alone. His cock stirred and his hands itched to grab her, stroke her, make her come apart in his arms once more.

Gone was the apprehension he'd felt before entering the room. The only thing that kept him from pouncing on her, and making her his, was her acquiescence.

His eyes finally adjusted to the dim lighting and he was able to see her gown lying across the foot of the bed. Her stockings and low-heeled slippers placed neatly to one side, almost completely hidden from view. The woman who stirred the embers of his lust lay on the bed in only her corset and chemise. Nash strode to the chair next to the armoire and took off his tailcoat before sitting down to remove his boots and stockings. He never let his eyes stray from the vision on the bed as he stood up and removed his waistcoat.

"You left your drawers in the garden. Would you like them back?"

"I thought them lost forever."

He gave her a wicked smile. "I should keep them as a reminder of your screams."

"If that is what you desire."

"I desire much more than that." He caught a glimpse of her tongue swiping a path across her bottom lip and his cock stood at attention, waiting and wanting. He grabbed his manhood through his clothing and brought her attention to where he needed it most. "Is this what you desire?"

The white of her eyes flashed in the light. A moment of shock or hunger, he couldn't say, until she leaned up on her elbows, turned to her side, and propped her head on one hand as she gazed at him. Her other hand ran down the side of her breast, her waist, her hip. Her bare foot created tiny circles on the coverlet as she bent her knee and exposed more of her shapely legs. "I find myself incapable of saying anything but *yes* to a night in your bed."

He paused for a moment, wondering at her words. Was she incapable because she was lust driven, or something else? She pushed up and leaned forward, the expanse of her creamy white breasts filling his line of vision, and all his doubts disappeared. He was on her in a moment, pushing her back into the mattress, devouring those plump lips that tasted like brandy and mint and everything feminine. His knee automatically separated her legs demanding she open for him. A whimper rose from her throat enticing him beyond his control.

He pulled away and her lips followed him as if she couldn't bear for him to stop.

"I must see all of you. No barriers between us tonight," he demanded. His hands traveled to her corset where the laces were tightly bound and nearly undid him as he struggled to free her. When the laces finally slipped loose, he pulled the garment from her body and threw it across the room, not caring if the damned thing landed in the fire. Her chemise was next, and he marveled at the woman in front of him. She looked up at him and for a moment he hesitated, his mind at war with the heat coursing through his veins.

As if sensing his hesitation, she reached for the buttons on the falls of his breeches. He watched as her fingers fumbled and his cock sprang into view. He was large and thick for her; he grew harder and harder as her mouth formed a perfect little *o*. In that moment, he didn't want to hold back the animal inside him. He wanted to thrust deep inside her pretty pink lips and fuck her mouth until she gagged.

"You're ... You're so ..."

"Trust me. I'm nothing you can't handle, Is—" He bit down on his cheek. "Take me in your mouth," he demanded.

She looked up at him in shock, as if she'd never heard of such a thing. It had to be a ruse, a very good ruse he refused to acknowledge. He didn't back down but waited.

Her tongue rang across her lips and his cock twitched with anticipation. He needed her to give in, heed his command, and when she did, his need nearly unmanned him as her lips drew closer, ever so slowly.

Torturing. Teasing, she licked her lips a second time and he couldn't stop himself from threading his fingers through her hair and moving his cock closer, probing her lips with its head. Her tongue touched his tip, and he groaned with satisfaction and frustration. He wanted more, so much more. He needed to fuck her. She was a witch, driving his body to the brink of madness, only to withdraw and make him wonder if the moment had been real.

This need was very real. His cock was as hard as forged steel, and her unhurried tentative pace was killing him.

She swirled her wet, velvety tongue around his head, gathering momentum as her warm mouth surrounded his tip and her eyes closed, a moan escaping her lips as if she felt as much pleasure in the act as he did. It should be his eyes closing in ecstasy, but there was something so beautiful about her hair glimmering in the firelight. Her breasts on full display with her dusty nipples taunting him with their tight buds. He cupped them as she swallowed more of him, her hand coming up to grab the base of his cock as if she wanted to control how deeply he fucked her mouth. He pinched her nipples letting her know that he was in charge, not her, and she moaned once more. An erotic sound of satisfaction that sent vibrations of bliss traveling through his body in sweet torment.

He grabbed her hand, guiding her to stroke him from the base to the tip in rhythm with her mouth, marveling at the way her small delicate fingers barely wrapped around his girth. Then he did the same with her head, pushing her to take more and more of him. In and out, out and in, until he felt the back of her throat and he wanted to spill his seed instantly.

"Fuck." He pulled out and pushed her back against the mattress, pausing only long enough to determine he hadn't hurt her with his impatient desire to be inside her. He kissed her harshly, roughly thrusting his tongue in her mouth the way he wanted to push his cock inside her, and she responded in kind. Wild and wanton, she pulled his shirt over his head and he momentarily pulled away to be rid of the barrier.

It was more than he could stand. Intimate. Sensual. Arousing.

His chest pressed against her soft, pert breasts, the pure exquisite feel of her body under his. He wanted to taste her, consume her, he simply had to have her. His cock needed to be inside her, stretching and stroking her sex. He found her entrance wet and wanting, heat emanating from her core. He pushed inside, her cunny so hot and tight around the head of his cock he was desperate to be all the way inside. She gasped as he bit her neck and grabbed her thigh to wrap her leg around his waist as he thrust all the way in.

Two sensations hit him at once. Pure euphoria at the way her body sheathed him, and utter confusion at the squeal of pain, not pleasure, forced from her lips. He'd never felt a woman's body so snug around his own. He was large, yes, but this was something utterly different. There was no room for him to move, to swivel his hips and hit that spot he knew she possessed. The spot he'd found in the garden as his finger slipped inside her. He pulled up and saw the pain on her face as he ran his hand along her thigh, attempting to soothe and caress her into feeling the same exhilaration he felt.

And that's when he realized it. She was untouched before him. The woman he'd wanted from the moment he caught sight of her a month-and-a-half ago. The woman he thought had been despoiled by Nithesdale and Lady Drake. The woman he recognized in Lady Drake's Garden as Iseabail Hancock, Duchess of Nithesdale. The woman he knew was in his bed the moment he opened the door to his room.

"Fuck." He started to pull out, but she grasped his buttocks and pulled him tightly against her body. Driving him deeper, his cock loving every goddamned bit of her.

"Don't," she whispered.

"Don't what? Fuck you? Cuckold a man I looked up to?"

She winced with pain, but he didn't believe it to be from anything but his words. And he knew his words hurt her in a way his body couldn't. Again.

"I can't do this."

"Please," she begged.

"Iseabail—"

"How? How did you know that it was me?"

"How could I not know it was you? Do you take me for a fool?"

"No, but it was dark."

"I held you in my arms in your garden. I would know your body anywhere." It was true.

It didn't take her scar, or the differences in their shoes, their shape, or their age. He would know this woman if he were blindfolded.

"Yet you came here to be with Phoebe."

"I came to the party to get information about your sisters from Lady Drake anyway I could, but the moment I saw you in the garden, I recognized you for the woman you are. The woman I desire more than any other, but this is wrong. Nithesdale was like a father to me."

"He married me on his deathbed to give me a future, but he said it was up to me to get with child."

"I'm the last person he would want to bury his seed inside you."

"You are the very person he wanted me to seek out."

He shook his head unsure of what to do. He knew what his body wanted, craved even, but this was insanity. He had never spilled his seed in a woman. Ever. Not once in his twenty-eight years had he allowed himself to potentially leave a bastard. He was not his father. "I can't."

She moved under him, flexing and tightening her sheath—it was beyond torture. It was perfection. The sensual way her fingers dug into his flesh was a completely new sensation for him. He'd never felt this sensation before ... of being consumed by the moment. He didn't want to stop—he wanted to drive into her until he found completion. Never before had his body overruled his thoughts when he was with a woman. He pushed into her, savoring the intoxicating desire she created. He'd had hints of this all-consuming want in the garden at Caerlaverock, had it on the tip of his tongue with her on the bench outside this very home, but nothing compared to being inside her. It was as if he had been searching for this his entire life ... and that frightened him.

Had he turned into his father after all? Would he be driven by his cock to seek pleasure like this for the rest of his existence? He would be no better than the other so-called gentlemen of the Ton who left bastards sprinkled all over the country.

His conscience wouldn't allow him to continue in this game.

He released her thigh and reached for her fingers.

"If you stop, my sisters will die in poverty." There was a desperation in her voice that he had not sensed before. Her gaze searched his, traveling back and forth between his eyes as if she would see a different answer in each.

"Nithesdale didn't provide for you?"

"He said you were the solution to my problem."

He cursed under his breath. "Tell me where your sisters are. I can protect them."

"No." Her voice was laced with steel. "If you do not wish to help me save them the way I have been my entire life, then leave." She dropped her hands from his body and he was instantly cold.

"Iseabail," he whispered, but despite her body beneath his, the woman who clenched his cock with her passion was gone. Her eyes as vacant as a whore's, and he could not have felt worse. He had taken away her home, tossed her future to the wind, and now her virtue was despoiled at his hand.

"Iseabail, let me help you."

She turned her head away to stare at the curtains, and he'd never felt more horrendous in his entire existence. When she lay there without a flicker of emotion on her face, he cursed his stupidity. His mind had lost interest at the sight of her despair, but his cock was harder than ever as it strained for more. He blew out a breath and moved inside her. A gasp escaped her lips and her gaze returned to his.

He stared down at her, memorizing every plane of her face and the glimmer of hope that blossomed in her eyes. It was as if she finally saw a sliver of what her life could be, what it should have been before the former Duke of Ross walked into her father's life.

He took her lips in a harsh and brutal kiss, uncertain if he was punishing their fathers, Nithesdale, her, or himself. He did not move. He just let her body adjust to his as he ravished her mouth, her neck, her breasts, until she squirmed underneath him, encouraging his movement. Her arousal, wet and hot, choked his engorged cock. He lifted up and looked down at her glorious body. The smooth creamy expanse of skin now marked by the day's growth of his beard. Her firm, ripe breasts were much smaller than Lady Drake's, but they were heavenly. Her waist was unfashionably slim yet completely intoxicating. The dusting of silken curls on her mound made him want to lick her until she could take no more.

He wrapped her leg back around his waist then slowly moved in and out. Teaching her the rhythm while gauging her pleasure. He grabbed one of her buttocks and lifted her to meet his body as he came down to fill hers. She gasped and moaned making him grind his teeth in an effort to hold back his release.

He moved his hand to the pearl between her legs and she responded the way he knew she would—wanton with abandon. This was his Iseabail. Not Nithesdale's. There was no other way to define what was between them. She wasn't the Duchess of Nithesdale, she was *his* duchess. At that moment, he cared about nothing else but making her his.

Their passion was outrageous and unprincipled, the way it should be between a man and woman. He had been with seasoned courtesans who had not made him feel ... this shamelessly wicked. Iseabail panted, her breath rough and ragged as he caressed and stroked.

"Please. Oh God, Ross, please."

He held back, denying her the pleasure she desired. "Nash, call me by my Christian name."

"Nash ... Nash." She sucked in a breath as he circled her point of pleasure and rotated his hips. "Oh ... oh!" She screamed her pleasure, her body pulsing around his shaft as he thrust into her with everything he had. Harder and harder as she milked his cock, the sensations so exquisite it nearly pained him. Then he was there, following her over the edge of rapture into oblivion.

Never had anything felt so right as when he collapsed on top of her, his seed deep within her womb, her small frame wrapped within his arms. For the first time in his life, he had experienced his completion inside a woman's body, something he had sworn he would not do until he was married to his duchess ... yet, as far as he was concerned, from the moment he put his cock in her cunny, the banns had been read.

Iseabail was his.

Fourteen

Dear Mr. Forrester,

The last time we were together, you advised me that you were at my service no matter how great or small my need may be—I am in need of your assistance with a matter of great import. I'm afraid it may cause you some distress and I would not ask it of you if it was not completely necessary. Please accept my sincere apologies with this request.

I require a copy of L'Arétin Francais Les Epices de Venvs published by Felix Nogaret Aux Depens des Fermier Generaux in 1787. There are only two copies known to be in London—one is in Prinny's possession, and the other is owned by the Earl of Astley. If you could obtain it from him on loan, I would greatly appreciate it. However, my identity must not be revealed.

The other book I would like you to acquire is a bit easier to obtain. Lady Benton was given a book by her husband as an engagement gift that he commissioned when they were betrothed, The Memoirs of Wanton Woman, London, printed for T. Benton. Lady Benton will be expecting you.

Your utmost discretion is needed for this venture as I do not wish for the Ton to hear of these acquisitions.

Respectfully,
Lady Phoebe Drake

—A letter from Lady Phoebe Drake to Mr. Joshua Forrester, Barrister of the late Edward Charles Hancock, Duke of Nithesdale, January 1811

It was everything she'd read about, and *more*. The 'more' was indescribable, so she understood why the books never expounded upon it. A writer couldn't possibly describe the ethereal out-of-body experience of sex. She wasn't sure how to put the act into coherent thoughts. The closest description she could come up with was pure, heavenly bliss. Or maybe, wicked heavenly bliss.

She would go to hell for comparing her experience with Nash with divinity. Yet the divine had created every erotic touch she'd experienced. Nash had simply peeled away layers of social mores and proprieties placed on her as a woman and unleashed the wanton within. Was that evil?

She didn't know.

The rapture of sex was in many ways comparable to her fall from the loft in the stable when she was nine years old. The hazards were very real—one could kill her, the other could leave her hanging in purgatory—unsatisfied. Luckily the first fall only left her with a broken arm and a scar on the back of her leg that gave away her identity to Nash.

Heart-stopping fear chased by heart-pounding ecstasy. In both cases, society would judge who was evil and who was holy. She was pretty sure she would never be placed in the holy category.

The fall from the hayloft and sex did have one thing in common—they both made her recognize her mortality. When her grip slipped at nine, and the ground came rushing toward her, she had a feeling of being robbed. Tonight, a part of her had died as well. She'd fallen over an erotic precipice and still she felt as if she'd been swindled. How did one go on, knowing it would never happen again?

The irony was not lost on her. She had given her virtue to the man she loathed most in this world. Her sworn enemy she wanted to destroy, and yet she had ended up begging him to bed her—and now she wanted more.

How cruel fate could be!

She glanced over at the sleeping form next to her. He didn't fear her in the least. The woman who had thought about, dreamt about, fantasized about destroying him for the past eight years ... and in the end ... She. Begged. Him.

Like a gentleman, he capitulated, gave into her pleas. To. Help. Her.

Then again, she wasn't the one he wanted to help. For some reason he was obsessed with finding her sisters. Helping them. At least that's what he professed. Was it possible for a man to change, for a conscience to grow?

She studied him. In repose, the arrogant aristocratic features she had despised softened, almost making her believe he was a man with honourable intentions. The straight line of his nose that had been a study of perfection when she was a teen, was now marred by a slight bump across the bridge. It spoke of the Duke going toe to toe with someone on at least one occasion since the day they'd met, and she wondered what would cause a duke to brawl.

His jaw had squared off since that day at Urquhart, and the deep shadow of his beard filled in with age. Not that he was old. He was in the prime of his life. His lips were soft and his eyes ... they had echoed the flames of fire she'd felt in the heat of passion. He was a different man in bed than he was out of bed. Gone was the aloof, uncaring blue blood, only to be replaced by a man who bared all as a lover.

She sat up and the sheet slipped from her body, exposing her breasts to the chilled air. She blushed and looked down at the Duke, expecting a comment about not being as lush as Lady Drake. Instead, she found him still sound asleep, his lips gently parted, a look of innocence ...

She rolled her eyes. She knew first-hand how wicked that mouth was, and she hated to admit she craved more of it. Even now, her body heated with desire despite the soreness she felt from the experience.

She had to leave. She wanted to stay. Pulling her gaze away, she slipped from the bed, careful not to disturb the Duke's slumber, and hurriedly dressed in her undergarments and gown. She had no idea where the pins for her hair were, probably strewn all over the bed and floor. She platted the long, messy strands of her hair and let it fall over one shoulder. Hopefully the halls were dark enough she could slip unnoticed into her rooms.

She stuffed her stockings into her bodice, giving her décolletage a more enhanced appearance and stepped into her slippers. Reaching for the door, she hesitated. She had to see him one more time.

Slowly she approached the dais where he lay in the large bed as if it were his throne, his body covered from the waist down. The moonlight still peeked through the window coverings, exposing a sliver of his jaw, but she wanted to see all of him—every last exotic inch one last time. She deserved the exquisite torture the memory would bring for years to come.

She turned and slowly pulled the dark velvet hangings away from the window, the moonlight falling across his broad chest one glorious plane after the other, as if exposing her to the glories of heaven. He was a masterpiece, sculpted and refined. Smooth skin stretched taught over cords of muscle and sinew. Michelangelo would take one look at him, and demand to cleave his form from marble.

She turned and walked away, slipping out the door without even a creak.

~

She had ruined him for all others.

She may not know what he had in mind for her future, but she would succumb to his desire to marry, even if he had to publicly seduce her to get the deed done. Then her sisters would be cared for and suitable matches would be made to secure their futures. The horrible deeds of his father would be erased, and his conscience would be clear ... with the added bonus of having a vixen for a wife.

What more could he ask for?

Knowing that she would never tell him what room she inhabited in the manor, he quickly donned his breeches, grabbed his shirt, and slipped out into the hall. It didn't matter that the floors were cold against his bare feet, without his boots she would not hear him following her, and at this point, that was more important than propriety.

He suspected Iseabail was staying in the family wing adjoining Lady Drake's rooms. In the light of day, there would be no mistaking the differences between the ladies, but at night they could easily fool an undiscriminating eye, provided it was dark.

He made his way to the family's wing without running into a soul, only to find all the rooms darkened and no noise emanating from inside. He looked up and down the hallway, waiting for something ...

A clock struck half past the hour somewhere down the hall and that's when he saw it. A candle flicker to life in the second room down on the right. He moved closer and put his ear to the door. Then he smiled as he heard her hum a lullaby, and retreated before whispering, "Sweet dreams, Duchess."

Fifteen

My Dear Lady Drake,

I am honoured by your faith in me. Please trust in my conviction to serve you, and know that I would never cause any damage to your reputation, nor would I allow another to impugn your character.

I have obtained the literature you requested without incident. Lord Astley was extremely curious as to which one of my clients requested it. Fortunately, I was able to assure him he was not familiar with the young married nobleman I represented. My response seemed to satisfy him and he was more than happy to assist another gentleman to obtain, as he stated, "Unparalleled bliss." He would, however, like the book returned to him once the gentleman has achieved his goals.

Since receiving your letter, I have found myself in a most uncomfortable state on a nightly basis. I hope that you can forgive my forwardness, but I feel we have come to a place in our relationship that my question must finally be asked, if not in person, then in written correspondence: Why have you not asked for my guidance?

Your servant in every request,

Joshua Forrester, Esquire

—A very inappropriate letter from Joshua Forrester, Esquire, to Lady Phoebe Drake, February 1811

S imon's valet was at the door on the first knock. He was starched prim and proper as he opened the door to a room much smaller than the one Nash occupied. "Your Grace, the Earl is indisposed at this time."

"At this hour?"

"He's bloody retching up his stomach contents," came a strangled reply from behind the door.

Nash winced at the noises his friend was making. "I'll come back later to check on you."

"Don't you—don't you dare—leave." Simon's warning would have been menacing if it wasn't for the godawful sounds he was making. The stench made Nash want to grab a chamber pot for himself.

Simon's valet sighed and opened the door further. Nash would have preferred he close it in his face. Instead, he made his way into the room. Simon lay in his bed leaning over the edge gagging and all Nash could do was wait. When he finally threw himself back on the pillows with the drama of a schoolboy, his valet handed him a damp cloth and removed the chamber pot.

Closing his eyes, Simon wiped his face and accused, "She did this to me."

"Who?"

"Lady Drake. She poisoned me."

Nash blinked. His friend had gone mad.

Simon's eyes flew open, anger seething from the depths. "Don't look at me as if I've gone mad. Lady Drake poisoned me."

"How did she poison you? She left the room before I did."

The valet approached the bed and began messing with the blankets as if Simon was a sick child and his valet a nursemaid. "You were utterly foxed when I found you, my lord. This is not your first experience with imbibing a bit too much."

Simon yanked the covers and shooed away his valet like an unwanted pest. The man bowed and quit the room. "The damned whisky. I think she put laudanum in my drink ... or hemlock ... or something."

"Do you have proof?"

"Of course I don't have proof, damn you. But I have never reacted to a drink like this before in my life."

"Your valet says otherwise."

"Damn him to hell as well for being a mothering nursemaid. You do know my mother hired him, don't you? It's like having a tattling younger sibling around."

The whine in Simon's voice made Nash's lip quirk. "Why would the lady poison you?"

"To ensure I didn't join you last night, of course."

"Unless I am mistaken, you weren't supposed to join us."

"Yet Lady Drake returned and flirted terribly before ... well, if I enjoyed the lady's company, I have no memory of it." Simon rubbed his forehead as if that would clear some of the fog.

"Then I'd say the lady didn't enjoy it much either."

Simon shot him a look that would kill a lesser man. "She came back after you left and said you never showed up in your room. She said the two of us may as well enjoy the evening and she poured us a drink. I wasn't sure what had waylaid your plans, but I thought, *what the hell*." His lips pursed. "I had one glass of whisky," Simon ground out. "One. The termagant poisoned me."

Nash had to give Simon credit. Even though he may have had a few drinks prior to the one he apparently shared with Lady Drake,

Simon could drink him under the table any night of the week. It would take a barrel of whisky to put him that deep in his cups.

A knock at the door stopped Nash from remarking. Before either man could say a word, the door opened and Lady Drake walked in as if she walked into gentleman's chambers every day of the week. Nash couldn't stop his brow from rising. Simon had a completely different response. He swore under his breath and purposely lowered his bedding to expose his broad bare chest. Since their time at Eaton, Nash had known of his friend's habit of not wearing clothes to bed. He had often grumbled for Simon to cover himself, but Simon had merely laughed and told him he blushed like a schoolgirl.

He may have shared a woman or two with Simon, but he certain didn't want to get familiar with his friend's manhood. At the moment, however, it took everything Nash had not to laugh at the blatant masculine gesture that was meant to intimidate the lady.

Lady Drake's lips broadened in a wide smile, not one hint of embarrassment in her expression. Her hands, however, belied her true state. They were too busy waving here and there, touching the buttons on her sleeves and dragging across her collarbone. She was not at all comfortable.

"Ahh, my lord, it is so good to see you feeling like your old self again. I was quite concerned last evening when you passed out on my settee. You must be careful with my Scottish whisky. It is said to be too much for the more *genteel* constitutions of the Ton."

Simon growled, his temper flaring. He looked as if he would throw off his covers and bare himself, just so he could storm across the room and throttle her. She was saved from that act, however, by the entrance of Mr. Forrester. Upon seeing Simon's bare chest, he closed the door behind him. Without a word he went to the wardrobe and pulled out a shirt and threw it at the Earl.

"Cover yourself, there's a lady present," Mr. Forrester said, as if Simon was a school boy.

"I would hardly call her a *lady*. Murderess is more fitting." Simon grumbled, his upset stomach clearly forgotten in his fit of pique.

"Careful my lord, or you will be facing my pistols at dawn." Mr. Forrester's low warning was enough to shock Simon into silence and make Nash wonder what Forrester's background was that he would even deem to think of such an audacious threat twice.

"For that ridiculousness, I demand you return my book at once." Simon pouted before turning back to Lady Drake. "Will you have your ruffian beat a man in his sickbed, my lady?" Simon's emphasis on the last two words were meant to taunt Mr. Forrester.

It did the trick. Forrester moved toward Simon as if he would throttle the Earl but Lady Drake stilled his advance with a calming hand on his forearm.

Lady Drake shook her head. "It's fine, Mr. Forrester. The earl is feeling the effects of our whisky. He won't repeat his error after his stomach is set to rights. Astley, you were ever so bold with your ... propositions for the evening's entertainment last night."

If a man could turn to stone, Nash witnessed Forrester do just that, but it was the promise of violence in his narrowed gaze that Nash found interesting. The barrister cared for Lady Drake much more than a man in her service should, much more than he'd displayed for Iseabail when he'd threatened Nash.

It was time to intervene. "We were both out of line, Lady Drake. May I offer our deepest apologies?"

"Speak for yourself, Ross." Simon scowled.

"May I ask for your forgiveness as well, Astley? You wouldn't be here if it wasn't for me." Nash smiled apologetically.

"I came here of my own accord. There is no apology necessary from you." Simon's casual tone belied his anger as he turned his glare on Lady Drake.

"Excellent," Lady Drake clapped her hands with glee and

turned toward the door. "Then we shall proceed with the house party."

The lady, however, despite her readiness to move on, had not even begun to atone for her sins and Nash wasn't about to let her leave without giving him answers. He stepped in front of her, blocking the door from her departure. "Where is she?" He demanded.

The feigned innocence on her face could have fooled a lesser man, but Nash knew of her involvement in the scheme. "Where. Is. Iseabail."

She tapped him on the arm as if he were a silly boy. "The Duchess is in mourning at Caerlaverock, Your Grace. Where else would she be?"

"In my bed, as she was last evening."

Lady Drake gasped and glanced over her shoulder at Mr. Forrester and Simon. His friend just looked on, his color returning as this turn of events gave him something other than his miserable stomach to think about. Mr. Forrester, however, looked as if he might now shoot Nash on the spot—no gentleman's agreement to the rules of engagement required.

"Watch your words, Your Grace. More than a lady's reputation is at stake." Forrester's warning came out clipped.

"I think he's talking about your head." Simon sat up straighter in bed.

"Not likely."

Simon looked around at the tight expressions in the room. "What else is at stake?"

It was Lady Drake's giggle as she lightly brushed some unseen piece of lint off Nash's shoulder that broke the tension. "I must confess that I am flattered to be compared to the young and vibrant Duchess of Nithesdale, but I assure you, the Duchess was not the lady in your bed." Her eyes flitted in a coquettish manner that had Mr. Forrester frowning even further, if that was possible.

Nash folded his arms across his chest and took on the ducal air he was born to wear, at least according to his mother. "She left her mark upon my bedding."

All the color drained from Lady Drake's face.

"Where is she? She did not answer her door this morning."

"You don't understand," she started.

Nash didn't care what excuse she was about to utter. "Where. Is. She." It wasn't a question. It was a demand to produce the woman he'd ruined the night before.

"She doesn't want to see you."

"I will not hurt her or damage her reputation." He promised, but it was obvious Lady Drake didn't believe him.

It was Simon who broke the silence. "I would think the lady wouldn't mind having a much-needed conversation with the Duke."

Lady Drake's jaw tightened. The seductress was gone, replaced by the protectiveness of an older sister with the ferocity of a bear. "An unwanted guest is to appear at my door next week in search of the Duchess. It seems Mr. Henry Jarvis is very curious about how the Duchess's pregnancy is progressing."

Jarvis. He'd nearly forgotten about Nithesdale's heir. Another boyhood friend, but whereas he and Simon had everything in common, he and Jarvis had the proverbial thrones as heirs to dukedoms as their only bond. Nash had befriended Jarvis out of his loyalty to Nithesdale, and although Jarvis had always been a prig, he'd been a harmless prig.

Until now. "Nithesdale's heir?" he asked. "Why is he coming here?"

"It seems at least one of the servants at Caerlaverock is in his pocket and reports everything the Duchess does to Mr. Jarvis."

"So, she came to you?"

Lady Drake nodded and then moved to the settee. She motioned for Nash and Mr. Forrester to do the same. She ignored Simon looking on from his bed, and once her back was turned,

Simon rose from the bed and slipped on a pair of breeches and the lawn shirt Forrester had thrown at him.

Simon slowly eased himself into one of the chairs by the fire, completely unembarrassed by his state of dishabille, his bare feet wiggling on the rug and the skin on his neck red from the exertion he expended in the minimal movements.

"The Duchess is attempting to survive the only way Nithesdale told her she could."

"She could be my duchess," he blurted out, catching Simon's attention despite his green pallor. Mr. Forrester seemed to be all ears. Despite his mother's machinations Nash hadn't planned to marry. His parents' marriage had taught him how unhappy the state of holy matrimony could be, but he was prepared to do right by Iseabail. She deserved this. Her sisters deserved it as well.

"She won't," Lady Drake insisted.

"She should," Simon surprisingly pushed.

"Gentlemen, I can appreciate that you want Ross to do the honourable thing, but Nithesdale and his duchess had a special relationship."

"Not that special," Nash muttered. Lady Drake ignored the barb.

"They decided this was the best course of action for Her Grace."

"*They* decided, or Nithesdale decided for her?" Because it definitely reeked of some scheme Nithesdale had come up with, not Iseabail.

"My point being," Lady Drake let the tension in the air ease. "Her Grace wishes to proceed with the plan she and Nithesdale had agreed upon, and I am duty-bound to grant those wishes."

"I am not." Nash stated. "Neither Nithesdale nor Iseabail consulted me regarding the use of my seed. I will not let my heir be raised as a bastard duke."

"Even if Nithesdale wanted you to do it for him?" Lady Drake's face appeared sad, and she seemed genuinely tired of the whole situation. "I know you were like a son to him. He spoke of you often. Nithesdale used to say he knew you would do better for the tenants and the Ross estate than the old Duke ever could. He had faith in you righting the wrongs of your father."

It was Nash's turn to tense.

Simon stepped in for him. "I think it is blatantly obvious that Nash is attempting to do right by the Duchess. He can give her a proper marriage that isn't in name only."

Nash gave a single succinct nod in agreement. If that's what it took to right the wrong of his father, he would do it.

"You have been very vocal in your opinion of not bearing an heir, Your Grace. If I'm not mistaken, they call you the *last* Duke of Ross." Forrester argued. "The Duchess wants Nithesdale's child."

"The child won't be Nithesdale's," he ground out.

"To the Ton and the world, it will be." Forrester responded.

"Gentlemen, let us not forget you are speaking for the Duchess, and as none of you are her husband, your guidance is misplaced." Lady Drake said.

"What does the Duchess want?" He asked.

"The Duchess is in mourning and would like to remain that way."

"I'm certain, after last night, the Duchess—"

"We spoke this morning, Your Grace. She expects to live out the remainder of her life as the dowager duchess."

"She's no more than two-and-twenty!" Nash exclaimed.

Lady Drake looked down her nose as if he had offended her. "And yet she is a woman who values her reputation and her marriage vows."

Nash scoffed. "She certainly didn't value them last night."

Mr. Forrester swore, his fist clenched, and he would have stood if not for Lady Drake's hand on his arm holding him in check once more.

"Her reputation is in a shambles. She is viewed as a bastard whore who stole a title from a dying duke on his death bed." Simon's words put them all on the defensive, as three sets of angry eyes turned on him. "Don't kill the messenger. If you don't believe me, bring her out of hiding. Let the lords and ladies at this house party speak for themselves."

Lady Drake's eyes widened in shock. "She cannot appear at a house party! Nithesdale just died!" She delicately rubbed the bridge of her nose as if she wished she could make all of this go away ... or at least the men in her company disappear. "Let us forget these pretenses and speak plainly, gentlemen. The Duchess of Nithesdale will hopefully bear the late Duke's heir. Period."

Nash ran his hand along the length of the carved arm of the settee. "And her sisters?" He asked.

"I will introduce them to society, of course." Lady Drake made the announcement as if the current scandal wasn't attached to her name as well.

"Your reputation will not help the girls gain acceptance, Lady Drake. Your name has been dragged through the type of muck one finds on the bottom of his boots in the Dials. You need a protector. Me." Simon's insult hit the room like a runaway carriage. It had been made to irritate Lady Drake and Forrester.

It worked.

"I have been courting Lady Drake for months. The Duke approved of the match." Forrester's proclamation was accompanied by a gasp from Lady Drake. Simon's jaw dropped awkwardly open.

Nash took advantage of the silence. "Then we will restore the reputations of both ladies with an immediate announcement of your engagement."

Forrester looked almost pained as the lady stiffened. If a betrothal was announced, Lady Drake would not travel in the same social circles she was accustomed to—if she was still receiving any invitations, they would stop after this house party. He would have felt sorry for her if she had not created such a scandal for Iseabail.

"Iseabail, the Duchess of Nithesdale, will become the Duchess of Ross."

Lady Drake recovered her composure. "No. She will not become your duchess. She has her sisters to think about."

"Sisters you can no longer introduce into society. As my duchess, no one would dare to snub them," Nash leaned back in the delicate settee with the pomposity only a duke could hold. At that moment, he hated how much he sounded like his father.

Simon held up his hand to stop the argument. "Enough. We have all had our fun, some of us more than others." The final comment was made under his breath and made Forrester stand. Simon pointed his still extended hand at Forrester before the man challenged him to a duel. "There will be no engagement, but the Duchess must make an appearance at your house party, despite how it may make her appear."

"She can't appear at a house party, she's in mourning!" Lady Drake protested.

"I understand your concerns." Simon continued. "It is less than ideal. There will be comments made about a bastard daughter of a climber not being up to snuff with the ways of society, but she must appear despite the animosity, if for nothing else, then to continue the ruse you set in place for Jarvis. When he arrives at the house party, she can decide if she will sneak out and return to Caerlaverock without Jarvis conducting his intrusive inquiry, or if she'll weather the storm right here, with us by her side." He gulped down a breath as if that would help him refrain from casting up his accounts, and continued. "It is the only viable option. And she must send word to Caerlaverock to have the bad seeds weeded out of the staff before she returns."

"Prior to the Duchess leaving Caerlaverock, she instructed the two servants she trusts to dismiss the staff she does not with letters of recommendation." Forrester added.

"I don't like it." Nash interjected. Simon's solution brought him no closer to securing Iseabail's future or her sisters'. He'd brought his friend here to aid him in obtaining the whereabouts of her sisters, instead, Simon's input did nothing to bring him closer to Iseabail or her sisters.

"You don't have to like it, Ross. I will take your concerns to the Duchess. If she decides to make an appearance, she will do so tonight during dinner." Lady Drake stood, and Forrester and Nash took to their feet. Simon, however, reached for one of his black leather boots and began heaving once more. Nash found he could no longer be angry with his friend. He had paid the price for his sins by ruining his favorite pair of hessians.

Sixteen

Miss Sinclair,

I have arrived at Caerlaverock and learned the most disturbing news from the staff. It seems you ordered a new roof and much of my estate to be refurbished while you are on holiday with Lady Drake. I have not authorized these expenditures and have instructed Paddington to cease and desist all current renovations occurring to the ducal estate. I will allow for the roof to be repaired, but that is all.

I have made arrangements for a doctor to meet me at Lady Drake's estate. We should arrive at the end of the week to put this matter to bed.

Henry Jarvis, Duke of Nithesdale

—A letter from Henry Jarvis, heir and presumed future Duke of Nithesdale, written to Duchess of Nithesdale, February 1811

T seabail crushed the letter in her hand. The man was a menace. The gall of him addressing her as Miss Sinclair and signing his letter as the Duke of Nithesdale!

Even she knew the proper address for written correspondence to a duchess. Instead, he chose to ignore her marriage, deny her parents' marriage, and deny the existence of her child's claim to the estate!

If she had an unborn child.

The last bit she should feel a bit guilty over, but she did not. This was Nithesdale's last wish. He didn't want Mr. Jarvis to become duke—if he had, he wouldn't have married her—right?

"Nithesdale believed the staff and the tenants would be better off if you oversaw Caerlaverock." Phoebe reassured.

"But what if Nithesdale had lost some of his faculties in his last days? It's not unheard of. Maybe the servants and tenants would be better off with Jarvis as Duke, because despite his odious and filthy suggestion about putting the matter to bed, he was raised to be the next Duke of Nithesdale."

"Until Nithesdale decided he wasn't. Don't question his motives, Iseabail." Phoebe's advice was filled with confidence.

She was not. "Blast it. Every man in my life has tried to run my affairs, and for once in my twenty-two years I'm in control. Yet somehow, I'm a mere wooden doll hanging onto the strings of their every word and whim. My father, Nithesdale, Nash, Jarvis, and now this ... this Earl of Astley is the one suggesting I show myself at the house party—it's utter madness!"

"He is rather mad," Phoebe mumbled.

Iseabail paced the floor in front of the hearth, unable to enjoy the warmth of the fire.

Phoebe sighed. "However, the Earl's plan is logical, crazy, and sound, despite the lesser societal pitfalls of being seen at a house party while you're in mourning. It makes sense for you to turn to your relations in your time of need. A roof repair is our excuse."

"Openly staying at Drake Manor during the very private house party is not. Jarvis was never supposed to know my current location."

"Paddington had no choice but to tell him once he showed up at Caerlaverock demanding to know your whereabouts."

"As if he had a right to know," Iseabail muttered.

Paddington had had no other choice. She knew that. They had prepared for it. She just hadn't planned on Jarvis arriving when he had.

"Now my excuse to use familial relations and their hospitality at Drake Manor during the repairs of my home will be public knowledge."

"You will have to rely on this new plan of feigned ignorance of the house party taking place, and make a very public second arrival."

Iseabail stopped in front of the fire and made up her mind. "Fine. Once it's dark, I'll go out through the servants' entrance, down to the stables, and have the carriage brought around as if I have just arrived."

"It's your best option," Phoebe agreed.

"If I had an *option*, none of this would have ever taken place."

Phoebe hugged her before saying, "I will see you at supper," and left the room.

Two hours later, with her maid leading the way, Iseabail traipsed across the lawn with her to her carriage. The night air was crisp and clear, the stars glistened down on them as if to mock her drab attire. Her navy cloak with the beautiful light-blue trim and lining she had adored was now black and gray, dyed for her period of mourning to a color that would disappear into the inky night.

"Quickly, Mary. We must not be seen."

"Yes, Yer Grace." Tall and willowy, Mary's shoulders slumped as she limped across the lawn. Mary had been purposely maimed as a child for her aunt to earn more money by the girl begging in the streets. The despicable practice that left many a child with no *options* as an adult, had given Mary few choices as well. Most viewed her lame leg as a sign she would not be able to do manual labor. As a result, Mary had turned to prostitution by the time she was mid-way through her teens. Now, younger than Iseabail herself, Mary had the look of a much older woman in her eyes, and although her limp was obvious, she was stronger than most of the other household maids. She was also grateful for her employment, which made her the most loyal servant Iseabail could ask for.

And she'd been taken in by the kindhearted Nithesdale. Jarvis would dismiss Mary immediately upon being named duke, of that Iseabail was certain.

They made it to the stables where Iseabail's young groom, Thomas, quickly moved forward to take their luggage. For his trouble, Mary scowled and cursed under her breath about not needing the likes of any man to do her work. He winked and gave her a smile as lovely as Iseabail had ever seen on the young groom's face. "That's what I'm here fer, Miss Mary." For his trouble, he got a deeper scowl that only seemed to amuse him further.

"Thomas, if you could get my coach ready, we need to pull up to the front of the house as if we just arrived."

"The Duke warned me to have it ready, Your Grace." Thomas was as jovial as ever, whistling a tune Iseabail had often heard coming from his lips. It was upbeat and jaunty, a song she had long suspected was learned with a pint in one hand and a willing maiden in the other. If he thought it would help him make headway with Mary, though, he was sadly mistaken. The young woman eyed him with distrust the entire time he helped them into the carriage, even sticking her head out the window to watch him load the luggage. A sleepy and somewhat inebriated driver was pulling himself up into the seat to take the reins, and Iseabail was thankful they weren't going farther than the front door, or she might doubt their ability to get there at all.

Within minutes she and Mary were exiting the coach at the entrance to Drake Manor, as if they had just arrived. They climbed the steps to the house slowly, not taking any chances that a guest might be looking out the window and observe too much energy emitting from their bodies. They were after all, weary travelers. Phoebe's butler's eyebrow quirked as he came to the door, but he said nothing of their bizarre arrival. Instead, he took her cloak, handed it to a footman, and then advised Mary where Iseabail's room was, as if the maid hadn't cleaned her room every day for the past fortnight.

"Your Grace, Lady Drake advised me of your possible arrival. At this moment, she is seated for supper with several guests."

"Oh, I had no idea."

The butler's lip twitched. "Of course. I could have a tray sent to your room—"

"Iseabail?" Phoebe's voice lifted with a feigned question, as if she couldn't believe her cousin had arrived at her residence. Oh, but to be able to act as well as Phoebe. The woman was born for the stage.

Iseabail turned toward the open doors of the dining room where every face seated at the table was turned in her direction. Silence filled the room as each of them quieted to shamelessly eavesdrop on Phoebe's conversation with her scandalous cousin. The men had retaken their seats upon Phoebe exiting the dining room, but one man remained standing. Nash.

Iseabail couldn't bear to meet his gaze as she addressed her cousin. She spoke loud enough for everyone to hear, yet soft enough for them to believe they weren't meant to. "I'm so sorry. I had no idea you were entertaining." Her eyes traveled to the dining room and its guests once again, and to the commanding presence of him—the man she hated, despised, and who had somehow creeped into her soul and turned her body aflame with wickedness. The Duke who was approaching her as if it was his right.

"Your Grace." He bowed elegantly over her hand, as if her station was much higher than his own. His actions were absurd and caused a flush to spread across her cheeks as his lips brushed her knuckles. She still wore her gloves, but the heat of his touch brought back searing memories of the previous night.

"I apologize for interrupting your meal—" she started.

"A beautiful woman could never be considered an interruption." His voice carried through the hall, and she felt the interest it garnered from the rest of Phoebe's guests.

She turned toward Phoebe, refusing to give his comment credence, or acknowledge the skip of her heart. He was the reason she was in the mess. "I have disturbed you long enough. I would prefer to retire to my room if that is acceptable."

"Of course—"

Nash interrupted Lady Drake and took Iseabail's hand, wrapping it around his arm. "Nonsense. You must join us for supper, Duchess. You have been alone in that dark dreary castle far too long."

She attempted to dig her kid heels into the carpet with no such luck. If she persisted, she would end up tripping herself and possibly him. She imagined the tangled mix of limbs they would make on the floor and her face flushed scarlet. Drat and double drat. The heat suffusing her face caused two ladies at the end of the table to exchange a knowing look. Now he'd given the guests even more titillating gossip to spread about London upon their return. No doubt they would report she was smitten with the Duke of Ross—why else would she blush so thoroughly when he escorted her to the end of the table where he sat next to Lady Drake?

Why else would he turn to Lord Bradbury and ask, "I'm certain you wouldn't mind giving up your seat for the Duchess of Nithesdale, would you, Bradbury? We can discuss business a bit later." The scandal was beyond the pale.

Lord Bradbury's lips quirked as he bowed and gave her body a less than respectful once over. She could have sworn she heard Nash growl, but when she looked up, he merely dismissed the lord with an absent nod as he held the chair for her to sit down. A footman cleared Lord Bradbury's plate and quickly set a new serving in its place. A chair had been brought to the other end of the table where Lord Bradbury was now sitting next to a widow who batted her eyes flirtatiously in his direction. He seemed surprised and pleased with the new seating arrangement.

Iseabail was not. Yet at that moment, she realized the seating had been off kilter upon her arrival. The Duke had been seated to Lady Drake's right with Lord Bradbury on his right and the Earl of Astley next to him. Now she was sitting in between the Duke and the Earl, and the table was set to rights. Every man had a woman on each side, and likewise for the women.

Iseabail felt as if she'd been purposely duped.

Her gaze flew to Phoebe who was addressing a gentleman on her left Iseabail didn't recognize. He had to be at least an earl, but her knowledge of the Ton was minimal. Bradbury had been to Caerlaverock to see Nithesdale about business in Parliament. She assumed it was the same type of business Nash had been discussing this evening.

A foot rubbed her own and she nearly jumped out of her chair. Nash. Her jaw tightened and she refused to look at him. Instead, Iseabail chose to engage the man on her right, Astley, but that encounter was almost as disturbing as it had been with her nemesis. The Earl was darkly handsome, holding his head with a sardonic lilt that said he knew he did not fit the societal mold of the Ton's pale skin and stylishly tousled hair.

"It is a pleasure to see you again, Your Grace."

"Thank you, my lord," she bit out, knowing he was referring to the parts of her he had seen in the garden.

Nash scowled at his partner in crime, but Astley seemed unfazed. His skin was naturally kissed by the sun, regardless of the season or how much time he spent out of doors. His hair was black as night, darker even, with none of the midnight highlights that made Nash's hair so alluring. Astley's hair was long and full. Sinful soft waves, as wild as the ocean he sailed, splayed over his shoulders. His brows were even darker, and yet he was beautiful in a masculine way. When he turned toward the lady on his right whose breasts were nearly falling out of her gown and onto her dinner plate, Iseabail had nowhere to turn.

She glanced at Nash to see if he was also mesmerized by the display. She was shocked to find his eyes glued to her own less-than-exemplary décolletage. A blush covered her cheeks once more, but this time, it traveled to her chest. Her entire body burned with the heat of his gaze. She heard, rather than saw the breath he released. It was as if he was just as affected by the exchange and memories of the previous night as she was.

"If you hadn't appeared, I was going to tear this house apart to find you," he whispered between sips of turtle soup.

"That would have caused a scandal."

"I am not above a scandal or two, Duchess." The way his voice turned to gravel, she had no doubt he knew exactly how to create multiple scandals at once.

It was then that she heard the whispers of the two ladies on the opposite side of the table who had eyed her upon her arrival. "Nithesdale couldn't even sit up in bed the last month of his life—how could he possibly sire a child?"

"I heard she got pregnant by a footman."

"I heard it was his barrister, Mr. Forrester, there at the other end of the table."

Nash's spoon froze half-way to his mouth. She didn't need to see his face to know the thunderous expression he wore. Anger rolled off him like a storm cloud roaring through the hills of Scotland and the ladies caught sight of it immediately. They silenced and sipped their soup, eyes downcast. The gentleman who sat between them, however, openly eyed Iseabail with the disdain the ladies' words had held.

And there it was. Exactly what Phoebe had described to her earlier. The table was silent. Everyone seemed to be counting how many sins she committed against Nithesdale. She wanted to scream and rant and rave.

It was the man sitting next to her who was reprehensible. He was responsible for an entire family's downfall. He was the reason she and her sisters were not living at Urquhart at this very moment. The reason she didn't have a Season. The reason Nithesdale had felt the need to offer for her hand in marriage before he died and the only reason she'd been forced to accept Nithesdale's ring to save her sisters. As nice as Nithesdale had been, she had always dreamed ...

No. Dreaming was for fools, and she was no fool. Phoebe laughed suddenly as if someone had told her an outrageous tale. All heads turned in her direction.

"You must forgive me, I was thinking of the last house party my husband and I threw." She was addressing the entire table as if it were normal for the hostess to allow her voice to boom throughout a dining room as she recounted a story about her husband spilling his wine all over his hunting partner—Iseabail's dead husband's—lap.

Iseabail didn't think it right to laugh at Nithesdale's expense, yet everyone else seemed to think it was quite acceptable, given how unorthodox the story and the manner it was told. Even Nash chuckled and she found herself drawn to that deeply masculine noise.

She smiled, but feared it looked as if she were choking on the turtle soup. She had to see this through. Her hand instinctively went to her flat stomach.

A ridiculous notion that was not lost on the Duke.

Nash leaned over in her direction as the table continued with conversations. "For most women it takes more than once." His voice was low and only meant for her ears. If anyone could have possibly heard, it would have been Astley, but he was too engrossed in what he was doing to the lady's décolletage to his right, as he wiped up a drop of soup that was quickly disappearing down the front of her bodice.

"I beg your pardon?"

"The chances of there being a babe in your womb are slim." He explained.

Her face flushed once more. Surely, he was not going to discuss this here? He continued as if giving a medical lecture to a pea-brained hen. She glanced about the table, but no one was looking in their direction.

"Think of it as you would a thoroughbred horse or a prized hound."

Good heavens, was he comparing her to a nag, or his favorite bitch?

"Sometimes it doesn't take, and you must bring the stud back around for a few more visits."

Or perhaps he was referring to himself as the stud? Oh, this would hardly do. "I assure you, Your Grace. If, and I emphasize that word most emphatically, *if* I am not with child, I will not seek your assistance again."

"No more visits to my bedchamber in disguise?" Although his face didn't show an ounce of emotion, she got the distinct impression he was laughing at her.

"No."

His tone sobered. "You dare risk your sisters' futures so carelessly?"

"Of course not," she practically hissed.

"Then I will come to your room." He sounded almost bored.

"I ... I have other options." Could this entire situation be more humiliating? She looked at Mr. Forrester.

Nash followed her gaze and snorted. "Over my dead body."

Iseabail worked hard not to grit her teeth. She was, after all, of the same station as he, and she wasn't about to let one of these prigs see her as anything less than a duchess.

It was at that moment she noticed the gentleman sitting to the left of Phoebe place his hand over Phoebe's. Phoebe pulled her hand away, but not before Iseabail heard a low grumble at the other end of the table. She eyed Mr. Forrester who was staring at the gentleman next to Phoebe as if he would challenge him to a few rounds at Gentleman Jack's Pugilist Club. It was rather eye-opening.

And to think she had asked Mr. Forrester to father her child. What a disastrous decision that would have been—for everyone.

Nash leaned over and whispered. "It seems Mr. Forrester is not an option."

"So it seems." Their soup bowls had been replaced with fish, and then the main course of venison and stewed vegetables. Iseabail took a bite of meat.

"There are so many things I could teach you." The gravel of his voice hinted at the manner of things he thought to school her on, and Iseabail nearly choked on the tender morsel in her throat. A warm, strong capable hand began to stroke her thigh under the table and she nearly jumped out of her seat. She calmly reached for the napkin in her lap but grabbed his hand instead as it moved toward the center of her being, the center she had not known existed until this man.

"Are you wet, Duchess?" He whispered.

Yes. "No."

A smile tugged at his lips. "I believe you are being less than honest with me."

Perhaps, but she was being honest with herself. No man had affected her in this manner and she absolutely detested her body's betrayal. He was the enemy, for goodness' sake. What was wrong with her? Her heart beat erratically as she allowed his hand to travel where she desired his touch. She nearly gasped when his fingers brushed her sex ... and didn't that turn her thoughts wanton. What had this man done to her?

"Will you surrender to the attraction between us, or must I remind you of how good we are together right here in front of everyone?"

She grasped at his fingers but only succeeded in driving them deeper into the folds of her gown and it took every ounce of control she possessed not to scream, *don't stop!* She blurted out the only thing she could think of. "Do you know how to play the game, Pope Joan?"

He took a drink of wine with his other hand, acting as if he wasn't driving her absolutely mad. "I haven't played since I was a boy."

"Ahh. Your tastes are much more sophisticated than those of us in the country, who only have the country squire as competition." The disdain in her voice was palpable. She had to get him to focus on anything but what his hand was doing to her.

"On the contrary. I've never held a house party of my own, and as a guest, I have always succumbed to the desires of my hosts." He let his gaze travel down the length of her body to let her know exactly what type of desires he was willing to please as his fingers found the spot she prayed he would not.

He was rewarded when her back went as stiff as his cock. He was willing to bet her body was ready to explode with the desire she wanted to deny.

"So, you will yield to my cravings as well?" she asked, as she picked up her fan and flitted it back and forth in front of her face.

He wanted to ask her to wave it in front of his, because the stifling heat in the room had drastically increased since the beginning of their conversation. "Duchess, I would bow at your feet and serve your every need."

Her smile was slow and sultry until she struck it down with the precision of a knight slaying a dragon. "What in the world could a duke possibly do at my feet that I would find praiseworthy?" She asked, her voice barely loud enough for him to hear.

"When I am finished, you will view my skills with exaltation."

She blushed prettily and he found himself wanting to see her do it again and again—without her clothing hiding the pink tinge traveling the length of her body.

"I'm not certain I know of the skills you speak."

"Give me the opportunity, and you will," he persisted.

"Perhaps we should place a wager on our game of Pope Joan?"

"Winner takes all?" he asked. "Name your price, Duchess."

She didn't hesitate. "One thousand pounds."

For a moment he was struck dumb. Had he heard her correctly?

"Are you afraid you'll lose, Ross?"

He scoffed. "Hardly, but I find that money doesn't interest me when I'm placing a bet with a beautiful woman." For a moment he thought he saw anger as hot as coal flash in her eyes, but it was instantly gone and a coy smile spread across her delectable mouth.

"Of course, money means nothing to individuals such as yourself with vast holdings."

He didn't hold half as much as his father had, but he wasn't about to share that bit of news. It might show weakness on his part. Instead, he nodded in agreement.

"What does interest you?" she asked.

Oh, but his cock stirred with her question. *She* interested him. Her lips. Her neck. Her breasts, her … everything. He wanted her more with every passing moment, and he found himself wanting to know her thoughts and desires as well as her body. It was a strange sensation.

"The next week of your company … in my bed. My bath. The stables, if I so desire. Anywhere I want you, you will bend to my will."

It was the first time he saw fear in Iseabail's eyes, and it was the first time she let her knowledge of his dark reputation slip. She'd felt comfortable teasing and flirting with him at arm's length. Anything more, however, was too much. He had no doubt she had felt *something* for Nithesdale, but they had not been lovers. The attraction Iseabail felt for him, however, was real. Very real.

Her fear disappeared as if it had never existed, and she held out her hand to seal their wager. "The pleasure of my company, versus your one thousand pounds. You have yourself a wager, Your Grace. I will give you a day to refresh your knowledge of the game."

"Oh, my dear, but this will be a sweet victory," he said as he took her hand and raised the back of her knuckles to his lips.

He felt the shiver run through her body. It was only then he noticed the absolute silence at the table. Not a piece of silver scraped a plate, nor a glass touched a lip. Every eye was watching their exchange. Every ear straining to hear their conversation, but if anyone could hear, it was only Astley and Lady Drake, and neither one of them would disclose a word.

Seventeen

Heir Apparent

Ladies and Gentlemen of the Ton,

It has come to the attention of this author that the Duke of N has met his maker, and although we are all saddened by his early demise, one cannot help but wonder if the bastard child of the late Lady S has not seized this opportunity to climb to the rank of duchess on her back. Will there be a child born of the Duke's blood as his solicitors are saying, or will another bastard steal a seat at your table? Only time will tell.

—The Whispers of the Ton, London 28th of February 1811 Published upon the death of Edward Charles Hancock, 6th Duke of Nithesdale

S he was cheating.

They had retired to Lady Drake's personal sitting room off her bedroom while the house party roared on, one floor below. Iseabail's deception at cards was evident in the quiver of her hands and the hitch in her breath. Every now and again he would catch her eying him as if her guilt was at war within herself. If that wasn't enough evidence, the sheen on her cheeks and brow was a definite sign of her nerves getting the best of her.

He leaned back and continued to watch her. When he'd first suspected she was cheating, he'd thought to call her out, but what would be the fun in that. Their wager would cost him a great deal of money, money he could spare and money he suspected she thought she needed despite the wealth behind her title. Iseabail bit her lip. Her tell before the double-cross.

"Duchess, you seem to be at odds with your cards."

Her gaze shot up from her hand and her lip slipped free of her teeth. He couldn't stop himself from being drawn to that mouth. Full and lush, the rosy tint of her lips had turned darker from the way she'd worked them moments ago.

"I'm trying to decide if I should leave you with a shred of your dignity or drag you through the mud for being the rake that you are."

"I have found that ladies love to use rakes in the gardens."

Her cheeks pinkened with his reference to their first and second encounters. He knew a woman's body. Knew how they moved. How they communicated. And everything about the Duchess's body language told him she wanted his touch. Unconsciously she leaned toward him. She brushed her foot against his as she concentrated on her cards. But what had driven him absolutely mad trying to control the lust coursing through his veins, was the way her nipples hardened when his forearm brushed the side of her perfect form as he'd escorted her into the room.

If Lady Drake and Mr. Forrester had not guarded her so intently, he would have taken advantage of the darkened alcove in the anteroom and stolen a kiss—and more. He wouldn't have taken her against the wall, but he would have reminded her of the passion they shared. The undeniable chemistry their bodies held for one another.

Iseabail lashed out with a kick under the table.

"Umpf." His brows drew together as he rubbed his shin. "I hardly think that was warranted, Duchess."

"Your behavior is beyond the pale, and it's your turn, Ross." Her eyes sparkled with fire as she slipped back into using his titled name.

Fascinating.

He pulled the ace of diamonds from his hand and Lady Drake followed with the two and three cards. Mr. Forrester played the four, five, six, and he caught Iseabail biting her lower lip. She was anxious for the cards to be played, yet she made no move with her own. He slowly pulled the seven from his hand, watching as she worried her lip and reached for the ribbon around her waist. She was a terrible cardsharp—even Mr. Forrester's eyes slipped over to catch her movement. Lady Drake made a move to reach for her drink and promptly rested her breasts on the table. Forrester couldn't help but be drawn to the display.

Nash was more entertained observing Iseabail slyly pull a card from under the ribbon of her gown. No one would suspect a small scratch of the ribcage as a diabolical ploy to win one thousand pounds from him. Her left hand immediately joined her right. If it wasn't for how quickly she laid down the eight and nine of diamonds, he would have thought she'd been making that particular move since she was a girl in the nursery back at Urquhart.

"Pope Joan," she announced with a shaky breath, her hand replicating the tremor in her voice as she reached for the counters in the nine of diamonds slot. In this hand, Iseabail had used the nine of diamonds, known as the curse of Scotland, to her favor and his demise.

Nash picked up his glass and downed his brandy. It was bloody difficult to allow oneself to be cheated, even if it was a desirable lady doing the job. "How very *lucky* for you, Duchess."

"Luck be with the ladies, tonight," Mr. Forrester added, as he returned his attention back to his cards.

"Luck or fate." He would lose and pay the Duchess her one

thousand pounds, but he'd be damned if he didn't collect a favor as well.

⁓

Iseabail pounded her pillow. She had retired to her room early. She'd taken the Duke's promissory note and he'd bowed politely in defeat. He had been an ever-graceful loser, but the glint in his eye was pure devilry. He knew they'd cheated. Forrester knew they'd cheated, but since he was somewhat involved in the ruse, that was to be expected.

She punched her pillow once more.

Instinctively her hands went to her flat stomach as if to will her babe to be safe. She was being ridiculous. She didn't even know if she was pregnant. Phoebe had confirmed that one time may not produce a child. Her friend had been married for four years with no conception. Yet it was Phoebe's lack of information about her relations with her dead husband that left Iseabail uncomfortable.

Was it always that way between a man and woman? The sensations and utter bliss the act had brought were unimaginable—until they weren't. Until they were all that she could think about.

She and Phoebe had discussed many things in the past several weeks. They'd studied the books Phoebe had obtained—how Phoebe had got ahold of such tawdry literature, Iseabail didn't know. Even as a widow, Phoebe had appeared shocked and embarrassed by the carnality of the text. Her cheeks pinkened almost as much as Iseabail's had, but the drawings and descriptions had been fascinating and titillating, if she was honest. She'd never dreamed there were so many ways for a man and woman to consummate a marriage. She just couldn't believe the manner in which she had lost herself the previous night.

How could she feel so much for a man she despised?

A sound at her window interrupted her reverie. The crack of a vine followed by the grunt of a man made her jump out of bed.

Someone was climbing the ivy on the side of the house. It was the dead of winter!

She looked around the room for something to use as a weapon to defend herself. She reached for her dressing gown and threw it on, the belt dragging loosely on the floor as she went to the wash basin and grabbed the heavy candlestick. She turned just as her window opened. Any hesitation escaped like the wind. Iseabail tiptoed across the rug, her body shaking as one long muscular leg was thrown over the sill. A dark head appeared, bent into the opening as he pulled his weight forward to work himself into her room. Iseabail swung, but the intruder was faster. The man twisted and grunted as the candle stick struck him.

"Ow! Dammit, Iseabail."

"Ross? What are you doing?"

Iseabail dropped the candlestick and reached to help him into the room, his weight pushing her to the floor as he toppled like a tree in the forest on top of her. The vibration shook her washstand as they landed in a heap.

He didn't move. Or breathe. Good lord, had she killed him? She didn't think she'd hit him hard enough to end his life. Her only intent had been to rattle his brains.

Her breathing short and crisp, her voice cracked. "Are you alright?"

A moan escaped his lips as his body molded to hers.

"Please wake up," she whispered near his ear.

He didn't respond. She could see his back rise and fall with even breaths and thanked the stars above she wasn't a murderess ... not yet anyway. She could very much see herself cracking his skull in two ... or kissing him.

She pulled on his shoulder to roll him over, but he didn't budge. His substantial size and form solid and hard.

Hard. He was hard and growing harder.

"You scoundrel, you're not even hurt." Everything she'd been trying to avoid, came dangerously to life. She bucked her hips to throw his hard length away from her, the movement only made her want to draw him closer.

He lifted his head and their gazes. "You hurt my arm."

"Your arm? You made me think I hit you in the head. You—"

He covered her mouth with his hand. She conveyed every ounce of hatred she had for him through her eyes. He chuckled. "Sweetling, is that any way to greet your paramour?"

The length of him trapped her body, and she hated how good the hard muscles of his thighs felt inside her own, the soft material of his trousers caressing the sensitive flesh now exposed from their tussle. How in the devil had he managed that?

"Can I release your mouth without you bringing down the house?"

She grudgingly nodded, knowing full well she'd give him an earful. His fingers slowly lifted as if he were testing the boundaries of her word. She would not scream. She couldn't. Her body was heating with the intimate nature of their position and it took every bit of her control to ignore the hard press of his cock.

The man was pure sin. Evil in every way, yet somehow her body wanted him, strained to be his.

When his fingers finally released their hold, she said, "What are you doing in my room?"

"You invited me."

She nearly choked on the words. "I did no such thing!" She wriggled underneath him only to feel his arousal push against her center.

"Just as your body is now. You want me, here." His voice was thick and masculine, just like his shaft between her legs, caressing her sex and making her want every inch he offered. "Whatever it is between us, you want this just as much as I do."

She wanted to protest but his mouth descended to her ear, his tongue doing wild intoxicating things to her senses. The words she wanted to spew at him were lost in his kiss, in the decadent way his mouth moved over the pulse point at her throat. Her back arched underneath him, giving him the access he sought. He groaned.

"You drive me mad with desire," he whispered, as he thrust his cock against the apex of her thighs.

He pushed her hands above her head and with one hand, held her, controlled her, owned her. God help her, she loved it. Her body came alive in his arms like never before.

He was right. There was an animal magnetism between them. One large hand held hers as his other began to explore her body just as his lips were devouring her senses—inch by inch.

"Please," she begged.

"What do you want, Duchess?"

She wanted to say, her home, her life, everything he had stolen from her, but her body betrayed her mind and soul with its wanton needs. "You," she panted on a moan as his lips found her breast through the much-too-thin material of her shift, while his forefinger and thumb rolled the taut, traitorous nub of her other breast. "Oh, God," she breathed. The things this man did to her could only be described as evil ecstasy. She understood why it was sinful, yet she found herself wanting to sin for an eternity.

"You taste divine," he murmured against her flesh, the wet heat of his mouth cooled with the puffs of his breath tantalizing her more than she could have imagined.

"More," she whimpered, and he gave it to her. His mouth moved to her other breast as his hand enticingly grazed down her side, lighting her skin on fire with his touch. He stroked her outer thigh, teasing her, taunting her, making her widen her legs of her own accord to give him room to touch her—there.

He chuckled against her distended nipple, his tongue torturing her, making her want to pull out his hair. She struggled against his grip, but he held her wrists tight and it was even more intoxicating. "Even you can agree, once is never enough."

It wasn't. She wasn't sure how she had thought one time would do the trick, but she prayed twice was enough to get this ...

this insatiable *need* out of her system. Her desire for him betrayed every devoir she had lived for.

"Stop talking and do what you—" Her breath hitched as his fingers finally found the spot of pure pleasure between her legs. Fire licked through her lower belly, spreading through her core, her limbs. The moan that escaped her lips was animalistic and wild.

"That's it, Duchess. Feel what I do to you."

She did. He ravished her in a way that wasn't possible. It was wicked—and more erotic than ever before. This man would be her downfall, yet at that moment all that came to mind was, "Don't stop."

"Never," he whispered, and then he was gone. His touch, his lips, his body. She was on the brink of falling apart only to come crashing down to earth to feel the hard floor against her back and the cool night air on her exposed flesh.

She blinked. Her senses confused and demanding she return to edge of rapture. Before she could understand what was happening, she was being lifted from the floor, a soft mattress was at her back, and her wrists were wrapped and bound tightly together with the sash of her dressing gown—the belt that had been meant for him. He spread her legs wide and her limbs were bound to the bed before she realized what was going on.

"What are you doing?" She yanked at her bindings.

"Something you will enjoy immensely." The wicked grin on his lips slipped when he picked up her discarded candlestick and candle from the floor, set it on the nightstand and lit it. His gaze traveled the length of her exposed body and his nostrils flared, his eyes flashing with his desire.

"God, you're beautiful."

She flushed from her toes to her head, unable to say a word as the commanding male looked his fill. His cravat was missing, she caught sight of it wrapped around one of her ankles along with one of her stockings on the other. Nash removed his jacket and waistcoat to toss them in the direction of her dressing table while his eyes devoured her. The next moment he was reaching over his shoulder and pulling his shirt over his head in one quick move. Dear lord, but the man was muscular and hard. His stomach rippled with so many muscles, it reminded her of the waves on the loch, smooth skin covering so much deadly power he could drag her under with no effort at all. And the large straining bulge in his breeches was more intoxicating than a bottle of the best malt Scotch. "What ... what are you doing?"

"What would you like me to do?"

Everything. Nothing. She didn't know. Being under his control was frightening ... yet she didn't fear him. No, it was rather exhilarating. It roused her senses to another level, a level she wasn't certain she could bear.

"I want ..." What did she want? He quirked an eyebrow, waiting.

"I want to see your cock," she said, with more candor and bravado than she felt. His lips curved at the corners and he took himself in hand through his trousers.

"You want to see what pleasures you so?"

"Yes," she breathed, because up until this moment, she had not seen him the way she would have liked to. She wanted to understand him, control his body the way he seemed to rule over hers.

He took his manhood in hand and stroked it through his clothing. "Are you sure you can handle it?"

Could she? She had last night, but ... she licked her lips nervously and saw heat flash in his eyes. Her sex had been wet with desire, but now she was dripping with need.

"Yes." She wasn't sure she could handle any of him. He was like nothing she could have imagined. She hated him—craved him, because in moments like this, she saw something else in him. Something tender and gentle, with an erotic heat that set her body on fire.

He unbuttoned the falls of his trousers and her mind went utterly blank. Lust took over. "Oh, my ..."

Nash smirked. "Do you like what you see, Duchess?" He stepped out of his trousers and she was shocked to see he wasn't wearing any smalls.

"You don't have on any undergarments?"

"No."

"Why not?"

"I find them dreadfully uncomfortable." He stroked his cock up and down and she could have sworn it grew before her very eyes.

She gulped. "Did it just ... grow? Will it get bigger?"

He chuckled. "Most ladies are quite pleased with my size, yet the virgin duchess is not."

With that one statement, he put their encounter into perspective. This was a tryst, a dalliance that would be over before it started. So why did it hurt that there would be more women after her who saw him like this? "I'm not a virgin."

"No, not anymore."

She couldn't tell if that was pride or shame in the deepening of his voice. She didn't want to hear either. Pride would mean he conquered her. Shame would mean he had a bit of a conscience, yet the man who had thrown six young girls out of their home had not felt remorse.

She needed to control this encounter. She pulled on her bindings.

"You're only making them tighter." There was that smirk on his lips as his hand touched her foot and began to move along the inside of her leg, reminding her just how much she wanted him.

The books she and Phoebe had read, however, had described a woman's power over a man even if she was tied up. She hitched her breath and brought his heated gaze from her sex to her face. She licked her lips once more and said, "I want to taste you."

He froze, his cocked twitched involuntarily in the direction of her mouth. "Pardon?" He nearly choked on the word, confirming everything the book had said.

"I want to taste you." She bit her bottom lip. His chest rose in a shuddering breath.

"Where?" he asked.

"Everywhere." She looked directly at his cock and lifted her head. "I want to feel your cock on the back of my throat as you pump in and out of my lips."

His disbelief was wiped away by the erotic image she spelled out for him, and before she knew it, he was straddling her body on the bed. His proud, rigid manhood with a drop of moisture leaking from the tip, just out of her reach.

"Are you certain? Like this, I will be taking all your freedom away. You will not be able to withdraw. I will control your very breath." Was there a hint of desperation in his voice?

"Yes," she whispered, and focused on the beautiful example of male nudity in front of her. She let her eyes travel down his strong jaw to the corded muscles of his shoulders and arms. His broad chest, sprinkled with dark curly hair, narrowed to the rippling waves of muscles of his abdomen that made a woman wonder what he possibly did to create such a magnificent sculpture. Even his lean hips were accentuated by muscles constructing the V-shaped frame leading to his captivating cock.

Goodness, but it was glorious. By the moonlight it had enticed her, but now it entranced her. Long and thick, with veining that should have been unattractive, yet made it vibrant with life and longevity, everything she yearned for. He brought the provocative pink tip to her lips and she flicked her tongue nervously over his seed, tasting him in a way she had never imagined she'd like, until the previous night when she'd developed an appetite for this—for him. She moaned with pleasure and leaned up to taste more of him. He was everything she desired, salty with pure masculine spice that made her senses tingle as she tentatively swirled her tongue around his head, tasting, and tormenting them both.

He grasped the headboard with one large hand as his other

held the base of his cock and he groaned, his pleasure causing his shaft to twitch between her lips.

"How the hell does a virgin learn to do that?" he ground out between clenched teeth.

Her lips turned up in a pleased smile right before she took him deeper into the recesses of her mouth, flattening her tongue to flick the tip of it along the length of the veining. A deep rumble traveled through his chest, and she felt the muscles in his thighs tighten against her torso.

"Fuck." He grunted, his hips moving of their own volition. She looked up and caught his gaze as he pushed in and out of her mouth at a slow pace. It was as if he couldn't decide what was more captivating, watching his member wrapped by her lips, or gauging the heat in her eyes as he pushed deeper. What had started as a way to enthrall him, now enslaved her with pleasure.

His hand moved from the headboard to the back of her neck, supporting her and guiding her mouth up and down the length of him as his hips rocked with the motion. His jaw tightened as his tip hit the back of her throat and her muscles spasmed in an attempt not to gag.

"Relax," he coaxed in a voice so full of gravel, she could have sworn someone else had had entered the room and whispered those words in her ear. She did as he instructed as he eased deeper into her mouth, into her throat. Her eyes burned with the effort and just when she thought she would lose control, he pulled back and allowed her to breathe before he was there again. His hard shaft taking control of her, dominating her body, her breath. Again and again, he pushed in and pulled out, his face a mask of savage ecstasy. There was something so intoxicating about the way his body reacted to the heat of her mouth surrounding him. Every inch of her sparked to life in a way that only he could ignite—until suddenly, he was gone, the flames of ecstasy doused to embers. Once again, right when she was on the brink of something completely intoxicating, he denied her the pleasure her body demanded.

"No ..." she whimpered, because she needed release. Needed him, now.

She opened her eyes, not realizing they had closed, and she felt the tears rolling down her cheeks. He was still there, between her wide-spread legs with his pulsing manhood poised to possess her. The head of his cock caressed her folds, back and forth, driving her desire and her mind to madness as he touched the center of her pleasure.

"Tell me what you want," he demanded.

In that moment her two worlds collided like never before. She wanted him ... the Duke of Ross. The man who stole her childhood and her home. The man who hadn't wanted to ruin her, yet took her tenderly into womanhood. The man she wanted to destroy brought her to her knees with want. However long it took, she wanted this man in her bed and his child in her belly. She wanted ...

"You, Nash." She panted. At any other time, the sound of desperation in her voice would have her running in the opposite direction. At that moment, she forged through every rule of propriety she'd ever learned, toward further ruination of her reputation and soul. "I want your cock inside me, Nash, educating me in the wicked ways of ecstasy."

A grin stole across his lips. "With pleasure, Duchess. I have become a glutton when it comes to you." He thrust inside her viciously, his previous caution unrestrained and thrown to Highland winds.

Iseabail gasped at the thick, deep intrusion. Her shock one of unadulterated bliss as the fires of satisfaction blazed through her body, from her toes to her fingertips to every inch in between. Her mind was lost to his touch.

His lips crashed down upon her own and his tongue plundered her mouth with feral abandon as his hips set a pace she'd never experienced before. His hands owned her flesh, commanding it to heightened awareness as he cupped her breasts and pinched her nipples, sending her over the edge. Her inner walls convulsing around him as she fell into the abyss of the fiery hell she should despise, yet coveted with everything she was.

It was true what the French said. In his bed of debauchery she suffered *la petite mort*, a little death—that was so much more. With Nash, because somehow her mind could no longer think of him as Ross, she had succumbed to the one deadly sin she hadn't committed until now—gluttony—for whatever this was between them, she couldn't give it up—not now. She was afraid she would never be able to escape the undeniable lure of intoxicating Nashford Xavier Harding, eighth Duke of Ross.

Eighteen

Duchess,

If you would like to join me for a morning ride, I will be in the stables at seven.

Yours,

—An unsigned letter to Iseabail Hancock, Duchess of Nithesdale, February 1811, left on her pillow at Lady Drake's house party

Iseabail crushed the vellum to her dressing gown and giggled. It'd been a week since she'd lost her virginity to Nash. A week of secret sex and laughter, sex and tenderness, sex and ... the best days of her life. At least the best days of her adult life. The past week had also been filled with guilt for being so weak as to fall for a man who could so callously turn his back on six young girls. When she thought of it, her chest began to ache. She could not fathom this funny, charismatic man was the same cold-hearted bastard who'd stolen her home eight years earlier. The Duke who continued to own her home to this very day and had never stepped foot into it since their first encounter.

Setting down the letter, she began brushing her hair while sitting in front of her dressing table. She was in quite the bind. Her feelings for Nash were growing, but her acceptance into society remained as Simon had forecast. Not one person at the party, outside her very small circle, addressed her or even acknowledged her existence at the breakfast, supper, or dinner table. Last night she had given up—opting for a tray in her bedroom to avoid their prying eyes and disdainful comments. Before her marriage to Nithesdale, very few visitors over the years had given her the time of day. Now her position was worse than ever.

A light knock sounded at her door.

"Come in," she called.

Phoebe stuck her dark auburn curls inside the room. "I haven't woken you, have I?"

"Not at all. Please, come in."

Wearing a lemon chiffon dressing gown adorned with a fern-green ribbon and slippers to match, Phoebe stood at the doorway.

"I think you become more beautiful by the day, Phoebe."

A blush crept up her friend's cheeks, the same way it would on a young maiden just out of the school room.

"The same can be said about you." Phoebe turned toward the maid. "Mary, if you wouldn't mind, I'd like to have a word with the Duchess."

Mary immediately stopped fussing with her bed linens and caught Iseabail's gaze in the mirror. Iseabail smiled. "A cup of hot chocolate would be most appreciated, Mary."

"Of course, ma'am. May I get you one as well, Lady Drake?"

Phoebe shook her head. "That's not necessary, Mary. Thank you."

Mary gave a quick curtsey and left the room. Phoebe closed the door behind her and turned the lock with a definitive click. Iseabail raised a brow.

"What's going on?" She whispered.

For the first time, Iseabail saw the hesitancy in Phoebe's manner. Instead of floating into the room as if she owned it, she approached as if she were walking on an iced-over loch. Worry lines marred her flawless forehead, and in her hands, she clutched what appeared to be a letter.

Iseabail turned toward the best friend she'd ever had. "What's wrong?" Had their ruse been discovered?

"He's here."

Phoebe didn't need to say his name for Iseabail to understand. The rightful heir to Caerlaverock had arrived at the house party, and with his arrival, the unwelcome weight of guilt seemed to tighten around her throat. She was committing the same crime against Henry Jarvis that Nash had done to her, stealing his inheritance as if it were her due—when it was not.

"He has more claim to Caerlaverock than I do."

"Nithesdale despised Mr. Jarvis."

"That may be, yet it doesn't change the fact that the man has more claim to the ducal estate than I do, or my child does." She shook her head and walked toward the window, longing for a glimpse of Nash making his way to the stable. "I'm not certain I can maintain this ruse in Mr. Jarvis's presence. It's hard enough battling my guilt when he's not here. His presence will be a daily reminder that I'm a fraud."

Phoebe rushed forward and grabbed her shoulders. "I can see the decision on your face, but before you hand the keys to the castle over to Mr. Jarvis, I have a letter you must read."

"I'm not certain a letter will change my mind."

"Perhaps not, but I implore you to read the letter before you do something drastic. Nithesdale asked it of you." Her last sentence was said as a whisper, as if saying Iseabail's late husband's name would conjure his appearance in that very room.

"Nithesdale?"

"Yes."

"But ... but ..." She searched Phoebe's face for a sign of what the letter could possibly hold. In the end she could not determine what manner of information her friend held back, nor why she would feel this was the moment to share it.

"Just read it." Phoebe said and held out the letter.

She had thought the reading of the will was the last time Nithesdale would speak from the grave. Looking down at the bold yet somewhat shaken script of her husband's handwriting, however, she realized she'd been wrong. Iseabail blinked back tears and read just how cruel life could be.

Nineteen

My dearest Iseabail,

I know your heart is questioning everything I have put into motion. I had every intention of finding you the perfect husband, until that ever-challenging lady named Fate stepped in and delayed my grand plan. I then had to set into motion a more devious and selfish plot. I married you and attached you to a dying man who could not give you the large family and security you so rightfully deserve.

Please do not fret over Cousin Henry's inheritance. He should have never been in line to the Dukedom, and he and his family have been compensated well in my will. Caerlaverock and all my estates should have gone to my son.

When I was a young man, I fell in love. She was the catch of the Season and I dare say she fell in love with me as well. However, a man stepped in and publicly compromised her. Her parents demanded a special license be procured and before I knew of the trouble she was in, they were wed.

To make matters worse, she was carrying my child, my son and heir. To my dying day, my beloved despised me for not *rescuing her from the clutches of an evil man. I don't blame her. From her perspective I took her virginity and abandoned her.*

I failed her and our son, and when I attempted to claim the two of them, she denied me. My only recourse was to remain friends with her husband, and in turn, be a part of my son's life as he grew into a man. I never told my son he was mine for fear that my own selfish reasons would haunt his mother. Only two people knew of my son's true heritage prior to the deterioration of my health. However, when a man faces his mortality, many things he thought he could accept in life, become completely unacceptable in death.

I sought Mr. Forrester's legal opinion on how my heirs might one day have their rightful inheritance. We decided it was imperative that one other person be brought into my confidence, as my plan would require her assistance. If you're reading this, the lovely Lady Drake is standing by your side and will explain all that I dare not put into writing.

I would ask this one thing: If you do find yourself to be with child while still bearing my name, please do not remarry until after my heir is born. I hope that fate has finally turned in my favor while I am in my grave, and that you will restore the proper line to the Dukedom of Nithesdale.

Your ever grateful husband,
Nithesdale

—A deathbed letter from Edward Charles Hancock, Duke of Nithesdale, to his wife, Iseabail Hancock, Duchess of Nithesdale, January 1810

Nash slid out of the saddle and patted Týr's sweaty neck. Hard and fast on a new path, his ride had been almost as exhilarating as the ride Iseabail had taken the previous night. A smile tugged at the corners of his mouth as he thought about the way in which she had ridden him. Wild and free, her hair flowing with the firelight glistening off the small beads of sweat forming on her body. Her beautiful breasts bouncing, she'd relentlessly challenged his stamina. She had been glorious. And perhaps a bit exhausted, otherwise she would have met him.

"Did you see Mr. Jarvis this morning?" Nash turned toward Mr. Forrester who spoke from the edge of the barn as if he was deathly afraid of the animals, or perhaps him.

"Yes, he's become odious." He'd been approached by Henry Jarvis while sitting at the breakfast table. Jarvis had made a glutton of himself at the buffet while making lascivious comments about Iseabail. It had taken every last ounce of his control to quit the room before he pummeled Jarvis to a bloody pulp. There was too much at stake to make that mistake. As he led Týr into the barn, his boots collected mud the entire way.

"He's the reason the Duke married the Duchess."

Nash turned to look at Mr. Forrester who was being more candid than he thought possible. "I thought he married her to give her a home and a chance at a future."

"That is true, but it was also his attempt to keep Mr. Jarvis from squandering the estates and placing the staff and tenants in the precarious position of having an irresponsible duke controlling their futures."

It was the exact type of maneuver Nash had been doing since he'd bungled the deal with the Blair family home at Urquhart. "He's protecting Caerlaverock."

Mr. Forrester nodded. "Exactly what he taught you to do with your estates."

He and Nithesdale had shared the opinion that the Ton had squandered enough money and ruined too many futures all in the name of pleasure. It was also a reminder of his own need to come clean with Iseabail. He owed her and her sisters an apology for his ignorance and the carelessness of his youth eight years ago.

"The Duchess has returned to Caerlaverock."

He spun around. "She what?" Her man of affairs had all his attention now. Týr nudged him hard, but he ignored the horse at his back who needed a good brushing down.

"It seems the repairs have been made to the roof at Caerlaverock. She received a missive this morning that said Her Grace may return home. Since Mr. Jarvis had sent for a doctor to examine the Duchess, she left before he could arrive."

He balked at the audacity of the man telling a duchess to do anything. "The man is not her husband, or a prince. He's still a mere mister."

Forrester sighed. "No. He is something much worse."

"What is that supposed to mean?"

Forrester looked at him as if he was a naive schoolboy, despite Nash being older. "One word from Mr. Jarvis, and the lineage of the Duchess's babe will be put into question. He has already sent for a doctor to run tests. Those so-called *tests* could cause her to lose the baby. She will not take that chance, Ross." Forrester pulled a piece of paper out of his jacket. He starred at it, turning it over and over as if trying to decide what to do with it, before he finally looked up and held it out to Nash. "She trusts that you will not be careless with this. I hope her faith is rightfully placed."

Nash bristled and took the letter with the reluctance of a condemned man approaching the gates of Saint Peter before he'd had the opportunity to atone for his sins.

She was *his*. If there was a babe, the child was *his*. To hell with everyone else.

He heard rather than saw Forrester retreat as he gazed down at the delicate scroll of his name written on the front of the correspondence. *Nash*—not Ross, not The Duke of Ross, but the name she used at their most intimate moments. Part of him was jealous she trusted Forrester with her most intimate secrets, yet he also knew it galled Forrester that she trusted Nash at all. That alone made him want to pound on his chest and claim dominance. No matter how much faith she had in Forrester in the past, the man hadn't shared her bed.

"Will you be going back to Caerlaverock as well?" he asked.

"The Duchess is a lady. She will not put her reputation at risk. She travels alone with Lady Drake." There was a warning in his voice that made Nash bristle once more. He was not to follow.

Nash turned away before Forrester said anything else as his groom approached. "Take care of Týr for me, would you, John."

"Of course, Your Grace."

John led away the stallion, who protested with a flick of his head and a snap of his teeth. The groom merely laughed and cooed right back at him. "Och, you're a mean beastie with a loyal heart, you are, Týr. Leave His Grace in peace for once, will ya?"

Nash tried to smile, but his lips wouldn't curve. Not with every one of his fears waiting for him inside the envelope in his hand. He took a long breath and let it out slowly before walking over to a copse of trees and sitting down on a fallen log. The cold damp chill in the air warned of snow coming in fast from the Highlands, and he could only pray Iseabail made it back to Caerlaverock in one piece.

He opened the letter, peered at the graceful scrolls of her hand-writing without taking in the meaning behind the words as he tried to absorb everything about this woman who had come to mean more to him than he thought possible. He blinked, and then started reading from the beginning, his blood freezing as if rigor mortis had taken over his body. His beating heart stood still in his chest, refusing to acknowledge the pain, the anguish he never thought he was capable of feeling.

She was truly gone.

Nash found himself at house party he no longer wished to attend while sitting at a card table with a man he despised. Jarvis was rubbish at cards. He always had been, and it seemed Whist was still a weakness his boyhood friend could not conquer. Since his earliest childhood memory, Nash could recall besting Jarvis in every game they'd played, despite Nash being younger. It had rankled the man's pride at every turn, and yet still he challenged.

"One thousand pounds."

Nash upped ante. "Two thousand pounds to the winning team."

Simon's brow lifted, and he smirked as he increased the bet again. "I'm feeling lucky. Three thousand."

Viscount Alford, sitting between him and Simon, coughed. "Too rich for my blood."

Alford's partner Jarvis, however, wiped his brow and then looked at the viscount. "We have them beat three to one."

"Ah, ah, ah." Simon waggled his finger back and forth at the two men. "No commenting about the game or your cards. That's against the rules."

Jarvis looked at his cards and then looked to Nash and Simon. "You're both bluffing."

Nash shrugged. "Perhaps."

Thoroughly enjoying himself, Simon took a drink of his brandy and sighed with appreciation. "This reminds me of our childhood."

"It reminds me of your arrogance," Jarvis snapped.

Nash pushed to get him where he wanted him. "The game, gentlemen. Are you in, or will you bow out?"

"Yes, Jarvis. Do you dare play without the dukedom in your pocket?" Simon taunted.

"It's a done deal, Astley." The sneer in his tone already betrayed his belief that he was better than Simon. A belief Jarvis had always held. At one time Nash would have dismissed the comment as male rivalry. Their antics had seemed harmless as young men, but now ... it seemed one of them had not known where to draw the line.

"I didn't see either of you willing to sneak into the Duke's study and pilfer some of his fine brandy."

It was Nash's turn to laugh. Not that he felt any humor in the situation. On the contrary. "You were the heir to a dukedom, what could possibly stop you from inheriting?"

"A damn climbing whore thinks she has a chance," Jarvis muttered.

Nash's fists knotted and Simon kicked him hard on the shin. It should have brought pain, he felt nothing but a desire to squash Jarvis like the maggot he now knew him to be.

"I'd say this brandy would rival the old Duke's. Wouldn't you, Nash?" Simon's question brought him into focus.

"Quite," he breathed through clenched teeth. "I understand you must wait to see if the Duchess is with child before you inherit, Jarvis."

"I have it on good authority she is not. Nor has she been able to bribe anyone into her bed to pawn off a bastard as the next Duke."

"Perhaps a female heir? If she had a girl, the child would inherit the estates and lands in Scotland."

Jarvis sneered. "She's not pregnant, but if she is somehow able to produce a girl, the little bastard will not live long enough to inherit." The table grew quiet and the viscount pulled at his cravat.

As if he suddenly realized he said far too much, Jarvis qualified his statement rather poorly. "We all know how many low-borns die after birth. It's the weak blood flowing through their veins."

It was Simon who broke the silence with his laughter. "Those damned bastards are sneaking their way into the Ton by any means necessary. I understand there was even an earl who brought a bastard home from every British colony his position as the regent's ambassador took him." He raised his brow. "And his Indian countess passed them off as her own."

Nash was the only one to laugh at Simon's jest even if he felt no humor in it. The first time he'd heard Simon mock his family's heritage had been at the Astley dinner table during a holiday break from university. The table of bi-racial children, along with the Countess, had roared with laughter. Nash had nearly choked to death on the piece of mutton he'd ingested. Tonight, he could only hear blood roaring a battle cry through his heart.

"I beg your pardon, Simon. I meant no offense." Jarvis cowed ever so slightly. He was after all, still a *mister* to everyone else at the table.

Nash somehow raised a brow, which did nothing to disguise the menace in his voice. "Did you mean to offend the Duchess, then?"

"Of course not." Jarvis cleared his throat uncomfortably, yet the sudden gleam in his eyes made Nash's skin crawl. "How about we make this game more interesting."

What was Jarvis up to now? Had Nash not raised the stakes high enough? "What could be more interesting than playing for blunt?" he asked.

Jarvis smiled. "Why don't you put the papers for that horse of yours on the table?"

He scoffed. "Týr? You can't even go inside the stables without Týr nearly breaking down his stable door. What makes you think you could own him?"

"Oh, I won't own him. I'll sell him to the glue factory."

Nash's stomach turned. Jarvis knew exactly how much Týr meant to him, but if Nash backed out now, he would not only look like a coward, he wouldn't be able to exact the revenge he sought. Yet to gamble money was one thing, to gamble with the life of his horse ...

"You love your horse as much as I love my money. Now you see my dilemma."

Simon interjected. "Gentlemen, I believe we have taken this a bit too far."

Nash gritted his teeth. It had to be done. He would not lose.

"Two thousand pounds *and* Týr against your four thousand pounds."

Jarvis sputtered. Alford looked as if he might suffer from apoplexy.

"You can't be serious?"

"I assure you I am." He was deadly serious about making things right within the world ... at least in Iseabail's world. His child would also be safe after this evening's events. Just one sleight of hand, and fate would intercede. For there were no bounds to Jarvis's narcissistic tendencies—he couldn't accept failure at cards any more than he could look in the mirror and see his true self. For Jarvis, both images would be warped into something far better than what reality exposed to the rest of the world.

As if sensing the pending drama, other members of the house party started to take notice of the play at hand. A crowd began to gather, and Nash cursed his error. He had not considered an audience, and now the idea he received from watching the Duchess cheat at cards, wouldn't work. The card tucked up his sleeve would have to remain out of play. Blast it all.

"Since this has become a Duke's wager," his lip quirked in feigned humor, "I propose the game be between you and me. I will give you the three-to-one score you currently hold, with the winner taking the pot when one of us reaches five. Simon and Alford are no longer a part of this game, or our wager."

"Now see here—" Simon started.

"I regrettably withdraw," Alford interjected while wiping sweat from his brow. He was up and out of his chair before Jarvis could speak.

Simon rolled his eyes and left the table to refill his glass.

At the age of sixteen, the three of them had relied on gin for most of their revelry with a stolen nip of the good stuff here and there. Since then, Jarvis liked the good stuff, and he'd never known when to stop while he was ahead. Each time they drank, Jarvis would imbibe beyond his capacity. He'd suffered the worst after their nights of drinking than any of them, thanks to his inability to decline a challenge.

If the past were to repeat itself—

Jarvis took the challenge in front of him. "Four thousand pounds it is," he spit out.

"Are you good for it?"

"I'm the heir to Nithesdale—of course I'm good for it."

"Just so, I think a marker is required. I'll of course do the same." His voice didn't reflect the queasy feeling in the pit of his stomach. He was putting Týr's life on the line, but it was either that, or his child's.

"Fine." Jarvis scribbled on the piece of parchment Simon handed him. "You're bluffing. Bluffing. I'll be two thousand pounds richer and your horse will be glue by the time the evening is over." Jarvis's expression held a maniacal element that would make a lesser man squirm.

The fool.

With a grand flourish meant to inflame his opponent's nervous tendencies, Nash turned over the last card of his deal—the trump card turned out to be a two of hearts.

Two heartbeats come together to create one. He would not lose his child to this man.

A crush of people surrounded the table to watch the high stakes at play. Jarvis immediately played the ace of diamonds and took the first trick. He played the king of diamonds and grinned in triumph. Nash nodded in acknowledgment of his success and watched Jarvis scoop up the trick. Simon was now at his back and muttered a curse.

"Feeling his loss already, Astley?" Jarvis asked.

"Actually, I just remembered a prior engagement that I don't want to miss. I'm afraid I must leave the two of you to *Duke* this out amongst yourselves."

Jarvis grinned. "I like the sound of that."

Nash rolled his eyes and focused on the cards at play. "Tell Marabella hello."

Simon grunted before leaving the room.

"Marabella DiSimone, the opera singer?" Jarvis nearly drooled.

"Yes." There was no need to feign boredom with talk about his former mistress. Nash had recommended her to Simon prior to his trip to Caerlaverock. Marabella had been a delight, but that had been before Iseabail.

Somehow the Duchess had changed him. Once she entered his life, he understood the difference between sex and making love. The passion between them felt deeper, more meaningful and real. It was like comparing gin to the best port Nithesdale had stashed away in his study. One was good when he didn't know anything better, but with one taste, the other was something he wanted to experience for the rest of his life. Funny how Nithesdale had hidden both from him, and now there was only one that he couldn't live without.

He wanted Iseabail for the rest of his life. He hoped she felt the same. But first he needed to ensure she was never put in danger again.

"Would you like an introduction?" Nash took two tricks without Jarvis batting an eye, his focus remained on thoughts of Marabella.

"You would arrange that?"

"I'm sure Astley would be amenable. That is, *after* you inherit."

Jarvis smiled and Nash took another trick. "I'm feeling very lucky, right now, Nash."

He nodded despite the familiarity grating his every last nerve, and said, "As you should."

Less than an hour later Jarvis was feeling anything but lucky.

"We have a winner!" Mr. Forrester announced as he clasped Nash's hand above his head, and the crowd began to applaud.

"It seems you owe me four thousand pounds." Nash picked up

the promissory note and waved it in the air for the crowd to appreciate. Polite applause turned into jeers. Pats on the back were plentiful, and Nash accepted congratulations with modesty.

Glass shattered as Jarvis wiped the table with a backwards swipe of his arm. Cards scattered, and a lady squealed as brandy splattered her gown. Jarvis raged as he knocked his chair to the floor in more of a drunken state than even Nash had realized.

"You coward—you—you—" Jarvis slurred.

"I wouldn't finish that sentence if I were you, *Henry*. Unless, of course, you would like to meet me at dawn." His tone lowered to a growl. Meeting Jarvis at dawn would be a dream. With his propensity to want to shoot at another person, Nash was certain Mr. Forrester would volunteer to be his second.

"Of ... of course not." As if suddenly realizing his mistake, Jarvis bowed his head. "My apologies, Ross." Jarvis glanced at the crowd who eagerly waited for more, their desire for blood palpable.

And Jarvis knew it. He leaned over the table. "If I might have a word in private."

"Of course," Nash agreed.

"Right this way, gentlemen. You may use Lady Drake's study," Mr. Forrester interjected, with more steel in his voice than Jarvis held in his entire body.

Nash pushed back from the table and allowed Jarvis to proceed him—the last position Jarvis wanted to be in. It was as if he was afraid Nash might strike him from behind. But a knife to the back was more Jarvis's style, not his.

Mr. Forrester opened the door to the study, the crackling in the grate and the sounds of Jarvis's heavy breathing the only sounds to fill the room. Nash couldn't have been more pleased.

"I expect the two of you will conduct yourselves as gentlemen in Lady Drake's home." When both men nodded in agreement, Forrester continued. "Then I will leave you to discuss business."

Nash nodded and Jarvis made a beeline to the decanter on the sideboard before Forrester pulled the two doors closed.

Jarvis turned back to him and downed a glass of brandy before speaking. "I don't have four thousand pounds."

"I didn't think you did."

"Then why did you allow me to bet?"

"I am not your mother or your father. You are a grown man."

"But I have children!" Jarvis wiped spittle from his chin with the back of his shaking hand.

"And a wife, yet that did not stop you from betting, attempting to take a mistress, or implying the Duchess of Nithesdale's unborn babe would die a premature death." The anger roiling through his body slipped through the cracks. Nash's fist blasted Jarvis's nose before he even realized he'd lost control. If the ass hadn't hit the floor on the first punch, Nash would have followed it up with another. Instead, he watched his childhood friend clutch his bloodied nose that was dripping on his cravat, waistcoat, and the carpet. He'd have to buy Lady Drake a new rug. He hoped it didn't hold any special meaning for her.

"What was that for?" The nasal quality of Jarvis's voice grated Nash's nerves.

Nash flexed his fist. "Stand up and I'll explain it again."

When it was clear Jarvis would not be getting up, Nash bent over him. He should have taken pleasure in the way Jarvis flinched, but all he truly wanted to do was pummel the man.

"Heed my warning, Jarvis. Regardless of whether the Duchess of Nithesdale is carrying Nithesdale's child or not," *his child*, "you will steer clear of her and Caerlaverock. You will not go there before or after the child's birth. You will not send an agent, a spy, a maid, or a footman to harm the Duchess or her child. Understood?"

"Y-yes."

Nash pushed Jarvis away with such force, his head hit the wall with a thud. "Then you will disappear to your country home with your wife and children and never say an unkind word about the Duchess or Nithesdale's heir again. If ..." Nash leaned in closer to get his point across and poked Jarvis in the nose. He whimpered, and for the first time Nash saw the blood on his hand from grabbing Jarvis's cravat. He suddenly had no stomach for the sight of it, or the man he'd once called friend. He wiped the blood from his hand on Jarvis's shoulder, smearing bloody fingerprints across the tan wool of his jacket.

"If you do, I will call in this marker and send you to debtors' prison."

"You wouldn't!"

The outrage in Jarvis's voice mirrored his own, but Nash's anger was on the verge of turning extremely violent. He took a step forward and grabbed the coward's cravat once more, to hell with the blood. "It's either that, or pistols at dawn. You choose."

The color drained from Jarvis's face. He knew exactly how good Nash was with a pistol. Nithesdale had taught them both. If Jarvis chose the latter, his blood wouldn't just be spilling from his nose, it would be pouring from his chest.

"I ... I will leave in the morning."

Nash pushed him away. This time Jarvis's head hit the floor. He winced but didn't utter a sound. "You'll leave before dawn or meet me in the mews. Your choice. Either way, you won't ever mention the Duchess's name or her child again. Understood?"

"Of ... of course."

He lifted a brow.

"Yes, Your Grace."

Nash turned and strode from the room. It was high time he took on the role of the Duke of Ross in more ways than one. Especially since he had a woman to claim, and hopefully a child on the way.

Twenty

Castle Under Siege

Ladies and Gentlemen of the Ton,

It has come to the attention of this author that the Duchess of N has banished the male members of the staff at Castle C in anticipation of the birth of an heir. One cannot help but wonder if the bastard duchess really is with child or if she's preparing for battle against the real heir to the duchy. Will there be a child born of the Duke's blood or will blood be spilled?

—The Whispers of the Ton, London, 5th of March 1811
Published upon the Duchess of Nithesdale's return to Caerlaverock

She shivered in the crisp evening air. Despite being inside the coach, the day had cooled the bricks at their feet and their breath formed little puffs of fog like clouds blowing in the wind. Already the trip was rough and bitterly cold. She felt terrible for putting the servants through such a brutal experience. If it had not been for Jarvis's arrival at Phoebe's house party she would have waited, but she could not risk the insinuations he would drop or the discoveries he could make if she remained at Drake Manor.

"He's going to follow you."

"No, he won't. I made sure of it."

Phoebe laughed. "You think a few words on a piece of vellum will stop the almighty and powerful Duke of Ross?"

"I think he will respect my wishes to raise my child as I see fit."

"It's his child, too, Iseabail."

"I don't even know why we're discussing it. I won't know if there's a child for some time."

"Your menses are due this week?"

Iseabail refrained from rubbing her belly. This was her only hope for a child. "Yes."

"And what will you do if you are pregnant?"

"I will raise Nithesdale's child to inherit Caerlaverock."

"The child is not Nithesdale's." Her words were not unkind, Phoebe had been in the wretched plot from the beginning, yet she suddenly seemed to doubt the reasoning for it.

"No one knows that but me."

"And the man who took your virtue."

"He didn't take it, I gave it. There's a difference."

Phoebe's voice softened. "The fact that you would even say that tells me you care more about him than even I had realized."

"There is no place for romance in this world. Love between a parent and a child, between siblings—yes. Anything else is just a fairy tale. Nithesdale loved Nash even more than my parents loved me and my siblings. I will honour that and love my child as strongly. Nithesdale would be very happy to see his grandchild grace the halls of Caerlaverock."

If nothing else, that was the one thing she knew in her heart to be true.

With the quiet lengthening between them, Phoebe's head

began to loll to one side as the carriage bounced in the ruts. They would be home soon. Their three-day trip had been long and treacherous. Each night she had made certain the servants received an extra share of warm food for their bellies and blankets to bed down for the night. Tonight, the men would not have to sleep in the haylofts as they had the two previous nights at the posting inns, and she was glad for that. The thought of sleeping in the hay did not appeal to her at all, until she thought of a particular large masculine body that knew how to keep a woman warm.

"You're dreaming of him."

Iseabail started. "Pardon?"

"You were dreaming of Ross."

"Hardly." To admit that to Phoebe would be like admitting it to herself. She wouldn't do it.

"I wasn't in love with my husband."

Iseabail stilled and tried to make out the expression on Phoebe's face in the glooming light.

"Mine, like most marriages, was one of convenience." Now in her late twenties, there had been twenty-five years that had stood between Phoebe and her husband. She'd cringed at the similarity of years between her and Nithesdale.

"Did you love Nithesdale?" She asked.

Phoebe's head whipped around to look at her in the darkness, and in that instant Iseabail realized her mistake. All this time she had thought Nithesdale and Phoebe were lovers. "I ... I'm sorry. I just assumed ..."

"If anyone knew the truth of my relationship with Nithesdale, I would have thought you did."

"You never—"

"Cared for propriety? Gave a fig about what the Ton thought of me?" Phoebe laughed. "You're right in that respect. The Ton has always seen me as a tradesman's daughter, grasping at what I would never be. I stopped caring in my first year of marriage.

Richard found me crying one evening over the cruel words of a countess. He told me I was made of better stock than any woman he had ever known. It was at that moment that I realized I didn't need to love my husband to be a good wife to him."

"It didn't bother you that he was ... was ..." Lord, but she was tongue-tied.

"Older? No. I mean at first it did, of course. Every young girl dreams of a love match, but Richard doted over me. I can't tell you how many of the girls I knew from finishing school who thought they had married for love only to find out that their husbands kept their mistresses after their nuptials were exchanged. The countess who treated me so poorly was one of them. I pitied her later that year when she tried to lord her station over me."

"You pitied her? Whatever for?"

Phoebe gave a sad smile. "Between the two of us, I was the lucky one. My husband was older and only a baron. Her earl was young and handsome and gave her the pox. Richard loved me. Only me, and he didn't take anyone else to bed. I thank God for him every day."

The sadness lingered on Phoebe's face, and it seemed blatantly obvious that she hadn't told the whole story. "And yet ..."

"Oh, don't get me wrong. In life, Richard took care of me beyond my dreams. I never wanted for anything. I rode in the best carriage, wore the latest fashions, had our house decorated with the finest luxuries, but he spent beyond what our coffers could afford. What Richard didn't count on was taking care of me after his death. It was out of the kindness of Nithesdale's heart that I have survived."

"But he let everyone believe you were his mistress," she said in shocked dismay. "Even I believed—"

Phoebe shrugged. "You don't understand. Before Richard died there was a public scandal involving Nithesdale. Let's just say a certain widow announced his inability to ... to perform in the bedroom."

Iseabail gasped. "What?"

"You see? The Ton can be quite cruel to men and women alike. This particular widow not only disparaged Nithesdale's manhood, but she did it in the middle of a ballroom ... and it was a lie."

"Who would do such a thing?"

"The very woman he loved with all his heart."

She wasn't sure she could believe it. "The Dowager Duchess of Ross?"

Phoebe's head nodded and even in the dim light Iseabail could see the sadness in her friend's eyes. "By all accounts, the Duchess had been in the worst of marriages. She blamed Nithesdale for being stuck in that marriage, and he blamed himself for her predicament, so he didn't even attempt to dispel her attack. That night, my husband and I watched as Nithesdale bowed gracefully and left the ball.

"And then he rescued me from financial ruin after Richard died. Everything we owned was mine before we married and then my parents died while I was on honeymoon. Everything we owned, the house, the estate, the family milner business was left to me, and I allowed my husband to take over everything. I was so young, and he was so mature. I assumed he knew better than me." She shook her head as if chastising her younger self. "He did not. After he died, I found out what a shambles our finances were. Nithesdale taught me how to run my company with a trustworthy business manager. The previous one had nearly run my family's business into the ground, thanks to bad business investments. When Nithesdale asked if he could fire Richard's solicitor, I agreed. I didn't like the man in the least. We hired Forrester on the agreement that the job was temporary until I understood the estate business and could choose for myself whom I wanted to assist me."

"You chose to keep Forrester on?"

Phoebe smiled. "You've seen how competent he is."

Iseabail suspected there was another reason as well, but kept her mouth shut. This was the most Phoebe had ever shared, and she didn't want to risk shutting her down, but the sudden stop of the carriage did it for her.

The driver knocked on the door. "We're home, Your Grace."

"Thank goodness." Phoebe said. "I was becoming as loose-lipped as a drunken sailor." She folded the blanket on her lap and pulled her hood down close to her face. "No better cure for garrulous chatter than some bright lights, good food, with a cozy fire and a pillow to lay my head."

Iseabail would have to agree, all of that sounded nice, but she wished she'd extracted more information about the Harding family before Phoebe stopped talking for the night. Yet did it really matter? The less she knew about Nash, the better. Her heart had already softened way too much for the man she should hate.

Snowflakes clumped to her eyelashes as she stepped into the frigid night air, and she couldn't help but think they were the tears from her frozen, troubled heart.

They hadn't been home but a few days when winter announced how very lucky they were to have reached Caerlaverock. The wind blew as if the devil's fury was sweeping through the castle. A shiver ran down her spine as the fire struggled to keep the chill of the storm at bay. Something felt wrong. It was as if the halls of Caerlaverock had been barren for centuries with only ghosts to inhabit the many rooms. She felt ... at risk. As if the enemy was camped outside Caerlaverock's walls, looking for the best possible place to breach the castle.

Leaving the library for her bedchamber, her futile attempt to locate a distraction only exacerbated her unease. With all the precious books within her reach, she hadn't found one to soothe her troubled thoughts. Iseabail was a duchess alone, stalking through the corridors of her dead husband's home with a possible babe in her womb that was not his.

Nothing made sense. Time was ticking by, yet her life was standing still, and with each passing moment, the thunder boomed through the night like an enormous clock echoing the passage of every second she had left at Caerlaverock.

Iseabail picked up her pace, sensing danger at every turn. Insecurity engulfed her as she looked away from the raging storm. On the opposite wall hung the portraits of dead dukes. Each staring down his nose in judgement of her misdeeds as if he was condemning her duplicity. *She* condemned her duplicity, why wouldn't the aristocracy who'd walked these halls before her? To them, she would be nothing but a grasping bastard.

Heart pounding, she increased her pace, nearly running for her rooms. She clutched her wrapper and night rail in one hand, while she clamped the flickering candle in the other as she ascended the spiral staircase. The sound of footsteps matched her own as she raced down the hallway. She slammed the door to her bedchamber harder than she'd intended. Leaning against the door, she looked around the empty room, the fire burning brightly as if having just been stoked. Despite the loud disturbance of her entry, the room remained silent, the crackling of the wood in the hearth punctuating the peacefulness within. Only the storm broke the silence.

Iseabail drew in a heavy breath and exhaled. "You're running like a frightened ninny," she chastised herself, her chest heaving as if she'd taken her mare out for a race across the Highlands.

Setting down her now extinguished candle, Iseabail slid into the cold bedcovers and thought of her sisters. If they were at Caerlaverock, she would have shared the large bed with them, the six of them giggling and teasing Caillen for the icicles she called toes. "I wouldn't be cold, if you were here," she said to the empty room.

"There's no reason for either of us to be cold," a menacing voice whispered. The promise of violence in those words stabbed like a frozen dagger to her heart.

"Leave!" she commanded. It was the only word she could

utter. Sitting up in her bed, she caught sight of the specter hidden in the shadows. Fear gripped her throat as if the malevolent man had a hand choking the air from her body.

"Why *Duchess*, after all the years I've served you, you're going to tell me to leave?"

She recognized the resentful sneer contained within the honourific long before she saw the form approaching her from Nithesdale's doorway. Then he made that noise she knew so well —the sound she despised with everything she was. Part brutality, part vulgarity, it was beyond foul in its intent.

"Take one step closer and I'll scream."

"Who will hear you? Your maid is abed in the attic and your husband is buried in the castle cemetery, rotting to dust as we speak."

"Don't you talk about him in that manner," she ordered.

Her former footman, Louis, laughed, an ugly sound without humor. "Would you like me to stoke the fire, Duchess?" He made that sound again through his teeth as if he was sucking on a juicy piece of meat.

Iseabail flinched and his snicker personified everything a woman should fear. Iseabail pushed the covers from her body and stood on the opposite side of the bed. "I dismissed you weeks ago," she said, her voice surprisingly steady despite the quaking of her nerves, and the shaking of her knees hidden by her night rail.

"Give a whore a little station and she'll forget her roots are in the working class. But then again, you were born to whore on your back just like your mum, weren't you."

She may have cowered before, but with his disparagement of her mother, Iseabail stood taller, her knees no longer shaking as she addressed the footman who had tormented her since her first day at Caerlaverock. "Louis, you were dismissed from service, perma-nently. I now withdraw my references. Leave at once."

She couldn't see his face with the glow of the fire behind him, but as he stalked across the room, the malice rolling off him was like nothing she'd ever encountered. This man didn't care about her rank or his job prospects. He cared about hurting—her.

Iseabail grabbed the pewter candle holder next to her bed, but he was there before she could swing. Stars flared to life in her eyes as pain exploded in her jaw, and the candlestick toppled from her hand. He shoved her back onto the mattress, and he was on top of her before she could scream. Terror tore through her body. She balled her fist and struck his head until he landed another strike to her temple and darkness shrouded her vision. She could hear him cursing her, feel his rough treatment of her clothing and body, and questioned if she would ever see the light of day again. A moan filled her ears and she realized it was her own voice rising through the dark rubble of unconsciousness.

He would not do this to her. Her baby would not suffer at his hands. If she was not pregnant, her future would be born out of choice, not force. It would not be determined by the likes of Louis.

With her hands now trapped above her head, the neckline of her gown was torn, exposing her breasts as he pushed her shift up to her waist and struggled to undo the falls of his breeches. He lay on top of her, dominating, defiling and degrading her, but he would not get any further. Nithesdale had prepared her for blackguards such as Louis in a manner her father had not.

Iseabail drove her knee up with more force than she would have dreamed possible and connected with his exposed flesh, driving him up and off her with a twist of her hips. An inhuman scream escaped his lips, the pitch reverberating off the walls as Iseabail scrambled across the bed and reached for the candlestick on the opposite side. Louis grabbed at her ankle, and she rolled on her back and brought the candlestick down on top of his head. The hollow thump was not enough to stop him.

"Bitch!"

He scrambled on the bed and grabbed for the candlestick, but missed and she swung a second time, connecting with his temple as he ducked. His cursing ceased. His body slumped.

Iseabail's chest heaved as she scrambled from the bed as if her life depended on it. She was quite certain it did. She ran through Nithesdale's open door, out into the hallway, not stopping until she was pounding on Phoebe's door. It was only then that she registered the cold against her bare feet as Phoebe opened the door in her pristine shift, her hair falling in a long braid over one shoulder.

"Help me." Iseabail could only guess what she looked like, and she knew she couldn't let anyone else see her looking the way she did. If any of the servants suspected she had been raped, her future would be determined regardless of what she said.

"Iseabail—" Phoebe froze, and took in the disheveled mass of curls, the swelling on her face, and the way her hands clutched her shredded night rail closed. Phoebe looked out into the hallway and then pulled her into her room and quickly closed the door. "Are you alright?"

"Yes, yes ... but I may have killed him."

"Who?"

"Louis."

"Louis?" It took a moment for Phoebe to understand who she meant. "The footman you released from service?"

Iseabail nodded, her body beginning to shake uncontrollably. "We must get him out of my bedchamber. If anyone sees him there ..."

"They'll assume any child you bear is his."

"Yes."

Phoebe hesitated before quietly asking, "Is it possible?" Iseabail shook her head, and the relief they both felt was palatable. "Then we must get rid of him immediately, but we can't do it alone. I'll need to call for Paddington."

"No!" She looked around the room for Phoebe's maid. Frightened that word would get out to the servants somehow. How could they possibly hide this?

Phoebe grabbed hold of her arms. "We need help. You said you trusted Paddington."

Tears threatened to spill down her cheeks as Iseabail nodded. She did trust her butler.

"Then I will be right back with him." Phoebe squeezed her arm before she turned and pulled a clean nightshift and wrapper from her wardrobe. "Change into this while I'm gone, then wrap yours into a tight ball and throw it on the fire."

When Iseabail nodded again in understanding, Phoebe said, "Lock the door behind me, I'll be right back."

It seemed hours before the soft tap on the door released Iseabail from the fear that threatened to grasp hold of her and not let her escape. "Iseabail, let us in," Phoebe whispered through the crack.

Iseabail opened the door to find Phoebe with Paddington, his face a mask of controlled anger. "Are you well, Duchess?"

Unable to do anything else, Iseabail nodded and he accepted her response without further discussion. In a low tone she could barely hear, he said, "Wait here, I'll take care of the rodent in your room."

"I need to see if I killed him," she whispered.

Paddington seemed disappointed when he said, "It's harder than you might think to bludgeon a man to death."

"Please."

He sighed. "Very well, Duchess, but if he's conscious, you must let me handle the blackguard as I see fit. Understood?" He looked to Iseabail and Phoebe, demanding each of their agreement with his plans. For a butler, Paddington seemed downright bossy, yet they both acquiesced.

The three of them made their way toward her bedchamber, the only light from the storm outside the window at the end of the hall. Paddington stopped in front of her door, but she guided them further to her husband's door which still stood open. She prayed no one else had come along in the middle of the night to discover what all the racket was about.

Once in her bedchamber, her fear resurfaced. Louis was still sprawled on her bed with a dark stain soaking into her bedding from the injury to his head. His flaccid manhood still exposed, she couldn't help but recall what it felt like with him on top of her, threatening to take away everything she held dear.

A snarl emanated from Paddington's chest. "He's lucky you knocked him unconscious."

"He's not dead?"

"No, but he won't be bothering you again. You can count on it."

"What will you do with him?" Iseabail wasn't certain she wanted to know.

"I know a man who will transport him, no questions asked."

She suddenly thought of a wife and children waiting for this man to return home. They would be left in worse straits than she and her sisters had been. "What about his family?"

"He has no family," Paddington responded, as he began tying the man up with the cord from her bed curtain.

Paddington tore the bloodied bed linen and then tied a piece around the footman's mouth just as Louis was regaining his wits. Paddington curled his fists in the man's stolen livery and said, "If you dare make a noise or look in Her Grace's direction, you will never see the light of day again. Is that understood?"

Louis nodded before looking to the floor as Paddington pulled him to his feet and pushed him toward the door, his limp manhood still exposed.

"As much as I'd love to have him paraded in front of all of the staff, his walk of shame needs to be at the docks, not here." Phoebe stated.

Paddington readily agreed and covered him with the remainder of the ruined bedclothes. "I'll cover him, but I can't bring myself to touch him."

Phoebe's grin slipped to the surface. "I wouldn't have it any other way, Paddington. You are a credit to your position." Phoebe stated.

Iseabail agreed, satisfied that a touch of *quid quo pro* was in store for her former footman. And that Paddington was the best of gentlemen.

Twenty-One

Dearest Emmaline,

By now word of my death has reached you. I know why you felt betrayed by me in life, I do, however, hope that you will forgive me in death and that you will listen to the plea of a man who has so many regrets, he cannot bear for you to experience the same. I ask that you indulge my last request, even though you owe me nothing.

I am not arrogant enough to believe that I know all the cruelties you have suffered to secure our son's safety and security, but I can honestly say, I love you all the more for it. I am also ever so grateful that you allowed me to pursue a relationship with our son, and yet part of me wonders why you did when you hated me so. I do not blame you for that hatred, no one despised me more than I did myself. I failed you in the worst of ways and deserved every bit of the animosity you held for me. You, however, do not deserve the harsh feelings our son harbors. I have attempted to calm his ire toward you throughout the years, but to no avail, and in that respect, it pains me that I failed you yet again.

I thought of taking my chances and confessing to your husband. I fantasized about how he would divorce you and attempt to ruin me. It was a battle I relished with every fiber of my being. Yet early on in your relationship, he made it clear that he would never let you go. He paraded you around to all the balls and house parties as any proud husband should, and I had no idea how evil he was until one night when he confessed all while deep in his cups.

His confession came on Nash's fifteenth birthday, the same night it is said he met a thief outside our club. What he didn't know was that it was not a thief he met in the night, but me. You see, I was blinded by my rage and nearly pummeled him to death with my bare hands. That he survived is just another cruel twist of fate in our lives.

The tragedy of our love, however, produced a wonderful man who deserves everything we could not give him. It is time he knows how deeply he is loved by his mother and father. If I know our son as well as I believe I do, he will forgive us our mistakes and want to form the relationship with you every mother should enjoy.

To the very end, my heart and love have been yours. My wife, Iseabail, knows what must be done after my death and I hope you will honour her path. She too was a victim of your husband's evil nature. She missed out on so much in her youth because of his greed. Orphaned at fourteen, she came to live with me. I will let Nash explain her circumstances since he is so deeply entwined in her past and how she came to be my wife.

I arranged for Nash and Iseabail to meet, and with any luck, by now they have fallen in love. I hope you will take over for me and arrange their happily-ever-after. They deserve in this life what I hope you and I will share in the next.

Forever yours,
Edward

—A letter from Edward Charles Hancock, Duke of Nithes-
dale, to Emmaline Harding, the Dowager Duchess of Ross,
January 1811

"The Dowager Duchess is here, Your Grace."

Nash looked up from his desk. "My mother?" What the deuce was she doing at his townhouse? He hadn't even been home an entire day. He didn't have time to deal with her now.

Before he could tell his butler he wasn't home to visitors, his mother burst into the room. If Mansfield wasn't as nimble and quick on his feet, Nash had no doubt his servant would have been knocked into the wall by the woman making her way across his office floor as if she were leading an army of dowagers hellbent on stopping his sinful ways. Yet this woman was not his mother ... his mother didn't look like *that*.

Her hair wasn't the severe dragon-like hairstyle he'd seen her wear his entire life ... it was beautifully curled. Loose ebony locks laced with strands of gray softened her sharp cheekbones and pointy chin and made him see the beauty his mother had hidden from the world. Nor was her mouth pinched in disapproval but rather turned up in a tentative smile. The unforgiving woman of his childhood, who had appeared in the nursery only when accompanied by his father, wasn't holding herself in the rigid posture he knew. She didn't look like the porcelain woman he'd imagined shattering into a million pieces if he'd attempted to hug her.

And her gown ...

Good God, his mother was exposing her décolletage. He suddenly preferred her normal fare of high laced collars. The men of the Ton would not, and it was as if she was comfortable in her own skin for the very first time in her life. Something *his* mother would never be.

What the devil was she up to? "Mother."

"I'm glad you allowed me to see you."

"Did I have a choice?" Nash waved his butler away and leaned back in his chair, clasping his hands over his taut stomach.

She ignored his rude comment and lack of decorum by not standing as she sat down across from him in the chair normally occupied by his solicitors. "I wanted to talk to you about ..." She glanced toward the windows as if she didn't quite know how to say what she'd come to say.

"Yes?" He prodded impatiently. He didn't have time for her machinations or her latest lecture about his lecherous way.

She met his gaze. "About the Duchess of Nithesdale."

"Iseabail?" Bloody hell, her Christian name slipped off his tongue like a confession. Which only made his mother's grin widen. That was the last expression he expected. Who was this woman?

"Yes, Iseabail." She said Iseabail's name on a sigh, as if it brought her great joy. "I know what you've done."

He was pretty sure no one knew exactly what he'd done, except Iseabail. He didn't respond.

"Your father was a beast." She confessed.

"Tell me something I don't know."

"He took away her family home and you tried to correct the injustice."

He stiffened. It seemed his mother knew more than he realized. "What exactly are you playing at, Mother?"

"I want to help."

"You? You want to help?"

She blushed. The act alone so out of character for the woman he knew, yet in that moment he saw the young vibrant woman she would have been as a young debutant. The one Nithesdale had spoken of with such reverence on more occasions than Nash had cared to hear.

"I have been known to do a few good deeds throughout my life."

"Tithing at church doesn't count, Mother. It's selfish hypocrisy." His words made the light in her eyes dim and somewhere inside him he felt horrible.

"I deserve your disdain, even your hatred, but there are five young women out there who didn't deserve your father's greed. I know you've been searching for them in an attempt to right his wrongs, and I admire you—"

"Don't," he interrupted. He was going to be sick if she continued. There was absolutely nothing to admire about his actions.

"Nash."

"Since when do you call me Nash?" She blushed again, only this time he suspected it was humiliation staining her cheeks. He did that to her, and once again something inside him flinched. He shut it down.

"Sorry. Ross, I've been a terrible mother to you."

"Yes." He agreed. It was true.

She continued undaunted. "I cannot make up for my mistakes."

"'*Mistakes*' is a kind description for the actions of a cold and absent mother." He really was a bastard in all senses of the word.

Her bottom lip quivered but she continued. "I cannot erase the past, but I can help you now."

He scoffed and pulled up to his desk, dropping all pretenses of giving her any more of his time. "That's enough, Mother. I am a grown man with little need for apron strings. I had a nursemaid for that when I was a boy. If you'll excuse me, I have work to attend to." He bent down over his papers and resumed his calculations.

"I know where the girls are."

A large ink blot stained the middle of his expense column. "Pardon?"

His mother fidgeted with her gloved hands in her lap. "I know where the Blair girls are staying."

"You know?" he said, nearly biting the words out of his mouth as he leaned forward and asked very quietly. "And you decided to say something now, instead of say, oh I don't know, eight years ago?"

She shook her head and held her hands up as if he were a rabid dog about to pounce. It was exactly how he felt. "No, no, you misunderstand. I just learned of their whereabouts yesterday, and I knew you would want to know immediately."

How did she know so much about what he was doing? He shook his head, it didn't matter. "Where are they?" He ground out.

"I have dispatched a gentleman to escort the young ladies here to London as we speak. I will be sponsoring Caillen, Máira, and Ailsa this season, and the two younger girls will come out next Season."

Stunned, he just looked at her. He had been searching for the sisters for eight years. Eight bloody years, and suddenly his mother wants to help, and she finds them in what? A month? A week? "How long have you been looking?"

"Since yesterday. I—"

"A bloody day?" he roared, surging out of his chair and knocking it over behind him in the process. He was getting very good at knocking over chairs, but he bloody well didn't give a damn. He had been searching and searching and now he suspected his mother, who pushed out of her chair and backed away from his tirade, was either behind their disappearance, or had known exactly where they'd been the entire time. He pushed his anger down below the surface.

"How long have you known where to find them?"

"Yesterday. I—"

He cut her off once more, rounded the desk and stood in front of her. "Do you expect me to believe you started looking for them yesterday and they are on their way to London today?"

"Ye-yes." She stepped back, but he continued his advance. It was only when she stumbled back into the wall and held her hand up in front of her face that he froze. "Please," she whimpered, her voice trembling as much as the arm she held up to protect her face. "I only meant to help."

He froze. His mother thought he was going to hit her. The cold, stoic woman he'd known his entire life stood before him, cowering as if he beat her on a daily basis.

A memory from his childhood flooded his thoughts. His mother coming into the nursery for her weekly visit. The one day he longed for destroyed before it began, as she reached down to catch him in her arms and was yanked backwards by her hair.

"What's the price for your betrayal, *Duchess*?" His father stood behind her, sneering in her face, her body bowed backward as he yanked on her hair. Her long curls Nash loved to bury his nose in when she read him a nighttime story. Nash grabbed his father's leg and hit him over and over.

"Stop! You're hurting her!" he screamed, only to find himself tossed through the air. His tiny body slammed against the armoire, his head splintering the looking glass. His mother screamed, terror for him filling her lungs. His head had hurt so badly he wasn't sure if it had been his mother or him screaming—until she was dragged down the hallway away from him. The nursemaid ran to his side, soothing and cooing as she applied pressure to the wound on the back of his head.

That was her last visit to the nursery.

Dawning struck him as hard as his head had hit the glass that day, rattling reality into something much different from what it had been a few minutes earlier. He stumbled back.

"My God, he beat you."

When her arm slowly lowered away from her face, her entire body trembling in fear, Nash backed away further. The past no longer crystal clear as he'd once thought. He rubbed at the scar on the back of his head and wondered how many scars *she* wore thanks to his father. "I wish he was still alive so I could kill him."

"The last thing I want is for you to be like him," she whispered.

Nash flinched and walked over to the sideboard where he poured two glasses of brandy. She took the glass from him hesitantly as if she didn't trust him not to turn on her and beat her anyway. That alone told him so much about the marriage she had never disparaged.

"Did you love him?"

"No." Quick and succinct, that one word spoke volumes about how this woman had felt about the previous Duke of Ross.

"Why did you stay with him?"

"Where would I have gone? My parents wouldn't take me back."

"Anywhere would have been better."

"How would I have taken care of you?"

He bit the inside of his cheek and exhaled slowly. She hadn't taken care of him after that day when he was four or five years old. Instead, she'd left him there in the nursery to be tended to by one nursemaid after another. He remembered each of them had been loving and caring ... until his father would see their affection and dismiss them unceremoniously. The only nursemaid who had been sacked by his mother had believed in the rod more than kindness.

But did she really believe replacing a mother's love with a kind nursemaid was taking care of him?

As if sensing his thoughts, she winced. "I know you didn't have the best of childhoods."

"No, it wasn't idyllic." Yet under the circumstances, he suspected it was the best she could have given him.

"We had a roof over our heads." Again, she seemed to think that made up for the lack of any parental affection. "You had the best education, and you were well taken care of."

The last part was debatable, but yes, the servants had treated him well and he'd had a good education. The camaraderie he'd felt at school with his classmates had filled the void his family should've occupied. His first year at Eton had been a whirlwind of activity. Fights he'd lost and won. Bullying he'd survived and grades that could have been better.

When the first holiday arrived, he'd foolishly thought he would go home and find two parents who had missed him, or at least realized their lives were better with him in it. When no ducal coach arrived to pick him up, he learned he was on his own in the world. The next holiday, he accepted the invitation to the Earl of Astley's estate for dinner. It wasn't the Earl, however, who invited him, it was his son, Simon Clark, the current Earl.

On his first visit, Nash had thought the house so very strange. It was blatantly obvious Simon was the only child related to the Indian Countess of Astley sitting at the dinner table instead of in the nursery. The rest were a rag-tag lot from around the world. Yet every single one of them bore the bright hazel eyes of their father.

There was also more love at the Astley holiday table than Nash had ever witnessed in his life. Laughter and teasing and the most deplorable manners he'd ever witnessed.

He'd loved it, and from that moment on Nash found it easier to accept the love that was given to him freely than to force himself where he wasn't wanted. He was better off visiting Astley Manor or remaining alone at school than returning to the ducal home for the holidays.

Now he wondered what those holidays had been like for her.

"What did he threaten you with?" From the look on her face, the way the color seeped from her cheeks, he knew his sudden epiphany was two decades too late.

The softness she had displayed earlier hardened to the cold veneer he knew so well. "He's gone. It serves no purpose to discuss the past." She downed her brandy with the experience of any member of White's, and then held the back of her gloved hand to her lips, the glass dangling from her fingertips. "I came here to tell you that you no longer have to worry about the girls. They will marry well, you have my word."

He had to give her credit, she was attempting to help him, but the question still lingered, how had she done it? "How did you find them?"

"Women talk, my dear. They will share information with another woman any day of the week, but a man must earn their trust. You did not earn their trust." She strode to the library door. "If you want to win your Duchess, I suggest you come to dinner next week and meet the Blair sisters. The Duchess won't be far behind."

She was gone in an instant. In just a few minutes she had turned his world upside down, shook out the cobwebs, and then turned it upside right again. Now she was giving him the opportunity to see Iseabail, to talk to her, hold her, win her. He never loved his mother more.

Twenty-Two

My Lord Duke,
It is done.

With much gratitude,

—An unsigned letter to Nashford Xavier Harding, Duke
of Ross, March 1811

Iseabail was pregnant. Iseabail was pregnant.

Never before had he spilled his seed in a woman—obviously that had been a wise decision. He could have bastards scattered across the country if he had.

Or a household like Simon's ...

He smirked. Two families like the Earl of Astley's weren't possible, but a home with Iseabail and their child ... a house full of children with Iseabail—that he could envision—and desire. For the first time in his life, he wanted one woman for eternity. Their time together had felt as if he was on the precipice of the best life he could ever live.

He folded the letter written in the same delicate hand he'd seen before. She didn't have to sign it for him to know it was her. Then he put the letter in his desk with the other two she had written him. It was dangerous to be certain, but he couldn't let go of the only thing he had of her. He wanted her in his life forever and he refused to give her up now—not after this.

Nash sent for his valet who appeared within moments. "Your Grace."

"Daniel, I need you to pack."

Daniel's eyebrow rose. Like the rest of his household staff, his valet had never quite managed to keep his facial expression under control. It was exactly why Nash had him. His father had despised Daniel immediately. What had been an act of defiance in hiring his valet as a young man of nineteen, had turned into one of the best decisions he'd ever made. That method of hiring with the rest of his staff hadn't failed him to date either. He didn't want a bunch of faceless servants in his household. As a child, the family staff had been the only family he'd had, and it had somehow translated into something much more as an adult. He answered Daniel's quizzical glance.

"We're headed for Caerlaverock."

Daniel grinned. "A wise decision, Your Grace."

"Thank you, Daniel." That little bit of approval meant more to Nash than anything the previous Duke could have possibly said. Daniel was a family man, after all. He had a wife who worked in the kitchens, and they were expecting their third child. If anyone knew how to make a relationship work, it was Daniel. Within the hour Nash was traveling across the city and headed toward the one woman who could make his life complete.

"No men are allowed in Caerlaverock, Your Grace."

Nash looked at the two footmen barring his entrance at the bridge over the castle's moat. "I must speak with the Duchess of Nithesdale at once." The footman on the right who barely reached his chin was shaking. If Nash said, "Boo!" the poor man would probably run for the Highlands. The other would be a handful. He was taller and much broader than Nash, but Nash's temper at being barred entrance was beginning to get the best of him, so the odds lay in his favor.

"We were given your name specifically, Your Grace, and told not to allow you entry." There was a bit of pity in the man's eyes, but that didn't mean he wouldn't uphold the orders he'd been given.

"Bloody hell."

The younger footman began quivering uncontrollably.

The castle door opened, and Paddington stepped out and closed the door behind him before he crossed over to where Nash stood. "Good afternoon, Your Grace. I am sorry to inconvenience you in such a manner. If you had written of your impending visit, I could have advised you that Her Grace is not accepting any visitors. However, since you are here—"

Finally, a bit of sanity.

"—there is a room in the village that you can rest at before heading back to London."

He looked at Paddington as if he were an ass—the kind with two ears and a tail. "I beg your pardon, Paddington?"

"It's been a standing rule since the Duchess returned."

Nash thought of her man of affairs, Mr. Forrester. He'd bet *he* didn't have to climb the castle walls to see Iseabail. "I'm certain if you take my card, the Duchess will see me."

Paddington nodded his head in supplication but refused the card. Nash nearly roared. He had known Paddington for years ... *years*! He'd thought those years were filled with loyalty and good cheer.

Apparently not.

He wanted to storm the castle with rapier drawn.

If he had a rapier, which he did not. "Are you telling me that you are allowed in the castle, the footmen are allowed in the castle, and I assumed Mr. Forrester is allowed in the castle, but Caerlaverock is closed to me?"

"No, Your Grace."

"Good. Then step aside."

"I mean the castle is closed to all men, Your Grace ... except me."

There was a smugness to Paddington's expression that made Nash want to plant a facer on the man for the first time in his life. "Who carries the wood inside for the fireplaces, who carries the water for the Duchess's bath? Who in God's name secures the residence?"

"Her Grace has been very creative since her return."

Nash crossed his arms and waited. "Explain."

"Once a day, the lads load a sleigh of wood and the maids drag the sleigh into the great hall. From there it is hauled up to the second and third floors by dumbwaiters." Paddington seemed quite proud of the process.

"I don't recall any dumbwaiters in the great hall." Because there hadn't been any.

"Those were installed the day after her return. Her Grace did not want the maids to be overly burdened."

"I see. Yet that must be exhausting work for them."

"Her Grace has hired more maids." Before Nash could ask about the footmen, Paddington continued. "The men are housed in the dowager house for the time being, and those who wished to move on were handsomely rewarded with severances and references or a pension. Others are being loaned out to neighboring estates until after the babe is born. Begging your pardon, Your Grace."

Paddington blushed as if talking about Nash's child being born was something he didn't want to hear. It was *all* he wanted to hear about, dammit! That and Iseabail's health.

Yet to everyone in this household Iseabail wasn't his and the baby wasn't his either ... they were Nithesdale's. Bloody hell.

"When does she meet with Mr. Forrester?"

"All communications with Mr. Forrester are done through Lady Drake."

Nash unfolded his arms. That did not seem like something Iseabail or Nithesdale would deem appropriate. Nithesdale had always had his hands in estate affairs. Nash had learned everything he knew from him. "And the Duchess trusts them with estate business?"

"Explicitly. She is learning the estate business and goes over the books on a weekly basis."

Well, at least there was that. "Why won't she allow men in residence?"

"It is not my place to gossip, Your Grace."

Now he'd had enough. There was so much gossip in town about Iseabail that it had to be coming from somewhere inside the castle. "Paddington, in all the years you've known me, have I ever impressed you as the type of man to gossip?"

The servant looked shocked and immediately replied. "Of course not, Your Grace. I did not mean to imply—"

"I know you didn't, but I am concerned for the Duchess. She needs a friend within the Ton, does she not?"

As if finally understanding his meaning, Paddington agreed. "Any help with her reputation would be greatly appreciated."

"So, tell me why every man has been cast out."

Paddington looked at the footmen who, with a nod from the butler, disappeared across the courtyard. Finally, Paddington reluctantly told the tale no one else had. "The last time he was in town, the Duke's heir, Mr. Jarvis, spread some nasty rumors about Her Grace allowing all sorts of men into her bed to ensure she became pregnant."

Nash had also heard some of this at his club, but knew it to be gossip from *before* he'd had his discussion with Jarvis. It was the ridiculous chatter of the bored, looking for entertainment to divert themselves.

"Her Grace drew the attention of one footman who had somehow gone undetected for the reprobate that he was."

Nash's hands turned to fists at his side. "Louis. I heard about him. I thought he had been dealt with." If Paddington had not dealt with the man, Nash would.

"Yes, the man in question was dismissed after the Duke died. Néill, the young lad you made shake in his boots, heard him bragging that he would be coming into a bunch of money once the *true* Duke inherited. He reported it to me, and the Duchess had me fire him. Except Louis was somehow able to sneak back into the castle after the Duchess returned from Drake Manor. He has since been deported."

Nash ground his teeth. "I wasn't aware of any incident."

Paddington nodded. "That is good to hear. Since that morn, no men have been allowed to enter the castle, except me."

If Paddington had been avoiding his gaze before, now he stood up tall and addressed Nash, man to man, not servant to Duke. "Had I known his true nature, he would have been dismissed from Caerlaverock years ago. I assure you, he is no longer in the Duchess's employ or a threat to her."

Nash wanted to deal with the blackguard himself, but the man being transported was probably better than Nash being connected to murder. "I need to speak with her." He wasn't quite pleading, but his tone took on a more beseeching quality than the arrogance of his station.

"If you would look up to my right, Your Grace?" Paddington looked over his right shoulder and Nash followed his gaze to the most beautiful sight he'd ever seen.

Iseabail.

She stood in the top window of the turret, gazing down at him. Her long hair fell over one shoulder and she was wearing a conservative navy-blue day dress that was like nothing he had seen her wear since the first day he saw her at Caerlaverock. Her expression was one he could only describe as blissfully sad, as her hand rubbed her midsection. She reached up to gently touch the glass. It was as if she couldn't believe she was truly witnessing him being barred entry into her cell—a prison of her own making.

For a moment he could have sworn a tear fell down her cheek … but then she walked away. The woman he loved walked away. Without looking back. He wanted to bellow her name. Yell loud enough for the entire countryside to hear him declare his love for her, but she simply walked away.

"I'm sorry, Your Grace." Paddington's voice shattered what little hope he'd held. Even the servants knew she was moving forward without him. It was humbling, to say the least. If his heart weren't shredded in tatters, his ego certainly would have been. As it was, he honestly didn't care if the staff pitied him.

"Congratulate the Duchess for me. I heard she is expecting the new heir of Nithesdale." Nash turned and walked toward the carriage, leaving behind everything he never thought he wanted, but now wanted more than ever.

~

"He's gone."

"Good." She rubbed her stomach feeling anything but good. His baby was torturing her body. Every morning she woke up to an even worse bout of morning sickness than the last. And everyone said that was a good thing—everyone but her.

"Don't you think—"

"No."

"You don't even know what I was going to say." Phoebe's voice was filled with compassion, but her words spoke of her impatience.

"You were going to plead his case as you have done every day since we arrived. Enough."

"Iseabail—"

She didn't wait for Phoebe to continue, she walked out of her chamber. "I'm going to the nursery where the views are more serene." Where she couldn't see the one visitor she wanted to see but shouldn't. "Besides if I continue to look out that window, Ross will just get angrier. As it is, he looked angry enough to break through every guard I posted at the entrance."

Phoebe followed close on her heels. "I disagree. His Grace looked vulnerable. He was staring up at you with such longing in his eyes that I have no doubt he loves you."

She wanted to believe she'd seen the same thing in his eyes. She shook her head in disgust as she entered the nursery. "If you believe that, then I have a story to tell you about Highland fairies."

She approached the window and let her gaze fall upon the trees and the wetlands beyond that led to the seas, and confessed her true desires. "I dreamt of a son with dark locks like his father's and his grandfather's, running through the woods chasing imaginary dragons back to the sea. I wish his father could be there with him, using sticks as swords in a pretend battle for the ages. Father and son battling the beast to set me free."

"That can all come true."

"No. It's utter rubbish. I don't need saving. I'm the only dragon slayer my child will ever need." She turned to look at her friend, an angry tear sliding down her cheek. "Not the servants. Not Nithesdale. Not Nash. Me. As God as my witness, I will slay any dragon, demon, or blackguard who dares to threaten my child."

"I understand your reluctance to trust—"

"Nithesdale gave me the opportunity to save myself and my sisters with our honour intact. It's up to me to seize that opportunity and raise our child." Not six children with the man she loved, but one beautiful child she would love to her dying day. She truly didn't need anything more than that.

And yet her heart ached for more.

"No one will challenge a duchess."

Iseabail rolled her eyes. "You are quite wrong about that,

Phoebe. I am already a duchess and I am questioned at every turn. Now, stop following me."

"Someone needs to knock some sense into your head."

"I'm fine."

"Not anymore."

"Phoebe, I am well aware of Mr. Jarvis waiting in the wings to pounce on the duchy, and only a blind person would have missed the disdain for me from the guests at your house party."

"You have the loyalty of the staff," she argued.

"That has been reduced dramatically, thanks to Mr. Jarvis's meddling." To think how close she'd come to missing out on the joy of the child in her belly. To missing out on Nash ... yet he was just a memory now. One she would cherish for the rest of her life. "I am giving birth to Nithesdale's heir. I will be here, at Caerlaverock, for our child. The Duke of Ross will have to find his own duchess in London."

Phoebe sighed and left the room. It was only a matter of time before she abandoned Iseabail as well. Like her husband before her, Iseabail would remain at Caerlaverock—alone—while the person who had captured her heart slept in another's bed.

He was truly gone.

Twenty-Three

An Heir is Born

Dear Reader—

From the dreary Uplands, word has reached this author that a certain Duchess of N has borne an heir. Simple arithmetic tells one the child could be the dearly departed Duke's, however, the castle remains in lockdown, refusing admittance to any man, including the Crown's doctor. It has been a veritable nunnery since shortly after the Duke's death. One would not question such an act of mourning if the Duchess herself had not been seen at Lady D's house party in February.

Is there a secret about the child the Duchess is desperate to keep?

—The Whispers of the Ton, London, published 15th of November 1811

Was it true? Had Iseabail born his child? Nash folded the scandal sheet and put it under his napkin as the giggles of Iseabail's sisters neared the dining room. He normally read the scandal sheet himself and then let his mother read it, she then passed it on to the girls. This morning, he would keep it hidden until he sent word to Caerlaverock and determined the truth of the matter.

The women reached the door, and their joy silenced as each one of them looked at him in that knowing way they had since his first day back in town. He rose and bowed. "Ladies. I trust you all slept well after last night's activities." He counted one, two, three, four ... was the fifth missing? There was a fifth, wasn't there?

His mother gently pushed the girls farther into the room, and Nash went through their names one at a time. Máira, Ailsa, Edeen, Robina, and ... who was missing? It was on the tip of his tongue but for the life of him, he could not recall the name of the missing chit. The blasted scandal sheet had scattered his brains and he couldn't think for shite.

From the day he had returned from Caerlaverock, these young ladies had been his focus, outside his estate business—unless his mind wandered to the babe growing inside Iseabail's womb.

A chorus of "*Ross*" went up as the women made their way to the sideboard to fill their plates.

He sat back and shuffled the food around on his plate. Until moments ago, he'd been a man lost in a sea of dresses and ribbons, shopping and parties, and gossip and lists of which bachelor was looking for a bride and which one was looking for a fortune. His only goal had been to see her sisters well placed, despite Iseabail dominating his thoughts.

When her sisters spoke her name, his ears magically tuned into their conversations.

"She gave herself to a decrepit old man for us."

"She sacrificed her future so that we would have one."

"I would never trade myself for the lot of you, and Caillen would probably marry a beggar just to spite all of us."

That was the missing chit's name! Caillen. He felt a moment of pride that he could process any of the conversation after reading today's gossip rag.

"Mother and Father would be so proud of her."

Thank heavens his mother had taken over the job of preparing the young ladies for the Season with more care and aplomb than he could have managed in a lifetime. The only thing he knew about the Season, was how to avoid matchmaking mommas and scheming debutants.

"We don't have much time, ladies. You are due at your fittings at half past one."

"Yes, Your Grace." The girls agreed in unison.

Dress fittings were the one thing the girls didn't argue about.

Nash took a drink of his coffee. "That seems to be the one thing you girls do agree on—spending my money on gowns."

Robina grinned. "We're more than happy to spend your money on new wardrobes."

"I thought your sister Caillen liked to spend my money on books," Nash interjected.

"That was *before* she met Lord Griffith," Edeen smirked, and another round of giggles traveled over the table.

"Ladies, mind your manners," his mother corrected.

"Before Lord Griffith, Caillen wanted no part of dressmakers or the marriage mart. All she cared about were bookshops and the lending library," Ailsa added.

Robina added two more pieces of fish to her plate, and his mother cleared her throat. Robina looked up to see the Dowager Duchess shake her head before she returned one. Out of all Iseabail's sisters, thirteen-year-old Robina Blair was going to be the biggest challenge to find a suitable groom. The bare feet visible at the edge of her gown were the least of the obstacles his mother would face.

Nash winked at the girl when he caught sight of her bare toes.

Robina grinned and quickly made her way to the table while defending her sister. "She planned to live with Iseabail at Caerlaverock as governess to the future heir. Then she could educate the future duke as to the worth of young women."

That had earned a collective eyeroll from her siblings and a nod of approval from him.

"Is Caillen not feeling well this morning?" He asked.

"She has locked us out of her room," Robina replied.

"Robina isn't wearing any slippers," Edeen tattled, as she daintily took a bite of eggs.

His mother leaned over and looked for bare feet.

"Caillen says some cultures bind young girls' feet to stop them from growing. All in the name of making her more appealing to a man."

"Big feet are rather unattractive. You should see my sister's." Simon entered the room as he shuddered in mock horror, sprinkling the area with water from his wet head. Then he grinned from ear to ear as he bowed to the room at large before running his fingers through his hair. The girls broke out in raucous laughter, but his mother was too busy greeting Simon to admonish them.

Caillen was the only sister who wasn't completely smitten with his friend. If anything, she was the one sister who might throw a dagger through Simon's heart. Or at least clobber him with a book from the library. Her absence probably spared him from having a bloody breakfast table. Simon winked at the girls and waited his turn to fill his plate from the silver serving bowls set out on the sideboard.

His mother closed her eyes and took a deep breath through her nose. Nash suspected she was saying a prayer for polite conversation.

"Corsets are definitely a torture devise," Ailsa chimed in.

His mother's eyes shot open.

Robina nodded. "They're to make a woman's waist appear smaller."

"And her bosom—"

"Enough!" Nash put up his hand to stop the girls from continuing the discussion before his mother died of apoplexy. The girls looked down at their plates and silently continued to eat like a group of hungry boys at university. He still couldn't fathom where they put all that food.

"Has Caillen's maid been in to check on her?" Nash asked, just to make certain the girls knew he wasn't angry.

"When Caillen is in a mood, no one wants to go near her," Maira replied.

Nash winced. He knew more about women's moods since returning to Harding House, and finding it overrun with femininity. He understood how raising six girls could be too much for their father to handle. He wasn't certain he would survive the next few years to see all of them married.

"Máira," his mother admonished, "Certain topics are not to be discussed in the presence of a gentleman, nor over the breakfast table."

"He hardly counts as a gentleman," Edeen added. "He's our guardian."

"I think you've been handed your manhood by a pack of she-wolves barely out of the schoolroom." Simon took a seat next to him with a plate full of food.

"Are you running short on funds?" Nash asked him.

"Nashford Xavier Harding!" his mother exclaimed, as if he was still in the school room.

The girls giggled behind their napkins. Simon winked again. If he didn't stop that, Nash was going to have to close that eye permanently.

"It's quite all right, Duchess. Nash and I have never shied away from talk of finances."

"I will have to ask that you do in the company of his young

wards who have impressionable minds," his mother warned, although by the batting of her eyes, Nash suspected his mother was just as smitten with his best friend as the girls. Simon could walk in the room smelling like horse manure, and every one of them would greet him as if he wore the scent of heaven.

Nash froze with the fork on the edge of his lips. Prior to the Blair sisters' arrival, Simon had only been an occasional breakfast companion at his townhome—after their nights out carousing with merry widows on their arms.

This was not the norm for Simon. For Nash it was a life decision. For Simon—Simon was taking breakfast at his table two or three times a week—sometimes four, with three young women on the marriage mart.

Simon looked toward the youngest, Robina. "So why is your sister locked away in her bedroom on such a fine morning?"

It wasn't a fine morning at all. Bloody hell. It was as if the frigid, wet weather finally woke him to what was happening right before his very eyes. Simon was besotted with one of the girls, and he was plying Robina for information! Nash had seen him charm a roomful of women, only to end up in the arms of the one woman he'd completely ignored throughout the evening.

Simon had ignored Caillen's snorts of disgust over his flirtatious comments for weeks. He'd kill the blighter before he'd allow him to seduce one of his wards.

"She was in quite the mood last night after the Farrington Ball. It seems her *beau* was not pleased with the Duke." Ailsa's description was rather politely put. From her tone, however, Nash suspected the young woman cared less for Caillen's suitor than he did.

"Did you really need to be so harsh with the young man, Ross?" his mother asked.

She was the last person he expected to question his judgement.

"Yes. I did."

"He was only interested in her dowry," Simon said, before taking a bite of toast.

Nash eyed his friend. He did not question the information Simon had given him about Caillen's suitor the previous evening. He did, however, now question why Simon investigated the newly appointed baron's background.

"I thought you were happy with Lord Griffith courting Caillen?" Ailsa questioned.

"Information came to light that I'd rather not discuss." Nash had initially thanked the bloody stars for William Griffith. The man had somehow captured Caillen's attention, despite the girl having no use for the Ton.

"Caillen was pretty upset with you, Duke." Robina buttered a piece of toast and appeared to mimic Simon's less-than-proper eating habits as she took a bite and began talking with her mouth full. "Ever since that article appeared in *The Whispers of the Ton* about our parents, Caillen didn't want to have anything to do with the Ton. Then she met Lord Griffith and she seemed to drop her emotional armor."

"Or he tore it off her body," Edeen added, with a wicked twinkle in her eyes.

Giggles broke out at the table.

"Girls! We do not discuss clothing being removed in mixed company," his mother admonished.

All four of the girls continued to giggle, and Nash glanced at Simon to see if the out-of-control siblings reminded him of home. He expected to see him hiding a grin. He was not. Simon sat staring at his plate as he swallowed his last bite of toast as if it were a stone.

God help him, he would not survive Iseabail's sisters.

"Lord Griffith has quite a bit of debt. Is that why you refused to allow him to continue courting Caillen?" Robina asked.

"Robina, that is not a topic for us to discuss." His mother took a sip of tea and looked at Nash over the top of her cup. If he didn't know better, he would suspect her of planning to leave Iseabail's sisters at a school for wayward girls.

"How did you learn that?" Simon asked.

The Dowager glared at him, but Simon was too interested in Robina's answer to notice.

Robina beamed under Simon's attention, and Nash swore under his breath. He'd have to kill him. He had no choice.

His mother turned her glare on him. "Really, Ross. You're not helping."

Simon repeated his question to Robina. "How did you learn about Lord Griffith's debt?"

Robina shrugged and took a bite of fish. "I have my ways."

"She digs in people's trash," Ailsa added to the conversation.

His mother sputtered her tea. "Robina!" She choked.

"Ow!" Ailsa blurted as she grabbed her leg.

Robina scowled. "Rat."

"*You're* the one digging in smelly garbage."

He was losing control of his household.

Robina changed the topic. "Griffith has been the source of many a scandal. Did he ask for Caillen's hand?"

"No," Nash answered honestly. He hadn't given the bounder the opportunity. Until the Farrington Ball, when Simon had set him straight, he'd thought it was a good match. Now he was finding out that Simon wasn't the only one who knew Griffith to be a rotter through and through who was only in search of an heiress.

Simon snorted, bringing Nash's focus back to the current conversation. He eyed his friend more carefully, unable to discern if his interest was in Caillen, or in the sister who seemed to need more supervision than he'd realized. Surely it wasn't the young Robina.

He thought of the entire written report on Griffith's reputation at the gaming hells and brothels which Simon had handed him less than twenty-four hours earlier. It was abysmal. Griffith was a violent drunk and nothing Nash would wish upon any woman, let alone Iseabail's younger sister, who couldn't see past the man's wit and charm to the scoundrel buried under the facade. Hell, he'd missed it.

"I think the baron is dreamy," Edeen said, with all the romanticism of youth.

Robina dismissed her. "You're blinded by his smile, just as Caillen is."

"You mustn't judge the worth of a man on his chemistry alone," Máira lectured. "Let me demonstrate."

To prove her point, Máira walked over to the sideboard and poured a cup of coffee. Nash bit back a smile and his mother released a sigh. Máira's obsession with scents had entered most of their dinner conversations, to the point where Nash knew exactly what she was about to demonstrate. So did his mother. He liked his coffee strong, without cream and sugar, a trait he learned from an American.

Máira took the steaming cup over to her little sister and let the fragrant steam waft in front of her face. "Breathe it in and savor the rich aroma." Edeen closed her eyes and took a deep breath, filling her lungs with the scent. "Don't you just love the bouquet of coffee? Can't you taste how wonderful and indulgent it will be on your tongue?"

Edeen nodded with enthusiasm. In front of the entire family, she was going to be introduced to a drink she'd been told was only for grown-ups. The look of expectation of Edeen's face as she accepted this rite of passage into adulthood was almost painful.

"Now take the cup, easy so you don't spill it."

Edeen nearly rolled her eyes, but caught herself when she saw Nash's raised brow.

"I've been serving tea for years, Máira. I think I know how to handle a cup of coffee."

Máira smiled. "Of course you do. You're a Blair. Now slowly taste it, but not too quickly so you can savor the experience."

Edeen did the opposite, as Máira, and everyone else, knew she would. She gulped the hot brew like it was an iced lemonade. Then spewed it across the table and onto Simon's face and cravat.

Nash couldn't stop the chuckle that escaped his lips. Her sisters openly laughed, while Edeen turned ten shades of red. If she'd had red hair, her expression would have been lost. As it was, her horror was quite visible.

"Girls, that's quite enough," the Duchess admonished. "Máira, get a damp towel for the Earl. The servants shouldn't have to clean up the mess you've made."

"Yes, Your Grace." Máira nodded, but leaned over the back of her little sister's chair and said, "Just because something appeals to one of your senses, doesn't mean it's good through and through. Men can be very appealing on the outside, but their hearts can be rotten to the core and leave you wishing you'd politely passed on the offer."

Simon wiped his face with his napkin. "Thank you, Edeen. I now have an aromatic scent that is a hundred times better than the pungent bouquet of wet man and horse that I arrived with." He followed it up with another wink.

Nash recognized it for what it was, comforting a girl's tender heart. It wasn't flirtatious in the least.

With that, the elder sister grabbed one of the extra napkins on the sideboard and wet it with water from the pitcher. Then she rounded the table and approached Simon. Nash watched his friend's reaction closely over the top of his cup of coffee. His own heart had been cold and black, until the heat he felt for Iseabail thawed it. The experience was exactly like the sip he took from his cup—searing and sultry to the very last drop. It heated him from his core to his fingertips. It was anything but rotten. It was vibrant and alive despite the months he'd gone without seeing her.

Simon, however, felt none of that for Edeen, Robina, or Máira. He'd had the perfect opportunity to look down the bodice of Máira's gown, and instead looked down at his cravat. No. His friend was not one to miss an opportunity, which made the situation even more odd. Until Simon turned to the Dowager and said, "Don't you think someone should check on Caillen? Ensure she doesn't need a doctor?"

His mother blinked as if noticing Simon as a man of the aristocracy for the first time in her life. An earl—interested in Iseabail's sister. A smile formed on his mother's lips, the likes he'd only seen on matchmaking mamas.

It *was* Caillen. His mother recognized it just as Nash recognized it. The very girl Simon had protected from a scoundrel.

"I mean ... I've never known her to miss a meal." Simon's stammer indicated his own recognition of the grin still lingering on the Dowager's face.

"Robina, darling. Go fetch your sister and ask her to join us at the breakfast table. I have something important to discuss with her."

Robina dropped her utensil, allowing it to clatter on the china before leaping out of her chair.

"Put on a pair of slippers while you're above stairs," his mother called after her.

"Yes, Your Grace!" Robina yelled, as she ran from the room, bounding up the stairs, no doubt two at a time.

"You have your hands full with that one," Nash smirked.

"*We* have our hands full, dear son."

Nash nodded and turned his attention back to Simon, while trying not to draw too much attention of the three remaining girls. "Would you like to tell me about your intentions?"

Simon nearly choked on the air. Dabbing at his cravat with the wet napkin, he refused to meet Nash's gaze. "I have no intentions. I was merely expressing concern."

"Concern for a young lady who happens to be on the marriage mart?"

That questioned garnered more attention than he desired. Máira nearly forgot where her seat was located, Ailsa struggled to swallow her food, and Edeen merely blinked in rapid succession. Simon stood up so abruptly his chair fell to the floor. There seemed to be quite a few chairs being knocked over since the Blair sisters had come into his life.

"Pardon me, Your Grace," Simon said to his mother as he righted the chair. "I seemed to have remembered a very important appointment that simply slipped through my thoughts in my haste to enjoy your breakfast table. If you'll—"

"She's gone! She's gone!" The sound of footfalls sprinting down the stairs and through the hall signified the level of panic in the young voice yelling out the alarm for everyone in the house to hear, and possibly the neighbors as well. "She's gone!" Robina yelled as she skidded to a halt in the doorway frantically waving a piece of paper in her hand. "She's really gone! What are we going to do? Duke, you must find C—"

Ailsa was by her side with her hand over her mouth before Robina could tell everyone within the block that her sister Caillen was most certainly ruined. "Don't scream. Of course, Ross will help locate your *cat* for you. We wouldn't want anything to happen to her. She has a litter of babies depending on her."

"Start searching for Robina's *cat*. We wouldn't want her struck by a passing carriage." His mother directed two footmen standing at the door, who bowed and immediately disappeared from the dining room.

"Ow! You heathen!" Ailsa hissed as she pulled her hand back, Robina's teeth marks evident on her index finger.

Any other time, Nash would have found the scene humorous. This morning it reeked of disaster. He took the letter Robina refused to let Ailsa read and scanned the contents.

Dearest sisters,

I tried to reason with the Duke, but he would not hear a word I had to say about Lord Griffith. I know that William does not come from great money, but I do not care. Dowry or not, we will live a happy life together as man and wife. The Duke does not understand what true love is, the Dowager does. It is filled with hopes and dreams of a better tomorrow, of challenges and sacrifice, of true devotion no matter what obstacles we face.

I will miss you deeply, but I must follow my heart, for I have found the love match our parents wished for each of us. I hope the Season is wonderful and glorious for you all. It was never a path I would have chosen to take for myself. How I found such an incredible man so quickly is beyond anything I have ever dreamed. Please wish us well on our journey to Gretna Green. I will write to you when we are settled.

All my love,

Caillen

"What utter drivel," Simon said from over his shoulder.

Nash scowled at him and then his mother. What nonsense had she filled the girls' heads with? Yet the stricken look on her face gave him pause. "Do not worry," he told the girls who now stood together as one. "I will bring her home," he promised. "Before anyone is aware of her disappearance. In the meantime, you must attend your appointments and the dressmaker's as previously scheduled."

"And what of the ball we have planned for Friday? If you are not there, and Caillen is not there ..." His mother left the question hanging in the air with the innuendo the Ton would create.

Nash cursed under his breath, every eye in the room looking to him for a solution. This was his family, and they were depending on him.

"I will head to Gretna Green and cut them off in your stead." The steel in Simon's voice was like nothing Nash had ever heard from his jovial friend. Yes, they'd been in fights and brawls, like all young men, but Simon had always laughed through the entire scuffle, making fun of their opponents and themselves. Now, however, his friend was more serious than Nash had ever seen him.

He pulled him off to the side. "What is it that you haven't told me about Lord Griffith?"

Simon bit his lip as if to stop from saying too much before he finally said. "I have picked up the pieces of Lord Griffith's past once before. It was not pretty."

Nash's heart stuttered for Iseabail's sister. "The pieces?"

"He was not kind to his last mistress. She has since retired to the country with her child, but not before she was permanently ... scarred."

"What did he do to her?" Nash didn't want to know, yet he needed the truth. He needed to be prepared for what Simon might find.

Simon glanced back at the women patiently waiting for their discussion to end. "Her beauty is no longer visible from the outside, but she is a good woman."

"You took care of her?"

Simon reluctantly nodded.

"Why?"

Simon rubbed the back of his neck and then said the most honest and forthright thing Nash had ever heard come from his lips. "My mother is a saint. She took my siblings in and raised all of us equally. How could that not have a bearing on the man I am today? You have my word as a gentleman, I will bring Caillen home safe."

Nash gripped Simon's bicep and patted his other arm in the most intimate embrace they'd ever shared. "Thank you. It won't be an easy task."

All seriousness disappeared from Simon's countenance with his grin. "Nothing ever is in your household. There's about as much drama in Harding House as there is in the Queen's fitting room." Simon shuddered, and once again despite the dire circumstances, the girls giggled. He performed a sweeping bow to the room and was gone before the sisters stopped blushing.

"Girls, go get dressed for the modiste. We leave at the hour."

The sisters left in a group as if they knew by standing together, they were stronger. Hell, he'd probably taught them that lesson when he'd taken Urquhart from them. Nash ran his fingers through his hair.

"I'm sorry." His mother's voice was full of regret.

"Did you tell her to elope with Lord Griffith?" He kept the accusation out of his tone, but it was there, hanging in the air between them.

"No! I told the girls that true love will find them, whether it's convenient or not."

"This is not true love," he informed his mother, angry with her despite his desire not to be.

"Of course it's not. Everyone knows Lord Griffith is on the hunt for a dowry."

"Did you tell Caillen that?"

"I dropped several discrete hints. I thought she understood my meaning that he was not a suitable candidate for marriage." She bit her lip, her eyes darting back and forth as if she were looking for a hole to escape to. "I made certain all the girls knew ..."

He walked over and took his mother in his arms, something he'd never done before. It should have been awkward. It was anything but.

"I'm sorry," she said into his chest. "You trusted me with them and I failed—"

"You did nothing of the sort. I should have told her what I knew."

"Do you think Simon—"

"Yes. Simon will get to her in time."

She nodded and then pulled away. "I saw *The Whispers of the Ton*."

He winced and turned away without acknowledging his mother's comment. What could he say? That he'd bedded the Duchess of Nithesdale and the babe she bore was not Nithesdale's child but his own? And if she had delivered this early, then the child was in danger? He couldn't focus on a stupid ball, or Caillen, when he was failing *her* at every turn.

"I fell in love with Edward my very first season."

That got his attention.

"Edward?" Nash stared at his mother. No one, not even he, called the late Duke by his Christian name. His mother's face expressed more sorrow and heartbreak than he would've thought possible.

She nodded. "He was the best of men. We planned to be married."

"You what?"

Her sad smile warmed. "He proposed to me toward the end of my first and only Season. We were so very happy ... and we, we did what most young couples do when they are in love and plan to marry, we anticipated our vows ... intimately."

"You what?" He sounded like Simon's family pet. The parrot, however, displayed a slightly more intelligent response, despite the lewd nature of the phrases it repeated over and over.

His mother went to the sideboard, ignored the tea and the coffee, and went for the decanter filled with brandy. She filled two glasses and turned back to him. "I think we'll both need this," she stated, as she took a sip and savored the way it went down her throat. Nash did the opposite. He tossed it back without preamble, just like Edeen had with her coffee. He did not, however, spit out a drop.

"Edward disappeared the next day. I didn't know where he'd gone. I couldn't go to his residence and my letters went unanswered. When I heard he'd left town, I was heartbroken. I attended the balls hoping he'd appear but found myself wandering the gardens, crying the hours away. It was on one such occasion that James found me—and I found myself compromised."

"You were already ruined," he stated the obvious. Nithesdale had been a reprobate after all.

"Yes, but society did not know I was ruined. Only I knew, and my hand was forced despite my denial that anything had occurred between James and me."

His chest compressed. "What are you trying to tell me, Mother?"

She took a drink and let out a slow breath before meeting his gaze. "My parents would hear nothing of my objections. I was publicly compromised and Edward was penniless—his father had run the estates into the ground. What I didn't know was that his father, uncle, and cousin were all killed in a carriage accident. Edward had gone home because of the accident.

"I didn't know. I didn't know." Her voice trailed off as a tear ran down her cheek and her gaze seemed lost somewhere over his shoulder. "I was wed to James by special license the very next week. I told him on our wedding night that I was not pure.

"It was the first time he hit me. He vowed not to bed me until he was certain I was not with child." The laugh she released was filled with anything but mirth, and he knew beyond a shadow of a doubt where this conversation was going. He wasn't certain if he wanted to run from the room or tell her to stop talking.

In the end, he waited for her to continue. His entire life held in the balance.

"My courses never came. I bore my first, and only child eight months later ... you." Another tear fell down her cheek. "The Duke was furious, he hated you from the day you were born and every day after, when I did not give him a son."

Nash fell in the nearest chair. It couldn't be. Nithesdale was his father? After all these years of viewing Nithesdale as the only man to admire and shape himself after, it turned out he not only took advantage of his mother, but he'd taken advantage of Iseabail as well. Maybe not physically but in the eyes of society she was tainted. And now his own child wouldn't be his, because his father stole his right to parent his child.

"I hated Edward for the rest of his days," she confessed.

He hated Nithesdale. Loathed him with everything he was.

"He tried to talk to me, but I refused to listen. On your fifth birthday, he was there, like every birthday before that. He was there. It made me angry. He'd repeatedly asked if you were his, but I'd always denied it. That day I told him he was your father, but he would never be able claim you or leave his estate to you because you had your own dukedom to maintain. In that moment, I think I destroyed him."

"Since the day you were born, James forbade me to visit you in the nursery more than once a week and on special occasions. Your birthday was always the best day of the year. James was never there to celebrate, but for some reason, after I broke Edward's heart on your fifth birthday, James appeared. He'd never attended our festivities before, I had no reason to suspect he'd show up on that day. I suppose it was karma slapping me across the face for being so cruel to Edward."

She poured another glass of brandy and held the decanter in his direction. He declined with a shake of his head.

"He was deep in his cups when he found me playing on the floor with you. It was behavior unbecoming a duchess ... and he beat me for it. For loving my son." Her lips turned up at the corners in a sad smile of acceptance.

"I wasn't allowed to visit you again. I received updates from your nannies. When Edward still wanted to be a part of your life, I allowed it for you, not him. I knew how good he was with you and I wanted you to know you were loved ... by someone. I still hated him for the fate he'd left me to. Luckily, James never knew Edward was your father. If he had, I have no doubt he would have ended his friendship with Edward long ago."

"Nithesdale was my father? You're certain?" He said the words for nothing else than to see how they felt on his tongue. They felt right—yet all wrong.

His mother nodded.

"Why didn't he come for you before I was born?"

"According to Iseabail, he did, but my parents sent him away. I believe he spent as much time with you as he thought he could get away with, without James suspecting anything."

"Iseabail told you? When? How did she know?" And why didn't she tell him?

"We've been writing since her sisters arrived, but that's all I'm going to say. You'll have to ask her what else she knows, but I need to know something, Ross." She hesitated, and he watched her throat work as she figured out how to ask the question that was so difficult for her to form. "Do ... do you hate me for not telling you sooner that Edward was your father?"

He should hate her. She should have told him. She knew how badly the Duke treated him, yet she also knew how much time he'd spent with Nithesdale. Time that was free of the drama that would have been there if he'd known. He'd spent more time with Nithesdale than anyone in his family—more than he had with the man society believed was his father ... and that wasn't such a bad thing.

He shook his head. "No, Mother. Nithesdale played an important role in my life. I admired him and looked up to him. There were days when I wished he was my father, and in many ways, he was. You did the best you could."

His mother's chin quivered, and tears rolled freely down her cheeks. Then she was throwing her arms around his neck and hugging him in a manner she never had before, harder than he had moments earlier. Nash felt his own eyes grow moist and had to clear his throat before he asked the next question.

"Why did he marry Iseabail?"

His mother pulled back and he handed her his handkerchief. "I can't say for certain," she said, as she dabbed at her tear-stained cheeks. "I can only speculate that he believed you would chase after her if he did."

It was his turn to nod. He did chase after her.

"Is the child his?" Her voice wavered as if she really didn't want to know.

"No, it's mine. Their marriage was never consummated." It was the first time he admitted it to anyone. Simon may have suspected, but his mother now knew the truth.

"And will you claim the child?"

"She refused me."

The Dowager Duchess finished her drink and put the glass down on the table without a sound. "Then it is done. Edward's heir will inherit the ducal seat of Nithesdale as he should."

Nash drew back, suddenly understanding Nithesdale more than he had in a very long time. Yet how was it possible? "And if it's a girl?"

"It's Scotland. Whether it be a boy or girl is irrelevant. If it's a girl, the title will, in time, go to the next heir, her son or grandson, but the lands and income immediately go to his female heir. I would say Edward planned that very well."

Nash snorted. "How could he have possibly known?"

"Known?" She laughed "My dear boy, even I knew how obsessed you were with the girl."

"The *girl*, Mother. I was obsessed with finding the girl and her sisters and making things right. I was not infatuated with her. I didn't know the woman Iseabail had become."

"And yet you are more than infatuated with her now. Perhaps Edward saw how perfect the two of you were for each other."

It wasn't a question. He answered it anyway. "Yes."

"What will you do?"

"Nothing."

His mother threw her hands in the air as if she'd met the dumbest man to walk the earth. "James would not let me love you, and by the time he died, I didn't know how. You know how to love. Your *real* father taught you that. I've seen it in the way you treat her sisters."

Nash ran his hand through his hair. "She doesn't want me, Mother." Some of the pain leaked into his words, and he wanted to curse his weakness.

"Do you want to know my opinion?"

"Not particularly." He was learning to get along with her and not resent her for the past. He wasn't sure he was ready to take advice from her though.

She ignored him. "Let her heal after the birth. The real birth. In the meantime, continue to take her sisters out into the Ton just as you would if she were standing by your side. And wait for her to come to you."

"And if she doesn't? If she hates me because I allowed Caillen to run off with a bounder?"

The grin on his mother's face held more feminine wiles than he'd ever known her to possess. "You trust Simon to take care of Caillen. As for the Duchess of Nithesdale coming to London? Leave it to me. By the end of the Season, she will be knocking down your door ... and I will spoil my grandchild like no other." With a swish of silks and muslin she quit the room and never looked back, the curls in her hair bouncing as they would have when she was a young woman in love.

A year ago, he would not have believed he could sit in the same room as his mother and have a meaningful conversation. Yet now, he trusted the Dowager Duchess. He also knew that Iseabail was on a mission to right a wrong, and she would stop at nothing short of achieving her goal.

Twenty-Four

A Wedding to Anticipate

Dearest Reader,

It seems the Ton has not one diamond of the ball, but three sought-after Sisters of the Season. The gentlemen have been seen tripping over themselves to get a slot on the dance cards of the beautiful sisters B. The Dowager Duchess of R is sponsoring the young ladies in what is deemed to be the most talked-about Season in ages. The Duke of R has been seen escorting the sisters to all the most important affairs, guaranteeing a certain amount of attention from those vying for his favor. It is said the ladies are keeping the Duke quite busy with callers, all of which he watches like a hawk.

I must warn you, however, Young Lady A may not have much time left on the marriage mart, for she has been seen on the Duke's arm for more dances than this author can say. Could there be a new duchess very soon in the realm?

And what of Lady C? She has missed the last three balls

and has not been seen in any of the bookshops she frequents. Where has this young lady disappeared? This author must further ask, what has happened to our scandalous earl? Could his disappearance be linked to hers?

—The Whispers of the Ton, London, published 16th of January 1812

Iseabail was going to kill him … if his child didn't kill her first. She tossed the scandal rag aside and gazed down at their beautiful son. Nash would certainly take affront to her calling his son beautiful, but he was. Edward Xavier Blair Hancock, seventh Duke of Nithesdale, who should be the eighth Duke of Nithesdale, was the most precious child she had ever seen. He had his father's eyes, and his grandfather's gentle smile. His father's temper and his grandfather's laughter. But most of all, he had her love—like both men, because without them, she wouldn't have Xavier. He was the reason she woke up in the morning and the reason she laid down her head at night.

"You really need to hire a wet-nurse."

Iseabail laughed at Phoebe who was staring at her wild, unkempt hair as if it contained bugs. "I wouldn't pass this time up with him for anything."

"Fine. Then let the nursemaid take care of him long enough to bathe."

"I assure you, I have bathed."

Her friend muttered something that sounded suspiciously like, "You couldn't tell by looking at you."

"My gown is clean as well as my body and hair. All my son requires of me he has, and more," she said in a hushed tone, as she laid the baby down in his bed.

Phoebe was right behind her, grabbing her by the back of her arms and dragging her to the wardrobe. "Look in the mirror, Iseabail." She gazed at her reflection in the mirror with

Phoebe. "You are in dire need of a brush and you have dark circles on top of bags under your eyes. Your cheeks are hollowed and your shoulders are slumped. You are hardly the young woman who captured the attention of a duke at my house party."

"I am a mother now. My son needs me, and if that means I must sacrifice my appearance, I will." She grabbed her brush and began brushing out her locks just to prove to Phoebe that she didn't let herself go completely. It was after all, only noon. By all of society's standards she should just be rising from her bed.

"Fine. What are you going to do about that?" She pointed accusingly at the scandal sheet on her bed.

"Nothing." She pulled harder on the tangle that didn't want to release her brush. It was as bad as Nash was on her heart. Wrapping around it and refusing to free her from his hold. "You're going to let him court Ailsa?"

"That's merely a rumor." The tangle gave under the pressure, and she nearly struck herself in the jaw.

"I have received word that the rumors are true." Despite how softly her tone delivered the blow, it still hit its mark right between her third and fifth rib. She didn't know where Phoebe got her information, and she really didn't want to know because most of the time the intelligence was spot-on.

She closed her eyes and swallowed down the bile threatening to choke the life out of her, then lied through her teeth. "If it's true, I wish them all the happiness in the world."

"You wouldn't mind Ailsa having a child by the same man you do?"

Yes, blast it! "No."

Phoebe took the brush she no longer realized she held and began gently stroking it through the length of her hair. "Don't you wish for Ailsa to have a man who loves her for the woman she is, not the woman he reminds her of?"

Iseabail stared at Phoebe in the mirror, but her friend ignored her glare and watched each stroke of the brush. "What are you saying?"

Phoebe finally met her gaze. "I'm saying Ailsa reminds him of you, and right now your sister is blissfully unaware of him being the father of your child, but if it came to light ..."

Iseabail grabbed the brush and slammed it down on her dressing table. The tone of her voice echoing the vehement denial of her words. "I don't know what you're talking about, and you will *never* disparage my son's birthright again."

Phoebe shrugged. "As you wish, but I, for one, would not want to play second violin to my sister."

"You don't have a sister."

Phoebe ignored the biting tone of her words and smiled. "True, but that doesn't mean I would want a man whose heart belonged to her. I couldn't bear it, nor could she." Phoebe left the room without another word as Iseabail's anger fueled to a boil.

She picked up her abandoned hairbrush and flung it at the closed door, taking no amount of pleasure from it ricocheting off the wood and clattering across the floor.

Xavier wailed, and Iseabail found herself taking three deep breaths before she walked over and picked up her son. "Shhhhh, darling. It's okay. Mommy's here. Everything is okay." She rocked her son in her arms, walking around the room, holding him tight. As Xavier calmed and began to fall asleep in her arms, Iseabail made her decision. "I think it's time for a reunion. Tomorrow we will travel to London for you meet your aunts."

～

Nash entered his home to the sounds of women giggling and cooing. Cooing?

The giggling was normal. He'd learned to tune it out as he stealthily entered his home without making a noise. Even the servants had begun to assist him. Mansfield was extremely adept to opening the door with his finger across his lips, alerting him to the ladies' presence. The footmen never asked to take his hat and coat, they silently held out their hands and nodded with a conspiratorial wink. Today, his butler was decidedly absent, and he had to open the door himself as the footmen were nowhere to be seen.

It was the cooing and then some ridiculous gibberish that sent his heart galloping through the entry and into the drawing room.

He didn't immediately follow it. Too afraid he was jumping to conclusions, he slowly removed his hat and coat and laid them on the entry table. Then he took two deep breaths, wet his lips, and marched through the doors with the command of a duke. When he entered the room, his exterior persona portrayed nothing of his inner anxiety. He held his head high and slowly perused the room. Trying not to let his heart leap from his chest because the neighbor had brought her nephew over for the girls to admire.

The cooing stopped before he could locate the imaginary neighbor amid the sisters and servants and his mother and Lady Drake and—

Iseabail.

He blinked. Cleared dry eyes that had taken too long straining and staring at every other woman in the room before finally finding *her*—more beautiful than he remembered. Her eyes were haloed with the fatigue of a new mother, a slight stain marred the bodice of her travel-worn gown, and her face and figure were slightly fuller than the last time he'd laid eyes upon her. He wouldn't have noticed any of it if he hadn't been cataloging every inch of her while trying to convince himself she was real.

Iseabail was here. Here. In his drawing room. Holding a baby. His baby.

He swallowed, an audible gulp unbecoming a duke escaped his person, but he didn't give a damn. Mansfield cleared the room of servants with a nod of his head, and then it was his mother's turn to get rid of the rest.

"Ladies, we have a ball to prepare for."

One of the girls, he wasn't certain which, began to object. "But Iseabail is here—"

"And she will be here tomorrow and the next day and the next," his mother interrupted as she herded the girls out of the room better than any sheep dog could have possibly accomplished. The door handle clicked and they were alone.

"Is—is—" He sounded like a babe learning to talk. The words unable to form, his voice lost somewhere in his throat.

"This is your son, Edward Xavier Blair Hancock, seventh Duke of Nithesdale. I call him Xavier."

He would have argued about their son's title, but she'd somehow included his name, his real father's name, and her father's name in one perfect bundle. The glorious smile on her face captivated him as he slowly walked closer. Afraid to disturb the babe, who stared at her with as much adoration in his eyes as his father's.

And then his son looked over and met his gaze. It was the most wondrous moment of his life. It was as if Xavier knew with that one look, exactly who his father was. The bond was like nothing he'd ever felt, but it wasn't just with his son, it was the connection between the three of them. Strong and unbreakable. He would gladly give up his life for this woman and their child, yet he would much rather share a future with them.

Iseabail slid over on the settee and then patted the cushion next to her. She balanced their son in one arm as if she had done such a thing her entire life. Perhaps she had with her sisters. "If you want to hold him, I think you should sit."

He met her gaze, shocked that she would agree so easily. "What if I drop him?"

"You won't."

"But if I do?"

"I'll be here to catch him."

Nash sat down next to her, amazed that he could be so close, and not want to ravish her. If he was being honest, he did want to bed her then and there, but their son ... how could any man pass up the opportunity to hold his son?

He sat down and held out his hands awkwardly.

"Relax. Sit back and I will place him in your arms."

Nash did as he was told. Iseabail after all was his child's mother and had been caring for him ... for how long? Before he could ask, she placed the small bundle in his arms, and dark brown eyes full of so much wisdom peered back at him. "He's beautiful."

"He looks just like his father."

A tear rolled down his cheek, but he didn't care. He wasn't ashamed of his emotions. How could he possibly hold so much joy and love inside him without it seeping out at the seams?

Xavier smiled, the dimpled grin every sane person would adore. "The papers said he was born in November. Is that true?" His son fisted his thumb in the most glorious show of strength he'd ever witnessed.

"No," she whispered. "December seventh, the same day as his grandfather. It's as if Nithesdale blessed us twice over with a reason to celebrate the day our son was born." He looked up at her to see the same wonder in her eyes as he felt.

"You knew that Nithesdale was my father?"

"I learned of it before you came to Caerlaverock. I owed it to Nithesdale to see the estate remain in his family where it belonged —where it would be kept safe."

"That's why you refused me?"

Her smile was a bit sad, yet he could tell she was content with her decision. He loved her all the more for it.

"Yes." She cleared her throat. "When did you learn? From the letter Nithesdale wrote me and from what Mr. Forrester has told me, the two of them believed you didn't know."

"When the announcement hit the newspaper of Xavier's birth, my mother told me. It was as if my life suddenly made sense."

"I see, and now that you know exactly who you are, do you plan to wed?"

Xavier stirred in his arms, his tiny face scrunching up like he'd had a bite of something distasteful, and he grunted. "Yes, I do."

"Do you have the young lady in mind?"

His son's face began to redden. "Is something wrong with him?" God don't let anything happen to his son.

"I believe he is soiling his diaper." Her tone sounded irritated, which made him wonder if he'd misunderstood.

"He's what?" The sound that emanated from his son was unmistakable. The feel of his backside against Nash's arm even more telling. "Oh."

"I'll call for his nursemaid." She was up and pulling the servants' bellpull before Nash even knew what was going on. There were parts of parenthood he could do without, and when the maid walked in and took the baby from his arms, he was more than happy to give him up for a little while. Yet at the same time, as he watched his son leave the room, he wanted him back. He could see himself growing accustomed to caring for his children in every sense of the word. Just not today, when the unwelcome smell of bodily functions would interrupt the very important task he had at hand.

He watched as the nursemaid left the room, the door closing behind her.

"Are you courting my sister?"

The question caught him off guard. He should have expected it, of course. The scandal sheets had hinted at it. He and her sister had planned it at his mother's urging. All to get Iseabail here, but he'd honestly never thought it would work. How could she not know where his heart lay? Yet she stood very still, her back turned toward him, waiting for him to answer.

"No." He watched her shoulders rise and fall as if she took a breath of relief before she returned to the settee and sat down in front of the tea service. She poured two cups, her hands slightly shaking as she put two lumps of sugar in her cup and left his plain.

All the while he watched her every move, mesmerized by her grace even when she was obviously uncomfortable.

"Then, why?" She handed him his cup of tea.

"Why what?"

Her nose twitched as she covered the corner of her mouth with her cup, hiding the smile threatening to form. "Why are you escorting Ailsa to all of the balls?"

"I've been escorting all of your sisters—well, the older sisters."

"Including Caillen?"

He knew that question would come. He'd just wished it had come later. "No."

"No? Where is she?"

"I don't know," he said honestly. He had not heard from Simon, nor had he heard from Griffith demanding her dowry. He had expected one or the other a fortnight ago.

"What do you mean? My sisters have been in your care for months." The panic in her voice was undeniable, and understandable.

"I turned down her suitor's offer of marriage. They disappeared later that night. She left a letter under the covers in her bed. Robina found it the next morning after she failed to come down for breakfast." He pulled out the letter for his jacket pocket. The letter he kept on his person, lest it fall into the wrong hands.

Iseabail unfolded the letter and read it. When she was done, she handed it back to him and closed her eyes. "Either way, she's ruined."

"I won't let that happen."

"You can't stop it. You can't stop her, and you certainly can't stop the gossip. The scandal sheets have made certain that everyone is looking for her. Neighbors will have their servants questioning your servants."

"My servants are very loyal."

She snorted an indelicate noise. "Not all servants are as loyal as they appear."

"You're speaking from experience." It wasn't a question. He didn't know exactly what she had gone through, maybe it was best he didn't know. He might have to take a trip across the ocean to kill the man.

Iseabail smiled. It wasn't coy or secretive, merely what was in the past, would stay in the past. Without her ability to let go of the past, he wouldn't stand a chance. His sins against her and her sisters were far greater than anyone else.

"I'm sorry," he said, and truly meant it.

The puzzled expression on her face brought him to his knees in front of her on the settee. He reached for her hand and pleaded in a manner he never had in his life. "I did you and your sisters a major disservice. I tried to find you, but you'd vanished into thin air."

Her smile once again said it all. She didn't care. How someone could have such a forgiving heart, he couldn't imagine—until she spoke.

"I am a duchess with the most beautiful son in the world. Where would I be, if you had allowed my sisters and me to stay at Urquhart? I would be a bastard spinster, shunned by society with no prospects of children. Your mother is sponsoring my sisters, and if worse comes to worse, Caillen can live with me at Caerlaverock."

"I was hoping that you would live here. With me. As my duchess."

She froze. It was as if she'd never thought of such a thing.

"Is it possible you don't know? I followed you to Caerlaverock. Tried to win you over with letter after letter. How can you not believe I want more? I want you."

"Are you offering for me, Your Grace?"

"I am, Your Grace."

"But Xavier—"

"Our son is the Duke of Nithesdale, and he will remain as

such. I will not take away what is rightfully his. Our next son, however, will be the Duke of Ross."

"And if it's a girl?"

"Then she will inherit Urquhart, I will make sure of it. Our children will not be robbed of what is rightfully theirs." Her smile grew and he asked again. "Will you marry me, Iseabail? I love you. I want to be with you, I want to grow old with you."

A tear slipped down her cheek, and before she could finish uttering the word "Yes," she was in his arms. His lips pressed to hers and the passion that had always been between them ignited.

He swooped her in his arms and carried her across the room. Throwing the door open, he nearly fell over his mother and her sisters, but not for a second did he stop kissing her.

Her sisters giggled. His mother gasped. "Nashford Xavier Harding!"

Iseabail laughed against his lips.

"I believe you've already met the next Duchess of Ross, Mother. Please don't be scandalized." Her sisters giggled some more as he took long strides toward the steps.

"Girls!" His mother said, but by now he knew her sisters wouldn't be corralled any easier than Iseabail. They would watch their ascent until he kicked his bedroom door closed behind them. "Ross!" His mother tried again. "You will ruin her!"

"He ruined me long ago, Your Grace." Iseabail smiled. "And I love him."

"But ... but the banns! We must have the banns read. What if *The Whispers of the Ton* gets word of this?" His mother sounded nearly panicked.

He probably should listen to her. He turned at the top of the steps and with every ounce of ducal authority he possessed, said, "Iseabail Blair Hancock has agreed to become my duchess. The honourable departed Duke of Nithesdale would have wanted his *son* raised in a loving family, and Iseabail and I plan to raise him to be just like his father *and* his grandfather. I will procure a special license, Mother, and to hell with the scandal sheets." He bowed slightly. "Ladies, if you will excuse us. What happens now is entirely between me and your sister."

"What about dinner?" his mother asked in a final effort to control the situation.

"We won't be joining you," Iseabail added with a laugh, and he did the only thing he could. He ran for his bedchamber before he educated her sisters on far more than a few passionate kisses.

Epilogue

Ross,

There has been a change in plans. I am taking Baroness Griffith to my family estate for her to recuperate. Baron Griffith has sadly expired from injuries he sustained during an attack by highwaymen when they were returning with their joyous news. Please let the Duchess know her sister is safe and will be well cared for by my family through Spring. She could not face her sisters while her emotions were so raw. I will see you upon my return.

Best,
Astley

—*A letter to Nashford Xavier Harding, Duke of Ross, from Simon Benjamin Clark, Earl of Astley, Gretna Green, Scotland*

The back of Iseabail's legs hit the bed before she registered they were in his chamber. The sound of the door slamming should have alerted her to their surroundings, but she was so happy to be in his arms once more, she was lost in the ecstasy. The rough calloused touch of his hands on the edge of her gown was everything she loved about this man. His lips tracked down her jaw, the lobe of her ear, and her neck where his tongue teased and tormented the throbbing beat of her heart. It was as if he had a direct line to her center. She was hot and wet, wanting him to hurry, and loving every minute he did not.

"You're more beautiful than ever," Nash whispered. The rough edge to his voice making her eager for more of his touch, his tongue, everything he had to offer.

"My body has changed," she gasped, as his finger trailed along the edge of the bodice of her gown and slipped beneath it.

"Every bit of it entices me," he said, as he nipped her flesh and exposed one of her breasts. He groaned at the sight and she felt his desire harden against her core.

His mouth was instantly on her breast as he plumped and kneaded her. She was used to looking down and seeing her son suckle her breast, but this was nothing like a nursing babe. It wasn't tender and endearing. This was rousing and erotic. She had never thought she would see this wonderfully bawdy and sensual view ever again. Yet she had to stop him before he realized she was breastfeeding—

Too late. She leaked, and he lapped it up as if he had done so his entire adult life. "Mmmmm." He looked up and grinned, that devilish smile no woman could resist. "I will not steal from my son. He has earned a small piece of you."

"I believe he's taken more than a small piece."

"I endeavor to teach him how to be more respectful of his mother in the future."

"You don't mind that I breastfeed?"

"I can't imagine you doing anything else. It's one of the things I adore about you."

"One?" She teased and reached down to rub the length of him.

"Minx, you have no idea how long I've waited—"

She laughed. "I believe I have been waiting just as long, Your Grace."

Nash stood up and flipped her over unceremoniously. "Sorry, love but I must free you from this contraption as soon as possible so that I may worship every inch of your delectable body."

Iseabail sighed. He could toss her on the floor if he continued to talk in such a manner. The fabric at her buttons tore and Nash swore. "Bloody bollocks." He tore the dress from her body and tossed it across the room. Next was her shift, undergarments, and stockings. He groaned and his mouth was on her backside devouring her flesh the same way he had her breast.

"You have the most beautiful arse I've ever seen," he whispered, as he plumped her flesh and made her squirm with delight. Yet she wanted more. A lifetime more.

She looked over her shoulder at him on his knees worshiping her. "I need you naked, Nash."

He spread her legs and licked her sex, and she nearly came with the contact of his warm firm mouth on her flesh.

"Now," she ordered, with more force than either one of them realized she possessed.

His smirk was pure masculine pride as he rocked back on his heels and stood in one fluid motion. Iseabail rolled over and watched him take off his navy riding coat with velvet collar and gold buttons. He folded it, then meticulously laid it over the trunk at the end of his bed. All of this while watching her.

"Touch yourself." Unlike her demand for him to undress, his was simply a request she could never deny. She ran her hand up her hip, slowly across her belly where a few lines of pregnancy told the story of how heavy with child she had once been. His eyes snagged on the scarring. "I bet you were gorgeous when you were round with our son."

Iseabail laughed. "I was as big as this townhouse."

"I won't miss our next child," he promised.

"No, you won't," she agreed.

"Even the birth."

"Even the birth. Although, I understand most men aren't able to handle it."

"I am not most men."

"No, you're not." She agreed and he took off his buckskin-colored waistcoat, its beautiful embroidery glinting golden in the sunlight. He slowly removed his cravat next, as she languidly moved her finger across her abdomen to her breast, each one of them savoring the moment their bodies would be reunited.

She circled her nipple the way his tongue had. Enjoying her touch that much more as he watched. He reached behind his neck and pulled his crisp white shirt over his head with one tug. God, he was gorgeous. How had she lived so long without the expanse of his chest and his strong arms wrapping around her? How had she ever thought to go on without watching the corded muscles of his abdomen ripple above her as he drove inside her?

He wet his lips as he sat down in the chair to remove his boots, his line of vision directed toward her sex. It was as if he had never seen another woman, yet she knew he was vastly experienced. Her cheeks flamed as she brought her fingers where his gaze was glued, the movement catching his attention, and he looked from the delicate exploration of her fingers to the gasping expression on her face as she found that little nub of pleasure.

"I have dreamed of you like this." He held her gaze as her chest heaved and he stood to take off his trousers in one smooth motion. He still didn't wear smalls, and she loved the way his cock stood up proud. The words of desire on his lips and the sight of his arousal pointing directly at where they both wanted it to be, sent her over the edge. Her eyes closed with the ecstasy of the moment, only to shoot wide open when she felt his mouth upon her once more. Lapping and licking, driving her mad with lust.

He knelt next to the bed and shoved her heels to the mattress, exposing her further. Her fingers curled in his hair, and she screamed with wonder at the way he worshiped her body. Only this man could drive a woman over the edge when she'd already fallen. He touched her everywhere. Squeezed her in the best of places, caressed her in the most sensitive. Her back arched as his wicked tongue did things she'd longed to feel once more and thought she'd never experience again. Yet every time was new. Every touch sent tingles spreading through her body like a new path to pleasure she longed to explore.

Iseabail screamed his name, over and over. This man she loved with all her heart.

"Keep calling my name like that and all the ladies of the Ton will be lining up at our front door."

She growled at him as he crawled up the length of her body. "You are mine, Nashford Xavier Harding, and no one else is allowed to touch you. Do you understand?"

His devilish grin spread across his face. "I serve one duchess. My duchess. No other lady shall ever scream my name again."

She smacked his chest at his incorrigible arrogance. "I don't want to know how many women have screamed your name in this room."

His face grew serious. "No other woman has entered my home."

She cocked a brow. She could think of a half-dozen other women living under this roof at this very moment.

"Your family and mine don't count. No other woman has entered my bedchamber or lain on my bed. Your voice is the only voice I care to hear echoing off the walls of this room. The library, my office, the parlor—"

She laughed. "My sisters need to be married before that happens."

"You'd be surprised at how much my mother loves to take them shopping. In fact, I wouldn't be surprised if she didn't round them up for a late shopping trip this afternoon after I carried you upstairs."

Her cheeks flamed. "I certainly hope so."

"I love you Iseabail Blair Hancock Harding. No other woman has captured my heart and soul the way you have." He nudged her entrance with his manhood. "No other woman has captivated my cock, either."

She lifted her hips and he drove into her as she grasped his hard, strong arms, the hair on his chest creating sensual friction across her breasts. He groaned deep within his throat, an enticing, purely masculine sound as he lifted one of her legs over his shoulder. His hips rocked into her, rubbing her sex as the length of his cock stroked that spot inside her she never knew existed before him. The muscles of his abdomen rippled, his hips thrust, and they both watched as their bodies joined and separated. Separated and joined as if showing them no matter how far apart they found themselves, they would always come together.

"I love you, Nash," she gasped, on the brink of rapture once more. His lips captured hers in a kiss full of promise for the future, for their children's future, and so much more as they reached for the stars of ecstasy together. It was a kiss that ruined a duchess for any other man and made a duke into the husband he was meant to be, as they collapsed in each other's arms, the sound of pure contentment resonating in their labored breaths.

And then a baby wailed from somewhere in the house ... and they laughed as one.

"Now that boy has impeccable timing," the Duke grinned down at his breathless bride-to-be.

"If you don't get him now, he will demand satisfaction," she teased.

"He waited for us to come together." His grin was full of

devilish innuendo. "I see no reason to make him wait any longer."
He rolled off the bed, taking the bedsheet with him.

"Where are you going?" she asked, because surely he didn't
intend to go out into the hall like that.

"To get our son," he said simply, as if it was something he said
every day of the week, and yet she saw his chest grow with pride,
and knew he couldn't wait to hold Xavier once more. "You better
cover yourself, Duchess."

She gasped and jumped from the bed, nearly tripping over his
boots as she reached for his jacket. She slipped it over her shoulders
just in time for him to open the door and march down the hall in
his nearly nude state.

"You can't do that while my sisters are in residence!" she yelled
after him. A giggle she had not felt in such a long time bubbled in
her chest and escaped her lips.

A moment later Nash returned, holding their son as if he had
done so since the day he was born. He was a natural at being a
father, and she couldn't have asked for a better partner to raise a
duke. He cooed at their son, momentarily distracting him from
what he wanted most—to eat.

"I suggest we purchase a new home where we can roam the
halls as we please." He looked up at her for a moment and grinned
his obvious pleasure at her wearing his jacket.

It was only then that she saw the piece of paper in his hand.
"What is that?" She asked.

"A letter from Simon."

"Simon? Is it about Caillen? Is she all right?"

"She is fine. She is a baroness now."

"No."

"Yes," he said, and then stopped her from asking more with the
staying of his hand. "She is also a widow. It seems they met some
highwaymen on their way back to London. Simon found them
and is taking her to his family estate."

"But she should be here, with her family." She insisted.

"She didn't want to be here. She's hurting. Let her heal." If anyone knew what it was like to need to heal, Iseabail did. She nodded and his gaze returned to the child in his arms who began to wiggle. "Don't you think we should be able to display the family jewels in all their glory anywhere in the house, Xavier?"

Iseabail couldn't help but laugh at his attempt to lighten the mood. "I'll make a pact with you, Your Grace."

"Go on."

"If you will cover the jewels while outside this room," she said, as he closed the door and dropped the bed linens at the same time, "then I will keep these two babies exclusively for the two of you." She reached up and plumped her breasts, the tips looking rather delectable peeking out of his jacket, if she did say so herself.

Nash growled as he approached her, exposed one of her breasts and snuggled their son up against her. "You drive a hard bargain, Duchess."

"I play to win."

"And yet I believe it is I who have come out on top."

She laughed as the three of them snuggled on the bed together. Their child in her arms, and Iseabail in his. Life in the Ton may not be everything she thought it would be, but she couldn't imagine sharing it with any more dukes than the two she loved most, and the one who blessed them with their future.

She smiled and looked up to the heavens. "Thank you, Nithesdale. I have never been happier."

Nash kissed her temple and agreed. "No father could have loved me more."

A Note From the Author

Dearest Reader,

If you're familiar with Scottish art and history then you will recognize many of the extra tidbits throughout the story I used to capture a wee bit of the Scottish culture.

First, I need to mention the castles. I absolutely love the castles of Scotland, more specifically the ruins. They speak of a people who have seen many battles and struggles for survival. Of clans and crowns fighting to occupy this beautiful landscape. While vacationing I fell in love with the two castles featured in **The Ruined Duchess** and on our journey across the country, my characters were born. Although the places are real, the stories, characters, and family names are a complete work of fiction.

- Urquhart, located on Loch Ness, is breathtaking. To stand amongst the ruins and gaze across the loch, one can imagine the fierce passion behind the battle cries and the devastation those wars brought to the people. Yet like the ruins, the people of Scotland persevere.

- Caerlaverock Castle was my very first castle experience. Like Urquhart, it has seen some restoration to ensure its longevity, but the original stonework is magnificent. The haunting artistry carved into the stone will mesmerize visitors. I was so glad to be on my own schedule and not a tour as I spent long hours exploring the keep. An hour would never be enough time to take in the mastery of this architecture. Maybe it's because it was my very first castle experience, but Caerlaverock will always be one of my favorite places.

My heroine, Iseabail, talked about a beloved piece of art her little sister painted on the walls of Urquhart Castle. Scottish artist Jacob More painted *Corra Linn*, the most famous painting of his three *Falls of the Clyde* collection. This incredible painting is on display at the Scottish National Gallery. The child's version is on the imaginary walls of the Blair's home at Urquhart Castle in my Scottish Brides series. ;)

Iseabail briefly compares Nash to a gallowglass warrior. I had not heard of these warriors prior to doing research for the Scottish Brides series. The word is anglicized from the Irish *gallóglaigh* or *Gall Gaeil*—foreign *Gaels*. Descendants of the 10th century Norse, these warriors were mercenaries from the western isles of Scotland who traveled to Ireland and fought for Irish nobles. They are a fascinating group of warriors who may require a story in the future. For a brief history, you can read about their origins at www.irishorigenes.com.

Iseabail and Nash place a wager on a card game called Pope Joan, a popular game in Scotland in the 1800's. It's not a play on Joan of Arc, but rather it was political propaganda during the Victorian era against Pope John VIII and his feminine features. The game first appeared in Hoyles in 1814 as Pope Julius. I placed it in my

Regency romance because of its popularity in Scotland, and it's similar to Hearts or Tripoli—a favorite of mine as a child.

Teaching a naive virgin how to seduce a rake wasn't an easy task to overcome, especially when the teacher in *The Ruined Duchess* is a widow who had been in a passionless marriage. I wanted to find the right type of book to assist them in their education. The two publications I found from the time period have some crude images included in the publication which offered something different than the Kama Sutra and seemed like they would be more accessible to Iseabail and Phoebe. The books were my way of allowing the two women to learn about sex and the art of seduction without asking anyone else for assistance—although Mr. Forrester did play a small role. You will see Phoebe and Mr. Forrester again.

- I found two references to this first book so I'd like to give credit to both publications of it. *L'Arétin Francais Les Epices de Venvs published by A Larnaka in 1782 and L'Arétin Francais Les Epices de Venvs published by Felix Nogaret Aux Depens des Fermier Generaux 1787*

- *The Memoirs of Wanton Woman, London printed for T. Benton*

I have wonderful memories of my girls' trip to Scotland with a fellow romance author and our castle hunt throughout the countryside. I hope I was able to bring to life a little of our experience and my love of Scottish history.

Warmest Regards,

Helene

Also by Helene Matheson

The Scandalous Sisters

The Ruined Duchess

The Rebellious Countess

About the Author

After following her childhood dream to serve and protect, Helene retired from public service and began a new dream—creating happily ever afters. First publishing in mystery and romantic suspense, she decided to add her love of travel and history to her personal oeuvre. From the first page to the last, Helene promises to take you on a journey to arouse your imagination and capture your heart.

When she's not writing or researching her next novel, she can be found rummaging through antique stores, estate sales, and flea markets looking for that next piece of inspiration.

www.ingramcontent.com/pod-product-compliance
Lightning Source LLC
Chambersburg PA
CBHW020357110726
47899CB00006B/1747